I0692005

Forged in Fire

by

C J Bahr

The Fire Chronicles, Book 2

Forged in Fire

Cover Art by *Debbie Taylor*

The Wild Rose Press, Inc.
PO Box 708
Adams Basin, NY 14410-0708
Visit us at www.thewildrosepress.com

Publishing History
First Fantasy Rose Edition, 2017
Print ISBN 978-1-5092-1787-8
Digital ISBN 978-1-5092-1788-5

The Fire Chronicles, Book 2
Published in the United States of America

On the floor, lying on its side

was a half empty decanter. Obviously it had fallen when he passed out. Dressed only in his breeches, his bare chest and arms with their outward scars were a testament to his hard life, but she worried more for his hidden scars. His tears stopped, and his moans turned into short panting breaths, legs and arms thrashing around. He was going to hurt himself if he kept this up.

"Kit! Wake up. You're having a bad dream."

He continued to twist, a grunt of effort escaped, followed by a cry of pain.

"Kit!" She reached out, careful of his whipping arms and touched his shoulder. In a flash Beth was grabbed and flung onto the bed. Before she could even react, he threw a leg over her hip, straddling her. Leaning forward, he grabbed her throat with both hands in a crushing hold. When he started to squeeze, panic set in. Beth bucked her hips off the feather-ticked mattress trying to throw him off, but she couldn't get much leverage. She slipped both her arms between his to try and break his hold. It wasn't working. Her lungs screamed for air as she pummeled him with her fists— striking blows to his shoulders and chest, but it was too hard to concentrate. Her limbs felt like wet noodles. Her hits became frantic pats. She had to wake him. With the last of her failing strength she managed to claw at his face.

Dedication

For Marla
Thank you for your belief and always being there

Acknowledgments

A story may start with a single person sitting at a keyboard, but it ends with a community. It takes a village to birth a novel, and my town is awesome.

First, a huge thank you to my first reader, critiquer, and co-conspirator, Marla White. As always, your insights and comments bring out the best. You challenge me to rise above my limits.

For my daring beta-readers, Jenn, Nahmi, and Tambra—Thank you for braving the rough version and your brilliant advice.

To my editor, Amanda Barnett at Wild Rose Press, for her amazing support and help in polishing and making *Forged in Fire* the best book it could be. I loved collaborating with you once again.

And of course, to the rest of the gang at Wild Rose Press, it's a pleasure and honor to be a member of the garden.

Last, but not least, thanks to you, my readers, for picking up this book. I love sharing Beth and Kit's story with you. Enjoy!

Chapter One

West Yorkshire, England, January 1795

The night pressed in around Christopher Locke. He hunched further into the warmth of his heavy black greatcoat as he stood beside his horse deep in the shadowy woods—blanketed in silence. A hush filled with expectation. The uncanny quiet struck a discord until the far-off yipping of a fox caused his horse to expel a soft nicker in return, breaking his moody reverie.

"Quiet, my friend." Kit stroked the gelding's neck.

His horse turned his head and nudged Kit's coat pocket with his nose, causing his slight frown to disappear. "Later, after the job," he whispered, aware sound traveled far on this chilly night.

A cold wind from the north swirled the leaves at his feet, as he glanced up at the broad canopy of the forest trying, to judge the hour of night. The thick clouds and trees hid the moon, but his internal clock told him it was time. Dampness clung to the wind foreshadowing rain on the horizon. He hoped the weather would hold until he was home, warm by a fire with a drink in hand. But at least the darkness would aid his endeavor.

Kit gave his gelding a final pat before placing his booted left foot into the stirrup. He swung himself up into the saddle with the agility born of living a lifetime on the edge of a blade. His prior mercenary life had honed his skills and reflexes, which played a part in his new one. He nudged Dante, his trusted collaborator, into a walk following a trail weaving through the trees. It didn't take long to reach the road carved through the forest. It was the perfect location, a blind bend to a straightaway with plenty of concealment where he had an appointment to keep. He halted Dante at the edge of the woods, cloaking them within the dark murkiness.

Thunder rumbled in the distance, drawing Kit's gaze upward again to the rush of menacing clouds revealed by the break in the forest. Were they a harbinger of the approaching storm or a message sent to turn him aside? Life was always a gamble. Was tonight the evening he would pay for his crimes? The thought was never far from his mind, living with him like a constant specter following him since he ran from his former life. If tonight he met the hangman's noose, well he'd had a good ride. At least his current occupation afforded him some thrills and riches, which is more than he could say for a soldier's pay. And he'd certainly lived longer than expected or deserved.

The sharp *clip clops* of hooves pounding on the dirt road from around the bend alerted Kit. He smiled and yanked the black cravat up, covering his nose and mouth and then straightened the high collar of his greatcoat. A quick hand pressed down on his tricorne hat to secure it tighter to his head and shadow his eyes from observers. His hair was secured in a tight queue.

Dante shivered beneath him. His friend knew what they were about this evening. With only the slightest pressure from his legs, his mount eagerly stepped out of the woods and onto the rutted road. Halting Dante, Kit dropped the reins, and pulled out a pistol, one of a matched pair. The double barrel flintlock was plain, the bare ivory inlayed grip smooth and well-used under his gloved hand—an old friend and a gift which tormented deep into his soul. He needed nothing fancy, only an accurate weapon with no misfires. The pistols offered him that comfortable precision, no matter how much he'd give anything not to own them. The pistols tortured him every time he looked at them, yet there was no possibility he could give them up, they meant too much. Verifying it was primed and loaded, he stood tall in his stirrups, as Dante held rock steady beneath him, and took aim.

The driver was trotting his four-in-hand dangerously fast in this bleak gloom by the echo of their hooves. Obviously the coachman was no horseman, but he was justified in wanting to hurry past. After all, the night was dark and full of danger. He was sure the coachman wanted rid of this isolated patch of road and into more civilized surroundings. The hairpin turn would correct the pace of the horses. Kit's lips curled up under his dark mask, his blood pumping through his veins, arm held steady as he waited.

He heard the horses break gait to a walk and shortly they appeared around the bend. Kit and Dante continued to hold firm as they waited for the carriage to complete its turn. Then with a loud roaring *bang* and a splash of sparks he fired, his shot glanced past the driver, taking the coachman's earlobe with it. The man cried out, slapping a hand to his injured ear while dropping a set of reins. The leaderless carriage horses shied left, but were halted by the dense woods edging the road.

Kit raised his second pistol, mentally marking the three shots left. Taking aim once more, he shouted his favorite words, the standard greeting of fellow highwaymen. "Stand and deliver!"

Chapter Two

Northern Scotland, Near Durness, July, Present Day

"I can't believe we're doing this! It's so exciting! So cloak and dagger-ish," Beth fidgeted next to her best friend. She was always up for an adventure, but she was usually the one dragging her friend into trouble, not the other way around.

"Hush." Laurel glared at her. "We don't know if Alex is out of town or not." Laurel reached the door and rang the bell to Sinclair House, waiting to see if he answered.

Beth had been thrilled when her best friend finally found time to escape her job in Chicago to visit. This past year, meeting and then marrying Grant Murray while studying Celtic design in Scotland had changed everything for Beth. She'd uprooted her life in the States as an interior decorator and moved into his home, Cleitmuir Manor, a whirlwind decision she'd never regretted, no matter how much she might miss her own family and best friend. But now, trying to steal a sapphire ring from Alex, her treasure hunting neighbor and most likely a killer—in the literal sense—got her blood pumping. It reminded her of all the fun times she'd spent with Laurel, minus the murderer of course. Beth, the normal instigator of adventures and

5

troublemaking, felt only pride in Laurel, who trumped all her past efforts by discovering a tortured ghost in need of help. *An actual flesh and blood ghost!*

"But I thought you said he'd be gone?" Beth hoped so. She really didn't want Alex to catch them.

"I said, Alex *thought* he *might* be gone. There is a difference." She rang the bell again, still no answer. "I think it's safe. Let's look for the key. He said he'd leave one."

She and Laurel didn't have to search long. It was in the first place they looked, under the doormat.

"Well, here we go," Laurel whispered as she unlocked the door.

"How do we know the ring's even here? I've seen Alex wearing it."

They slipped inside and shut the door behind them. Laurel dragged her toward the front parlor.

"He wasn't wearing it yesterday, and it was sitting on the mantel in the same place he put it after it snagged in my hair a week ago."

"Oh good, then this should be easy," Beth replied as she followed closely behind. "Though it's hard to believe he'd leave an heirloom sapphire just lying about. I mean, it is valuable." She couldn't stop babbling. "How cool is this? We're treasure swiping from a treasure hunter. I can't believe Simon never noticed Alex wearing it. And wait until we give the ring back to Simon. He's gonna be speechless. And when he finds out it's the missing key, double rainbows all the way! Oh, and can you imagine what Alex will do if he ever finds out he had the key all along—oof!" She slammed into her best friend, since Laurel crashed to a halt directly in front of her.

"Shit."

"What? A little warning about the stoppage next time, friend."

"The ring, it's not here."

"So much for simple."

"Damn."

"Maybe he's wearing it?" Beth suggested.

"Let's hope not. We need to search the house." Laurel looked around. "Crap, this place is huge. We've got to think about this logically." She closed her eyes while thinking out loud. "If he's not wearing it, where would he keep his jewelry?"

"Either a safe or his bedroom," Beth answered without hesitation.

"Good, we'll try his bedroom. I don't even want to think about locating a hidden safe. Any idea where it might be? His bedroom, that is."

"Of course. I had a tour of Sinclair House eons ago. He never took you to his bedroom? Some seducer he is…Yeah, right, probably a good thing. Follow me." She couldn't believe she'd tried to match-make her best friend with a killer. The thought had invisible ants crawling all over her skin. After they got the ring and helped Simon, they needed to find a way to bring Alex to justice.

Beth led Laurel up the grand stairs, then down the hall to its end. She paused at the open door on her right.

"Here you go. Now what?"

"Get searching. We split up."

"Aye, aye, *mon Capitán*!" Beth decided to head directly to the nightstand next to the bed, while Laurel went straight to the dressing table near the mahogany wardrobe.

"Wow! Black Code by Armani. No wonder he smells so good. I wonder if he's a boxer or briefs guy? Oh, or maybe commando!"

"Beth, focus," Laurel called across the room. "We don't know how much time we have."

"Sorry." Beth couldn't help herself. She tended to babble and crack jokes when nervous. Laurel was right, they needed to speed things up. She turned from the nightstand and gasped. Alex MacKenzie stood lounging in the open doorway, leaning casually against the frame, with one arm behind his back.

"And just what are you lasses doing here?"

Beth caught the quick glance Laurel shot across the room, warning her to keep her mouth shut. No problem there. What the hell were they going to do now?

"Um, Beth dropped by while I was researching," Laurel lied. "We got to talking about the house and when she found out I hadn't toured the place, she offered to show me around."

Beth smothered the sigh, which almost escaped at Laurel's plausible explanation. Quickly, she nodded in agreement, keeping her mouth shut before she said something stupid. Like possibly accusing him of multiple murders and getting in his face. Probably not the best time to confront him on his own home turf, but damn, she really hated the unfairness of not being able to.

Alex let out a low chuckle. "Is that the reason you're pawing through my personal belongings? Don't get me wrong. I've always wanted you in my bedroom and with a friend. I'm open for doubles." He glanced at Beth.

Ewww. That's just gross. She met his gaze directly,

hoping her thoughts were apparent on her face.

"It's boxers, by the way," he replied, proving he had been there long enough to eavesdrop.

They definitely were in trouble. How were they going to get out of this?

Alex finally tore his gaze away from her and locked it onto Laurel. "However, you seem to be on a mission. What are you searching for?"

"Nothing. Honest." Laurel held up two fingers in the Boy Scouts' pledge and then dropped her hand. "Chalk it up to curiosity. I wanted to find out more about you. So I was snooping. I'm sorry and truthfully, quite embarrassed. I apologize."

Again, Alex gave a throaty laugh. "You're a horrible liar. Now, I'll ask again, what are you looking for?"

Laurel kept her mouth shut, and Beth followed suit. Best to be quiet and let the mind work on swiftly figuring a way out.

Alex *tsked.* "I warn you, I'll only ask so many times. I'm not stupid. I know you figured something out yesterday. Where's the treasure, lass?"

"The gold? Surely you don't think I was going to find it in your bedroom. After all, I would have thought you'd have noticed a horde of Jacobite gold lying about, you being a treasure hunter and all."

He shook his head. "You and I both know it's not gold." Anger leaked into his voice.

"I—"

"No!" He interrupted Laurel. "One and only one more time. What are you searching for?"

Ants started creeping across Beth's skin again as Laurel shot a worried glance her way. This was so not good. Maybe if they coordinated their attack the two of them could jump and overpower him? How to communicate it...

"Alex," Laurel soothed. "It's nothing, really."

"Wrong answer." Alex's hand swept out from behind his back, holding a sleek matte-black gun complete with silencer. Straightening his stance, an evil smile curled up his lips.

Beth froze as panic and sheer terror held her rooted to the floor. This couldn't be happening. He wouldn't shoot. He was just trying to scare them. And he was doing a good job at that too. They had information he needed. The dead don't tell tales.

"You'll learn I mean what I say."

"Alex, no!" Laurel pleaded.

A muffled pop filled the sickening silence when Alex fired the gun.

Beth felt the sudden punch to her chest, at the same time Laurel's scream reverberated through the room. She peered down and watched a bloodstain soak through the lavender cotton of her shirt. The stain would be hard to remove. The odd thought skittered across her mind until pain lanced through her, and she felt her knees give out.

"Beth, Oh God, Beth. Hang in there. I'll get help." Laurel caught and cradled her as she collapsed to the floor.

She couldn't reply. She couldn't get enough air, her breaths came in short, sharp gasps.

"No, Beth, please." Laurel pressed her hand to the wound, trying to staunch the blood.

She tried to scream as fire spread through her limbs from the pressure. The world went black and Beth fell into a dark void.

****

The pungent smell of moss and damp dirt filtered through Beth's nostrils as awareness crept upon her. She cracked her eyes open with effort. Her chest ached, making breathing difficult. It was dark, almost pitch black. She forced herself to sit upright from lying prone. Swaying, she placed a hand on the wet ground and the other to her chest.

Where was she? What had happened? Beth's eyes adjusted to the minimal light to discover she was sitting in a small clearing in a heavily wooded forest. *What the hell?* She rubbed her chest, trying to relieve the deep pain—pulsing in time with her heartbeat.

She plucked at her T-shirt and peered down through the murkiness. Her eyes widened and with a sharp exhale, she discovered the neat hole in her shirt directly over her heart.

Memories crashed back. Alex had shot her. My God, what about Laurel? She scrambled to her feet, but her vision tunneled, and sweat broke across her brow. Her knees crumpled, and she was back on the forest floor. She had to find her friend. Laurel was in danger. Beth tried to slow her gasps, but when she inhaled for a deep breath, pain pierced through her chest once again. A sob escaped her. *What the hell was going on?* Tears slid down her face. She curled into herself, pressing her knees to her aching chest, and wrapped her arms around her legs and gave in to her misery.

A bright flash followed by a clap of thunder directly overhead brought her back to her senses. She emerged from her cocoon, urging herself back to her feet. She wasn't a quitter. This mystery was hers to solve.

First things first, she studied her bullet-torn shirt again. There was no bloodstain, which was impossible, just as these woods were. She had marked the spreading stain at the time of impact. Her shirt should be crusted with it, but except for the hole and the dirt clinging to the material from lying on the forest floor, the cotton was unmarred.

Beth twisted her shirt up and away from her chest to survey her bared skin above her lacy bra. It was too dark to really see, but there definitely wasn't a corresponding hole in her flesh, or blood on her skin. With her other hand, she fingered a raised lump, which aligned with the hole, tender to the touch—bruised but not broken. She yanked her shirt back down. Too many questions and not enough answers.

Another rumble of thunder rolled out, and this time Beth felt a fat drop of rain hit her head. It was time to find some shelter before the storm struck. She didn't recognize these woods. In fact, there were no big forests near her home. How had she gotten here? Another drop of rain plopped on her. It was freezing, and the temperature continued to drop. She needed to pick a direction. At this point any would do since she was clueless.

She spun in a circle searching the clearing. An owl's hoot drew her attention to a tree, and she spotted what appeared to be a path. It seemed to be the only way out through the ring of trees. Beth started walking.

Chapter Three

West Yorkshire, England, January 1795

The rhythmic clang of metal striking anvil pulled him from the woods to the blacksmith's shop at the far edge of the town. He hadn't wanted to be rude and just pop in on his brother, especially since he'd just done him a solid favor. It was why he was here.

The raging blaze of the forge splintered the stormy night, beckoning him inward. He stopped barely inside the entrance, just as his brother put down his hammer and lifted a glowing hot blade, which he flipped and submerged into a bucket of water, causing a thick column of hissing steam to rise into the open-spaced room. He pulled the newly forged blade from the water and placed it on the bench behind him, before turning to greet him.

"Uri, you needn't have come." His brother wiped at his sweating brow before gesturing him farther into the room.

"I know." He joined him and took the freshly poured mug offered to him. "Blessings upon you." He clinked the crockery to his brother's before taking a careful sip. One had to be wary of what Remy would offer. His mouth curled upward into a smile. The ambrosia of a good single malt scotch warmed his pallet and continued downward when he swallowed.

"I wanted to thank you."

"You have done so already," Remy replied, before taking a sip from his own clayware mug. "Your request was simple as I watched over her soul. A resolution for the benefit of us both. A win-win situation. Yes?"

Uri sighed. He owed a debt. What he and his brother had done was close to breaking the rules of free will, but the situation in Scotland had been a bitter pill to swallow, especially having to watch from the sidelines. The woman was a causality that shouldn't have happened.

"How is she?"

"Alive."

"Obviously." He pointed a finger at Remy. "You know what I ask."

Remy smiled as he glanced up at an owl perched in the rafters. "Her feet are walking the path of her destiny. It is hers to embrace or reject."

"True." Uri took another sip before placing his empty mug on the table. "You will help as you can?"

"What is allowed to us." Remy smiled again. "And maybe a bit more?"

"Careful, brother." Uri admonished before gripping his brother's arm in a warrior's clasp, hand to elbow, which was met in return.

"I will be. This is a brilliant solution to a long and vexing problem of mine. As I said, a win-win."

"Only if Father sees it that way. Good luck, brother."

The Archangel Uriel gave his brother Remiel's arm a farewell squeeze before leaving the blacksmith's shop. Walking into the night, his bronze wings unfurled, and he launched himself skyward.

Chapter Four

Kit kept his quarry in sight. The driver and two passengers appeared docile enough, but he had his eye on the dark-haired bloke. One couldn't be too careful in his line of work, and the back of his neck itched every time he stared directly at the man. He trusted his instinct, which had kept him alive thus far.

"Once more, toss your weapons to the ground." Kit swung a leg across the pommel of his saddle and dismounted, landing lightly and steady on his feet. He kept his pistols leveled and met the gaze of the stubborn black-haired fellow. The coachman and other passenger had already nicely complied. There was always one who thought to challenge him. "I do not have to kill you to make your life miserable." Kit tilted his head in gesture toward the driver with the missing earlobe. "Disarm yourself, now!"

The gentleman glared as he tossed his pistol aside then unbuckled his sword belt letting it drop to the ground at his feet.

With a mental sigh, Kit squared his shoulders. "Gentlemen," he spoke, while keeping his guns steady. "I am sure you know what comes next. Out with the goods, please."

The second passenger grabbed his purse, which clanked promisingly, and lobbed it to land at Kit's feet. Too bad they couldn't see his raised eyebrow hidden by his hat. If they thought he'd be fooled by such a simple display, they were greatly mistaken. Kit had intimate knowledge as to what treasure they were hiding, and a bag full of coins was not it.

"You are holding out, gentlemen. The gems, if you would be so kind."

The roar and discharge of sparks from Kit's left-handed pistol spoke louder than any words. The ball gouged the ground in a spray of mud, barely missing the dark-haired man's foot, which was edging toward his sword on the ground. No doubt in hopes of flipping it up with his foot.

"Touch the sword and you die." The man's foot ceased moving. Kit now had one shot remaining in both his guns, plenty to hold off his prey.

"Do not make me kill you," he warned. "This transaction can be done with minimum fuss. The jewels, now!"

The men exchanged glances as Kit continued to hold them at gunpoint. He expelled a soft sigh as the difficult man reached into his open coat to withdraw a velvet bag. At last.

"Toss it here, sir. Right alongside the other generous donation."

The bag landed with satisfying weight next to the coins.

"Right. Gentlemen, into the carriage, please. Leave your weapons. You can regain them after I leave. Move along," Kit gestured with one gun toward the open door of the coach.

The coachman entered first, followed by the compliant passenger, leaving the black-haired gent glaring at him.

"How did you know?"

Kit's smile was hidden under the mask at the irate question. "A poor highwayman I would make if I did not know my gains." His amused tone angered the man further.

"I'll have those jewels back!"

"You will need the luck of the Almighty Himself to regain what you lost tonight. Now, into the carriage before I decide you are not worth leaving alive."

The dark-haired man glanced once more at his weapons lying useless in the mud before he stepped into the coach and shut the door behind himself.

Kit holstered one pistol while keeping a watchful eye on the carriage and then bent down to snatch the jewels and coins, dropping them into a pocket of his greatcoat. The wind gusted as lightning flashed followed on its heels by the deep rumble of thunder. He made quick work mounting Dante and settling into the saddle. Not immediately wanting to turn his back to the coach, because he had no doubt more weapons were inside, he nudged Dante into a canter, riding past the coach with its closed door. He was about to enter the forest on the opposite side of the road from where he entered, when he looked over his shoulder.

The carriage's door flung open, and less than a heartbeat later a pistol fired, illuminating the dark night. Kit flinched and immediately changed direction, urging his horse to gallop up the muddy road, heading for the bend, putting the carriage between him and the shooter. It took him a moment to realize he wasn't hit. In fact, the lead ball hadn't come anywhere near him. He risked another glance over his shoulder just as a second shot blasted out from the coach toward a figure on the edge of the woods where Kit had first emerged. The figure gave a high-pitched scream and dodged to the side, her long hair flying in the wind.

Bloody hell, it's a girl! Kit wheeled Dante around. He charged up to the carriage, slipped his foot from the stirrup and slammed it on the open door, knocking the gunman back inside. He thundered past and leaned off to the side, holding out a hand. The girl grabbed his arm and swung up behind him onto Dante. They galloped into the woods.

No answering shot followed them as Kit's mount took them deeper into the oak and pine. His pace slowed to a lope as the path narrowed and darkened. Kit leaned lower on his horse's neck to keep from getting whacked by lower tree branches. The mysterious girl clung tightly, her body pressing against his back from neck to seat, her arms wrapped around his waist.

He eased Dante into a trot then to a walk, stretching up to sit tall in the saddle when they reached a clearing. The girl loosened her rigid grip and lightly placed her hands on his hips. He didn't stop, just kept his horse walking through the clearing onto another deeply shrouded path. *What the bloody hell had he just done?* She had made the perfect distraction for his getaway. Instead, he rode right back into the thick of things. He wasn't in the profession of rescuing damsels in distress, though he had doubts about her damsel-ness. What was she doing this deep into the forest and scandalously dressed like a man? He rode in silence, trying to decide on a course of action. Currently he was in possession of a stolen coin bag, and of course the jewels. The black cravat still covered his face and it was dark, so he doubted the girl could identify him. He even went so far as to disguise Dante's splashy markings and coat with blackening ash. But adding two and two together was easy. If the occupants of the carriage he robbed lodged a complaint, the girl might be able to place him, or at least back up their claim.

Damn and hell. He should dump the girl and gallop away as fast as he could. But the weather had turned for the worst. A large crack of thunder rumbled as the heavens opened. The deluge of rain hadn't reached them through the overhead canopy, but a few stray fat drops did, and one managed to drip down his neck and reach under both his greatcoat and shirt.

He expelled a harsh breath, billowing his mask in frustration as Dante continued to pick his way through the forest. *Blasted English weather.* If it got any colder, the rain would turn to sleet and God forbid, possibly snow. Rain muddied his trail, but snow would leave his path glaringly obvious to even the idiots of the Watch.

There was a light tap to his shoulder. "Excuse me, where are we going?" The girl behind him asked. "I mean, um, thank you for your help back there. Did someone actually fire a gun at me from an actual horse-drawn carriage? And what's with you? Great costume. And I love your horse. Did I bumble onto a movie set? I mean, I was shot at! I don't think those were blanks. What the hell is going—"

"Hush," Kit growled. *Movie?* The girl babbled nonsense. His head ached from trying to follow her words. Was she simple-minded? Her accent was strange. He really should just dump her off Dante right now and not look back. Another drop of rain splattered onto his covered nose, back-splashing into his eye as he looked upward for guidance.

Tredford was in the direction he was headed, not too far off from the turn to his home. It would barely be a detour. Mind made up, he took the path to town where he'd leave the odd girl before heading for home. She could make the rest of the way there easily on foot. In no time, Dante would be snug in his stall, and Kit would be in dry clothes by the fire with a well-deserved drink in his hand.

Chapter Five

Beth pursed her lips. Needle pricks of frustration with the flaring heat of anger rose at his admonishment to be quiet. Well, she had been babbling. Again. But what did he expect? Her life was turned upside down, and she had no answers. When she'd emerged from the woods it had taken her a moment to realize the tableau in front of her. It was straight out of Regency novel. A highwayman cloaked in a trademark tricorne hat and a greatcoat fleeing a carriage with irate passengers. She really had thought she'd ruined a film shoot. But then a gun fired at her. *A gun! Again!* Like she hadn't had enough people shooting at her already. Huffing internally, she might have laughed at the irony if past consequences hadn't been so dire. She needed to find Laurel.

And who was this costumed actor, horseman? She tapped his shoulder again.

"Seriously, where are you taking me?"

"If you like," his British upper crust accent purred out, "I can leave you here."

As more rain managed to break through the trees and fall on her, she frowned. "You can't just dump me in the middle of nowhere during a storm."

"Can I not?"

That shut her up. He certainly could. Just like he could have left her to the gunman on the road. She bit her tongue to keep quiet, not wanting to give him an excuse to leave her in these strange woods.

They rode on, the horse sure-footed even in the worsening conditions. The path was beginning to become slick with mud, and the temperature significantly dropped. It was July. Why was it so cold? Beth shivered in her thin, damp T-shirt and jeans. She cautiously inched closer to the man. He radiated heat even with the lowering temperature. Hard muscles flexed beneath her hands, sending a jolt of awareness through her, reminding her of his strength.

It was odd how safe she felt, how she had no doubts when he galloped his horse at her and offered her a hand up. She didn't think, just grabbed and swung up hoping she'd make the jump onto the tall horse without falling, getting shot, or dislocating her shoulder. Then the crazy insane ride, dashing through the pitch-dark woods. It had taken all her concentration and equine riding skills just to stay on. She was surprised her rescuer hadn't complained at her death grip as she held on tight.

Beth, for the thousandth time, wished she knew what was going on. Another shiver racked her body, and she pressed herself tighter to the stranger in front of her, relishing the warmth sinking into her chest. Now if only the rest of her could get warm. Hopefully, Grant wouldn't take umbrage to her cuddling with another man. She wondered where her husband was at the moment. She wished he were here beside her. The moment she found a phone she was calling him to come get her. She was all for adventures, but this day/night was bordering on the extreme. What happened to the nice, comfortable, safe life she had? Her muscles grew slack, and she slumped forward as exhaustion claimed her, weariness seeping deep into her bones.

A moment later her eyes snapped open. Beth couldn't believe she was falling asleep. But then again, she'd been shot, woken up in a dark forest only to get shot at again. She had the right to be exhausted. Her eyes slid shut again, and it took longer to will them to open again. Falling asleep would probably be a bad idea since she was utterly ignorant about her current circumstances.

Beth forced herself upright, relinquishing the warmth the man provided and let the cold and the wet shock her awake. She needed a phone. Oh, wait a second, maybe the actor guy had one. They'd been riding quite a while. How big was this movie set anyway? Bracing herself against the certain grumpiness of her fellow rider, she tapped his shoulder once again.

"Um, can I borrow your cell phone?" She hesitated as the man stiffened before her. "Just a quick call. I can pay you for it." Well, she hoped she could, since she had neither her purse nor wallet.

"What language do you speak?"

Huh? "Um, English, just like you, dude."

"I doubt it." He relaxed and reined up his horse. He swung his leg across the front of the saddle and slid lightly to his feet with only a slight squelch from the wet ground. He turned and met her eyes as she sat on the horse.

"Do you need assistance?" The man held up his arms in offer.

She shook her head and grabbed the back of the old-fashioned high-cantle saddle, leaned a bit forward and swung her right leg up and over the horse's hind end, dismounting while facing the horse. It was a long drop for someone only five feet two inches tall and the horse was big, like seventeen hands tall. She stumbled on landing, but her rescuer was once again there, gripping her hips to keep her from ignominiously landing on her butt in the mud.

He didn't release her. In fact, he stepped closer, crowding her against his horse. She pushed against the gelding, but the stubborn and apparently well-trained equine didn't budge. Her heart rate increased. She suddenly found it difficult to breathe. She had to calm down and not panic. He hadn't hurt her so far, she reminded herself. Beth pressed her forehead against the damp yet warm flank of the horse and waited, trying to stay passive, which was so not her strong suit, but he did have the upper hand at the moment. He moved his hands to either side of her, pressing them against his horse, effectively trapping her.

The warmth of his breath caressed her ear, giving her the only warning before he spoke, low and quiet.

"So…" he drew the single word out.

She shivered. He was taller than her, but almost everyone was. He had to bend to whisper in her ear, his body enveloping her.

"What are you doing out alone in the woods, this dark and dreary night?" His soft words tickled her ear. "Dressed as you are?" He slowly removed one hand from his horse. The hand came to rest on her waist, just above her jeans. She felt a light caressing of his thumb on her cotton T-shirt. "So soft," he murmured.

Beth wasn't sure if she was meant to hear his last remark. His hand began to stroke upward until she felt the light brush of his fingertips against the side of her breast.

"Hey!" Beth spun in his embrace so she now faced him, plastered against his front with the warmth of his horse seeping into her back. "Knock it off! I'm a married woman." She held up her left hand and showed him her wedding rings.

He chuckled and grabbed her hand and started to slide off her rings.

"Stop!" She yanked her hand from his grasp. "What in the world do you think you're doing?"

"What I am very, very, good at," he replied from behind his mask while reaching for her hand again.

Beth whipped her hand behind her back. "You can't have my rings."

"Think of them as payment for services rendered."

"I...no...you can't..."

"Here now, give me your rings. I do not want to hurt you."

"I won't. They're mine. I won't give them up."

"Now, luv," he tucked a strand of her hair behind her ear. "I am sure your husband will understand, especially one who lets his wife wander the woods dressed so..." He deliberately drew his gaze leisurely down her body, then back up to meet her own gaze. His eyes shadowed under his tricorne hat.

His hat was pulled low on his brow, and the dratted black mask covered his mouth and nose. All Beth could see in the dark was the glint of his eyes. She couldn't even make out their color. Why was he dressed like some highwayman from one of the historical romance novels she loved to read? She couldn't have interrupted a film shoot. After all, it's not like she'd seen any cameras, but maybe it was one of those unlicensed gorilla films? Cameras were so small these days she could have missed them. But then why had he left the set? They had ridden for a while. At least thirty minutes, probably longer. The ants she left behind in Sinclair House started crawling over her skin again. She was so lost.

"The rings, please." He straightened to his full height. The top of her head just reached his shoulders. Beth always felt short so it was hard to judge height accurately, but he was somewhere around six-foot, was her best guess, only slightly taller than Grant. Thinking of her husband caused her stomach to clench. She needed to get back to Cleitmuir, find Grant, and dear God, Laurel. She had to stop MacKenzie. Any port in the storm. Decision made, Beth pulled her hand from behind her back and tugged at her rings. She had to twist and pry to get them past her knuckle, but eventually the bands, one a plain white gold, and the other a simple one carat oval cut diamond dropped into her hand, and she closed her fist around them before meeting his eyes.

They seemed to laugh at her, probably just her imagination, or maybe not. He raised a gloved hand and opened it palm flat. With a grimace, Beth unclasped her fingers, held above his hand, and let her rings drop into his leather embrace.

With a nod, he slipped his hand into his coat pocket, depositing his ill-gotten gains somewhere in its dark depths. He took a step away from her and made a sweeping courtly bow.

"It has been my pleasure doing business with you. But alas, the hour has grown late and the weather worsens. Fare you well, my lady." He tipped his hat and walked to the head of his horse, taking the reins, and started walking away.

"Hey, wait! You can't leave me!" Beth called out to him and jogged to his side. For her efforts all she received was a disdainful glance, and then he lengthened his stride.

She kept pace. "What's your name?"

He snorted. "I think not, madam. Most unwise, at least on my behalf, and I do always look after myself, first."

"But—"

"If you must," he interrupted. "You can tell everyone you have met the Knightmare and survived."

"The Nightmare?" She laughed. "You're kidding, right?"

He tossed her what she suspected was a dirty look.

"I mean, why not use Mysterio, or better yet, Nightmask, if you're going all Marvel?" This was ridiculous. Maybe he was mentally unstable? After all, he was out in the woods in costume, but then again, he did just rob her, so who was crazier?

They reached a turn from the main path, and he led his horse onto a narrow off branch, forcing her to fall behind, since it was barely wide enough for the horse. Abruptly he stopped, and Beth slammed into his horse's hind end. Luckily the well-mannered equine didn't kick her. She quickly rebalanced herself and stared at the masked man who disappeared in the dark woods with his black clothing, only his eyes glinting like a cat's in the slim light available.

"I would not follow me if I were you," his voice dropped into a menacing octave.

"Really? How dramatic of you." Beth brushed her

wet hair out of her face. "If you haven't figured it out already, I'm lost, soaked, and tired. You're the only game in town."

He stayed silent for long enough, Beth wondered if he would even reply or just stand there staring at her until she took herself away.

"Look." Beth sighed. "I need your help." She swallowed her pride. "Please."

His glinting eyes disappeared, and he vanished into the dark. She corralled her panic. His horse was still here. He wouldn't leave without his horse, right? The cat's eyes returned and bore straight into her. A shiver coursed through her, which Beth blamed on the freezing cold rain and not fear. She was *not* afraid.

"I have helped you. More than I should have." His voice was as intimidating as ever.

"Well, help me some more." She copied his harsh tone. Stubborn was her middle name. She would not give up. "Let me come home with you, just so I can use your phone, then I promise I'll be out of your hair." She held her breath, hoping his gallant side would return.

"No."

"But—"

"No." He sighed. "Turn around and continue on the main path. It will take you to Tredford. The rest is up to you. Be gone."

This time she stared at him in silence. Was he telling the truth? Or just trying to get rid of her? Beth had never heard of Tredford, but then again, she'd never seen woods like these. Not even growing up in Wisconsin and certainly not in the far north of Scotland where she was presently living. And of course, the comic-con cosplay escapee wouldn't want her to know the whereabouts of his secret *lair*. Dear God, what was going on? She thought she was losing her mind.

Beth nodded, realizing she didn't have much choice. She wondered if he witnessed her capitulation or decided it didn't matter. Either way, he and his horse were disappearing into the night. With a frustrated sigh, she spun and walked back to the main road, if you could call the muddy dirt sinkhole a road. Pausing at the cross roads, she risked a look over her shoulder. There was nothing to see but darkness. Her erstwhile rescuer and his equine partner were gone. She contemplated following him, but tossed the idea aside. He was wearing weapons, two old-fashion looking pistols and a sword. Nut job. She was better off on her own.

Hoping he hadn't lied, she followed the path. Beth trudged on. She put her hand to the hole in her T-shirt and pressed hard, not even feeling a bruise anymore. Had she really been shot? She couldn't have, because she'd be dead instead of freezing cold, wet, and hiking in the middle of the night. Right? Maybe MacKenzie somehow dumped her in these woods? Or, was this all a dream? More like a nightmare. A smile tugged at her mouth, as the masked *highwayman* flashed across her mind. Yeah, nightmare was more likely. Wrapping her arms around herself for warmth, her sneaker-clad feet squelched in the heavy mud, leading to God knew where.

Chapter Six

Edmond Renweard drummed his fingers on the arm of the plush leather chair sitting next to the roaring fire. His courier was late, and he hoped it was only due to the storm. He clenched his hand in frustration, and he listened to the rain lashing against his polished glass windows. With a sharp exhale, he opened his hand and shook out the stiffness in his fingers, before reaching for the cut crystal tumbler, filled with imported French brandy, on the table beside him. He took a moment to savor its heady earthy aroma, before taking a sip. He needed those gems, one in particular. Edmond took a larger swallow, feeling the liquor burn down his throat. So help him, if Ashton didn't arrive soon, he would greatly regret it.

He placed his glass down on the side table and then removed his pocket watch from his vest, flipping the gold cover open. Three in the morning. More than two hours late. Edmond snapped it shut and let the watch fall from his hand. Secured by its chain, it landed on the chair beside him. He ran his hand over his smooth, shaved skull.

Little Anna. Asleep upstairs, but not safe. Time was running out for his little girl. There was not much left for him to try. Modern medicine had not helped, and as his desperation grew, he reached out to the far East and their heathen remedies. When those too failed in curing his little girl, he turned to mysticism and finally the dark arts of the occult. He spared no expense. The jewel Ashton couriered was his final hope.

Edmond lifted his glass and took another sip. He needed to protect the last of his family. He hadn't been able to save his wife or son when they had died of smallpox, but by his solemn vow, Anna would live. He would not lose her to this wasting illness, more devious than the pox, attacking her. He didn't care how he achieved his goal, as his past actions proved. With the aid of his trusted head-servant, Charles, they had crossed many forbidden lines, spared no one, in his search to heal his daughter. Having long lost faith in an unforgiving God, some might call him a monster now, but he thought of himself as a father who would protect his child at any cost.

A floorboard creaked in the hallway, drawing his attention. A moment later his faithful servant lurked in the entrance to Edmond's study.

"Yes, Charles?"

Clearing his throat first, Charles replied, "Mr. Ashton has arrived, sir. Shall I send him in?"

Over two hours late, he had better be shown in. "Yes, with all due haste."

"Very good, sir." Charles gave a slight bow before disappearing down the hallway.

In short order, booted feet trod the floorboards to his study. At the entrance, Oliver Ashton paused before stepping in.

Edmond gestured. "Come in. You're late." He didn't bother hiding the disgust in his voice.

Ashton entered and stopped before Edmond's

chair. The tall man pushed the black, wet strands of hair off his face and swallowed before meeting his gaze.

"The gems." Edmond held out his open hand.

Ashton swallowed once more. "Sir. Lord Renweard, I am truly sorry—"

"The next words," he glared up at Oliver, "had better be regarding the lateness of the hour."

"It's not my fault…"

Edmond placed his crystal tumbler down and rose slowly to his feet, while tucking his watch into a pocket. Ashton took a sudden step back. Though not tall, Edmond held a presence which intimidated. Still having to look up to meet Oliver's gaze, he was pleased with the fear now glistening in the brown depths of his eyes.

"Choose carefully your next words."

"It was the Knightmare! He was there on Woodfall Road. How did he know?" Ashton rattled out, the words tumbling upon each other.

"The Knightmare?"

"Yes! Not only did he know when and where we would be, but he asked for the jewels, specifically."

"So you shot him? Or cut him down with your sword?" Edmond began to circle Ashton, fully aware of the answer to his questions. When Edmond was hidden behind Ashton, he quickly palmed a decorative dagger off his desk.

"He had us dead to rights—"

"So you gave him the gems? You handed over all the jewels, including the Viper's Eye?" He walked into Ashton's view.

"I had to. There was nothing I could have done."

"You could have died trying to keep the gems,

could you not?" Edmond paced another circle around the distraught man.

"I'll find him—"

"When others have not? When it has been more than a year and this highwayman has eluded all who have sought to trap him?"

"He had a partner!" Ashton spat out. "I almost shot her."

"Her?"

"Yes! I thought she was a boy until she screamed," he declared. "I know I can find the Knightmare. I'll find him through her."

Edmond stopped his circular pace to stand in front of Ashton. "And pray, what did this woman look like?"

"She had long hair and was dressed like a boy, but strangely. Her clothes were odd."

"How, odd?"

"I don't know. It was dark. The rain had started. I do know she had light-colored hair. It is probably blonde," he rushed to add.

"Hmmm." Edmond placed a finger against his lips, tapping. "Mr. Ashton, you expect to catch the Knightmare, when no one else had, by finding a girl you can barely describe?"

"Sir…I…" Ashton looked down at his boots.

So disappointing. "Oliver, look at me."

Ashton lifted his head and looked into Edmond's eyes. He raised a hand and laid it gently upon Oliver's shoulder. "You have served me well in the past, but this failure I cannot overlook." He shook his head. "I'm sorry it has come to this."

Striking faster than a snake, Edmond clamped his hand tightly to Ashton's shoulder and raised the dagger he'd hidden in his other hand. He forced the larger man forward and onto the blade. Ashton's eyes bulged as Edmond drove the ornamental weapon between his ribs and upward, striking his heart, with purely brute strength. With a choked cough, blood leaked from Oliver's mouth while his warm blood seeped out around the dull blade in his chest and over Edmond's hand and arm, soaking the sleeve of his French linen shirt.

Tightening his hold on Ashton, Edmond watched the life leave the man's eyes. With a shove and grunt, he pulled away the blade, and the body fell to the floor with a dull thud. The blood dripped from the blade held in Edmond's hand onto the Oriental rug. The candlelight highlighted the glossy red, giving him pause. He'd just stabbed a man through the heart. Snuffing out his existence as quick as blowing out a piece of tinder. But Anna was his heart. He must get those jewels back.

Edmond stared at the mess at his feet. The Knightmare had picked the wrong man to rob. The highwayman's days were numbered. He would exact his revenge and retrieve his jewel. Anything for his little Anna.

Chapter Seven

Beth shivered as she slogged through the mud. Tredford had better appear around the next bend, or she would personally hunt down the crazy actor dude and kill him. The trees had thinned, which allowed the pelting rain to drench her. She was freezing. It felt like winter even though it was July. Her thin T-shirt afforded little comfort in the storm, clinging to her like a wet T-shirt. She longed for warmth. Looking down, she checked to see if her feet were still attached to her legs. They were so numb from the cold and mud she wasn't sure. Her teeth were chattering. Beth had to get out of this storm or she just might die of exposure. Stupid cosplay boy! Arrogant jerk! How dare he leave her out in the middle of nowhere during a freak cold storm.

The wind picked up and howled, carrying voices. No…wait. Not voices, but a voice. Someone was singing. She forced herself into a jog, about as fast as her tortured body could produce at the moment. As she rounded the corner, the view down the path was lit by a flickering glow. Sanctuary at last, or at least she hoped. She needed this nightmare to end.

Her numb feet carried her closer and through the storm, she could now make out the clang of metal on metal and a man's voice. He was singing and she knew the tune. Journey's "Don't Stop Believin'" was like a lure drawing her in, a bit of normality in the surrealism her life had become since Alex MacKenzie shot her.

Beth halted at the entrance to what her exhausted mind decided must be a blacksmith shop, like she'd once seen in Williamsburg, Virginia, and it included a raging forge. The blacksmith, whose back was currently turned toward her, was tall, well over six feet. He was dressed strangely for someone singing a Journey power ballad. Getting to the chorus, he belted out a strong baritone, which was such an odd, juxtaposition with his attire. *What the hell?* Had she stumbled into some reenactment town, like Colonial Williamsburg? But it was late…really late. Shouldn't the park be closed? Or was everyone here fanatic method actors? He had the clothing down pat. But at least he knew the century he was in. She always liked that song.

Reaching the end of the song, the blacksmith put down the sword he was working on and slowly turned around.

"Are you planning on lurking in my doorway, or would you like to come in out of the rain?"

Beth darted in and edged up to the flaming forge, holding out her frozen fingers to the hot blaze. She studied her second rescuer of the night—anyone who would let her thaw out after being frozen by the storm ranked as a hero in her book. He was handsome in an edgy way. His face was all sharp angles, as if it had been a block of clay and someone had taken a sharp knife to cut facial features. Crystal blue eyes gazed back at her, highlighted by pitch-black hair. His coloring reminded her of the ghost, Simon MacKay, who haunted her hotel. And of course, he towered over her, just as Simon had.

"Thank you. I think if I stayed outside a second longer I'd become an icicle."

He smiled. "You're most welcome. However, to truly warm up, you should remove your wet clothes."

Beth raised an eyebrow. As a pickup line, it had its directness.

"No ill intent implied," he said, as if reading her mind. "There are clothes in the corner behind the screen you can change into. Go." He made shooing gestures in the direction of the screen.

She gave him, then the fire, one last longing glance, but the idea of removing her soaked clothes was too much of a temptation. Beth started walking toward the corner. "You're not some perv, are you?"

He laughed. "And if I were, would I be confessing such a thing to you?"

"You have a point. Do you have a name?"

"You may call me Remy."

"I'm Beth." She went behind the screen and saw a small cot with a bundle of clothes lying on top. She picked up the first garment and shook it out. *What the hell?* It looked like a nightgown. Putting it aside, she grabbed the next item. It appeared to be a corset, and the other a dress and a skirt with cutouts. There were thick hose and fuzzy short boots. Apparently, she was to dress as a cast member in crazy re-enactment land. She sighed. No way in hell she was wearing a corset. Besides, what was he doing with woman's clothing?

"What's the deal?" Beth pulled off her wet T-shirt and decided her damp bra had to go as well. She started to peel off the wet denim, which was frustratingly hard. "What's with the costumes? Is it method-land, twenty-four seven?"

She heard Remy's deep chuckle. "Something like that," his reply reached her as she pulled the nightgown over her head. Plopping onto the bed, she yanked on the thick leggings. Yawning, Beth felt her face straining at the size of her yawn. Feet like icicles, she thrust them into the fuzzy boots, wiggling her toes inside the furry comfort. Another yawn escaped, and her eyelids drooped. God, she was exhausted. Beth glanced at the pillow beside her. It looked so inviting, but Remy, a complete stranger, was on the other side of the divider. What to do? Her eyelids closed of their own volition. Beth just needed a moment. Her head was on the pillow before she knew it.

****

Remiel appeared around the divider and smiled. On silent feet, he crossed the short space and crouched in front of Beth, who was sound asleep. Gently he removed the boots and lifted her legs to place them on the bed so she was lying more comfortably. Next, he stood and grabbed the folded blanket at the foot of the cot and covered her. Beth burrowed into the blanket and straw-ticked mattress with a satisfied exhale and slipped into a deep-seated slumber.

He studied her sleeping form a moment longer before bending and picking up her sodden clothing. Making sure he had everything, including her shoes, he quietly left the enclosure. Stopping in front of the forge, he stared intently at the raging fire until its flames shrank and the fire was banked to glowing warm embers. Satisfied there was no danger, he gave one last glance to the divider hiding his hope for humanity before walking out of the smithy. Embracing the stormy night, he unfurled wings of cobalt blue as a clap of thunder crashed overhead. Lifting off into the storm, Remiel disappeared.

Chapter Eight

Beth stretched and cataloged all her aching muscles, but her sore legs beat out the twinge in her right shoulder, as the cold seeped in through the coverlet. Rolling over to her side, she reached for Grant, her personal heating device. When her hand hit nothing but air, her eyes snapped open. This wasn't her bed, not her bedroom, or even her house. Reality crashed back in. She had to find a phone. Grant would be worried sick and had probably called everyone from the local police to Scotland Yard. How long had she slept?

Throwing off the blanket, Beth sprang to her feet. Quickly glancing around, she couldn't find her sneakers, jeans, bra, or T-shirt. So, with a futile sigh, she slipped her feet into the wool-lined boots. Next, she tugged the pale blue dress over her head, and smoothed the ankle length cloth down her body, and then tugged on the dark blue skirt over it. Beth grabbed the corset, and came out from behind the screen holding it before her.

"I am so not wearing this," she stated, while glaring at the offending piece of clothing. "Woman have fought long and hard not to be tortured by corsets, unless by choice. I don't care how many actors I insult, I'm not squeezing into this piece of medieval bondage."

Beth drew up short when she saw the empty smithy

and cold forge. Where the hell did he go? Clutching the bodice to her chest, she crossed the room to the entryway. She studied the muddy lane, heard the chirps of birds, and noticed the bright clear sky with white puffy clouds. The storm had passed. There was no one in sight. Her stomach growled. Blowing out a breath, which misted in the cold morning air, Beth made a choice. She shook out the dark blue and gray striped corset, took a moment to glare at it again before slipping her arms through sleeveless openings. Snatching at the long black cord, she started lacing the infernal contraption. There was no way she was tying it tight. She missed her bra, but the corset was better than nothing, since she couldn't let the girls go bouncing about unsupported. Beth tied it all off with a sloppy bow, then stepped out of the smithy. Turning left, she continued down the lane she traversed last night.

Rubbing her arms to generate heat, Beth wondered if she would ever be warm again. She desperately wanted a shower, and a toilet wouldn't be refused either. A toothbrush. Her stomach growled again. Food. Beth mentally added to her list. A phone. A transporter to zap her back home to Cleitmuir.

She rounded a bend, and the world changed, stopping Beth in her tracks. The trees disappeared, and a town lay magically spread out below her from her vantage on top of the hill. This must be the Tredford her erstwhile rescuer told her about. Glancing down, she was pleasantly surprised at its size. It was a right proper town—multiple streets and alleyways with businesses and residences. Someone down there must have a phone.

Beth was about to run down the muddy road when

her brain finally registered what her eyes had seen or not seen. *Oh, hell, no.* No cars. No satellite dishes. No electrical lines. No paved roads. It couldn't be. She saw plenty of people, horses, and even carriages. She shook her head and started downhill on the path leading to town, mentally praying this was Europe's version of a reenactment village and the participants weren't hard-core method actors.

Entering Tredford, Beth stayed to the wooden walkway running in front of the buildings and joined in the foot traffic. She kept her mouth shut and her eyes open. Not a single out of character actor, no one was on their cell phone talking or texting. Shivers marched up her spine. Beth had a sinking suspicion something was very wrong. The farther she walked into the heart of the city, the more she felt out of place. Odors assaulted her nose from unwashed humanity, rotting food, and passing one odiferous alleyway, the stench of urine. This wasn't right. Not even diehard actors would forgo bathing, and wasn't it unhealthy to leave food spoiling in the streets? Her stomach growled. How was it possible to be hungry with all these rancid smells accosting her?

Beth had walked the length of the main street and was almost back to where she started on the opposite boardwalk when an elaborately carved and painted sign caught her attention—a black bristling boar with tusks, carrying a red rose in its mouth. The scent of freshly baked bread wafted from the open door—quite the lure to her starving self. She didn't resist the temptation and entered the building. The interior was dim, lit by a few candles and a roaring fire in a central hearth. Various sized tables made from dark wood had benches or chairs around them. The wood plank flooring was a slightly darker stain then the furniture, and all showed loving care in their worn polished age. The fire drew her to the middle of the room where she held out her hands trying to thaw them out.

"Welcome, Miss, to the Boar and Rose," a thick English accent greeted her.

She turned toward the voice and saw what could only be described as a grizzled old man with a bushy full head of gray hair and matching beard with a face so wrinkled it reminded her of a Chinese Shar-Pei dog. He wasn't much taller than Beth. With his warm smile and a twinkle in his eyes, he resembled a shrunken Santa Claus.

"Would you be having a meal?" He broke into her musings. "Or are you here for the work listing?"

"Um." Beth's stomach let out a huge growl.

The man laughed. "It must be food. Right. Take a seat where you'd like." He gestured through the room. "As you see, we're not so busy at the moment."

Beth smiled and stood a little straighter. "I'm in a bit of a bind. I'm sorry to bother you, but I was wondering if I could use your phone? I really need to make a call."

His face scrunched up, at least she thought so through all the facial folds. "Young Miss, I don't understand. What is a phone?"

She sighed. "Look, I know you don't want to break character, but I'm in trouble. It's an emergency."

"I apologize. I wish I could help. Maybe if you described what a phone is, I'll be able to figure something out for you." He shook his head while holding his hands out by his side.

The man was really taking his role-playing to a whole new level. But Beth would play along if it got her a call. "You know, a phone. A device where you can communicate with another person long distance, instantly."

The tavern owner's eyes practically popped out of his face. "Well now, isn't that something? Maybe they might have a phone in London, but we're not so advanced here in Tredford."

Dear God, would he not stop? "How about a computer? Or a wire service?" Beth prayed there had to be something, somehow, to contact Grant.

"No," he shook his head. "Are you well? Perhaps you should sit down."

Frustrated, Beth's eyes burned with tears she refused to shed. There had to be an answer. The man *tsked* and walked over to her, witnessing her distress. He put an arm around her shoulders and guided her to a bench.

"Now, now." He patted her shoulder as he settled down next to her. "There's no need for tears. Tell me what ails you and I will do my best to help."

She sniffled and brushed a hand across her eyes. *Damn it*. She would not cry. "I need to get home. A friend of mine's in danger. I have to help her." Beth cringed as her voice cracked.

"Well now, where's your home, girl?"

"Scotland. Cleitmuir." Seeing his confusion, Beth clarified. "It's near Durness, Northern Scotland."

"Ah, you're a long way from home."

"Um, where exactly am I?"

He raised a single bushy eyebrow. "You don't know where you are?" The man studied her intently.

"You're in Tredford, northwest of York." He stared at her before adding, "England."

Holy crap! How in the world had she gotten here? The room spun, and Beth braced her hand on the table to steady herself. It didn't matter. It *doesn't* matter. All she had to do was get home. "What about a train, or even an airport. Is there one nearby?" She had no idea how she'd pay for a ticket with no money, but Beth didn't care. She'd figure it out.

He gave her another pitying look and a slight shake of his head. "Again, Miss, I don't understand your words, but if you're looking for transportation, the next coach to arrive heading north is in a fortnight."

Coach? Fortnight? Her anger rose to the front. "Enough!" She leapt to her feet to tower over the man. "Cut the crap. Drop the act. There are lives in danger."

He sat there, eyes wide in his wrinkly face, and gaped at her.

"Fine, I'll go somewhere else." She stomped off, but stopped just beside the door when a paper caught her eye. She reached for the oversize sheet as invisible ants began to march across her skin. The York Gazette was emblazoned across the top. Her eyes traveled downward to the date—January 15, 1795. It couldn't be. It was impossible. Her gaze was drawn out the door, the proof before her eyes. Somehow, she had traveled back in time. Beth wasn't surrounded by actors. She was the one who was lost and misplaced. Her vision tunneled to black, and she collapsed to the floor.

Chapter Nine

Kit rapped his knuckles against the wooden door of number 204. A creak of flooring behind the barrier was the only warning before the door opened a sliver's width. Eyes the color of expensive dark chocolate blinked back at him.

"Oh, it's you."

The door opened wider to admit him. Kit stepped into the room, his gaze searching the simple space, and found only a rumpled bed, wardrobe, and a single table with two chairs. He strode across the bare wood flooring and flung open the wardrobe, finding nothing inside except articles of female clothing. She sighed behind him, but he ignored her and continued his search. Next, he went to the water closet and made sure no one was hiding inside. Once he was assured they were alone, he paced back to the door and turned the key, locking them inside. Only then did he turn his attention to the woman in the room. He must have awakened her. She stood barefooted in her nightrail, her waist length, chestnut hair tantalizingly mussed, blinking those sinfully dark eyes at him.

"Ah, Sophie, my apologies. I shouldn't have arrived so early. Late night?"

She gave him a cheeky smile, then yawned. "It's always a late night, Christopher, as well you know."

Kit cringed knowing the use of his full name was

the chastisement he earned for waking her. Sophie sauntered across the small space to stand directly before him. She raised her hand and gently trailed a finger down his chest.

"However," she drawled. "Being woken by you, even at this hour, I can always forgive."

Sophie stepped closer, pressing her lush curves flush against him while entwining her arms around his neck. She tilted her face up in invitation for a kiss. Ever the gentleman, he obliged.

One of his hands gripped her waist, while the other dove into the soft strands of her hair to grasp the back of her head. He lowered his head and first pressed a soft kiss against her full lips. The chaste kiss didn't last. On a soft moan, Sophie opened for him, and he answered in kind, delving his tongue deep, tasting her as they dueled for control.

Kit's hand slipped from her waist to grasp her arse and lifted, pressing her closer to his hardening length. With a last swirl of her tongue, Sophie broke the kiss but stayed within his tight embrace.

"A very good morning to you, my Lord Locke," she greeted him, followed by a husky chuckle.

"You undo me, wench. You make me forget my manners." Kit teased her.

"Manners are highly over-rated, sirrah."

He gave a firm squeeze to her soft round butt cheek, before releasing her and taking a step back.

Sophie frowned then gave him her back as she took the few steps to the bed to reach down and take up a thin cotton wrap. Covering herself, she turned and plopped down on the bed.

"Seeing you don't want to play," she winked up at

him, "I assume there is more urgent business for you to be calling on me before the noon day meal?"

Grinning, Kit reached into his gentleman's coat pocket and withdrew the black velvet bag from his profitable adventure last night.

Sophie whooped and leapt to her feet, clapping. "You did it! You got the gems!"

"I did, indeed. They arrived exactly as you said they would."

She crossed the room and stood before him, hands clasped behind her back, her bare feet bouncing, eyes twinkling. "Ashton is a great bore, but he does like to brag, hoping it improves his performance in bed," she said.

"Well, my dear." Kit's free hand cupped Sophie's face. "You deserve a profit from your hard-earned labors." He felt a twinge of guilt from his inability to convince her to quit her trade. "Sophie—"

"No, Kit."

He dropped his hand and bowed his head.

"You know a girl's got to work."

"But you don't," he growled, before striding away from her, stopping at the lone window. His fingers toyed with the flimsy lace curtain as he stared down at the gem bag clutched in his other hand. Corralling his anger, he replied in a more reasonable tone. "You needn't sell yourself every night, Sophie." He looked up, trapping her gaze from across the room. "I am more than capable of providing for you...caring for you. If only you would let me."

She shook her head. With a saucy grin she asked, "Are you proposing? You want to marry me?"

Chill dread crashed through him as the shock of her

question lanced him. Marriage? *God, no.* He only wanted to protect her, set her feet on a better path. He was done caring about others. His emotions must have been splayed across his face because Sophie started laughing.

"That's quite enough," he muttered, which set her off all the more, causing her to gasp and send tears trickling down her face from her mirth. "Sophianna."

"Gad!" She slapped her hand against her thigh. "The look on your face! You might as well have been shot."

She crossed the room and patted him on his arm. "Oh, my lovely, handsome Christopher. I appreciate your concern, but I make my own way, as well you know. Now show me the gems."

Kit tugged at the leather drawstrings until the pouch was opened. He turned the bag over. She squealed in delight as the three gems, followed by a fourth larger jewel, tumbled into her palm, and she needed her second hand to keep them from falling to the floor.

"Oh, my precious baby Jesus." Sophie clutched the jewels closer to her chest before crossing to the bed to sit and toss her treasure against the off-yellow coverlet. Kit followed and joined her on the bed, the wood bracings creaking under his added weight as she separated and organized the treasure.

Three rough uncut gems of the traditional nature—one sapphire, one diamond, and one emerald—were all the size of a chicken's egg. But it was the fourth jewel, polished to a shinning glint and larger by twice the other jewels, that drew the eye.

This gem was a rare black opal. Held up to the

light, the translucent dark canvas of the stone held the reflections of much brighter colors in a play of fiery red, burnt orange, and deep violet.

Passing over the priceless rough gems to grasp the larger finished black stone, Sophie turned it over in her hand and studied it. "I can't believe you did it. The Viper's Eye. I've never seen anything like it."

Kit smiled. Neither had he. The unusual jewel had caught his attention as well, when studying his ill-gotten gains in the very early hours of this morning.

"It has a story," Sophie stated, as she fondled the precious gem.

"Do tell." Kit raised an eyebrow.

"The Viper's Eye comes from the far South, past Africa itself. It's supposed to contain a supernatural nature. It absorbs thoughts and feelings of people, and amplifies their emotions, and apparently provides protection to its wearer." She continued to stare raptly at the opal. "Ashton claimed it granted its owner great power and steals the souls of your enemies." Sophie finally looked up at him, eyes bright. "Do you think it's true?"

Kit doubted it. The more expensive and rare a jewel, the larger the myths were surrounding it. It was a way to increase an already priceless item. "No, my dear." He took the priceless gem from her and dropped it back into the velvet bag. "Wipe the covetous smile from your face. You can't keep it. It's to be sold with the rest." He scooped up the remaining gems, slipped them into the bag, and tied off the drawstrings, tight.

"But—"

"No. We've remained free by not being too greedy. It's not like you can wear it about town."

Kit rose. "Same routine, right, my sweet?"

She nodded, and Kit handed her the bag of gems. "There's a coach headed to York, I'll be on it tomorrow. I'm sure Feinstein or at least Geoffrey will be able to deal with these for a fair price in exchange. The usual, aye?" Sophie asked.

"Yes." He stepped forward and dropped a kiss on her head. "Let me know when you return. I do believe a celebration is required."

A sly smile curled up her mouth. "I do like how you...celebrate, my Lord Locke."

"Indeed." He gave her one last admiring, lingering gaze before turning on his booted heel to the door. He paused and said in a low voice, "be safe," before he left one of the few women he'd trust with such a prize.

Chapter Ten

Beth sat on a wooden stool, and stared out the third story window, her thoughts racing as she tried to make sense of everything that had happened to her. Was she really in the late eighteenth century? At the moment, too many instances pointed in this direction, but where was her scientific proof? Or could this still be a dream? But deep down she knew this wasn't a dream, and science for damn sure didn't know everything.

Trapped in a coma, set in motion from MacKenzie's shot? This last thought made her pause and review every detail. She remembered the pain and shock of being shot, falling to the floor as her legs failed her, Laurel's scream and then darkness, only to wake up in a forest outside of York, England over two hundred years in the past. Simon MacKay would be alive in this era; maybe he could help her? But then again, he wouldn't know her in this century. What the hell was she supposed to do if she wasn't stuck in a coma but actually traveled in time?

Her heart galloped faster, and her skin turned clammy. A full-blown panic attack was in progress, when a startled gasp escaped her, as her mind jogged a puzzle piece loose. Beth couldn't have time traveled. When she first arrived on the outskirts of Tredford, it was the song the blacksmith, Remy sang, which had drawn her in. "Don't Stop Believin'" by Journey hadn't been written yet, not until the early eighties. Therefore, since he was singing the song, unless he had futuristic premonitions, she couldn't be in the eighteenth century.

Beth leapt to her feet, grabbed her cloak, and ran across the small room Richard Landon, the owner of the Boar and Rose, had kindly given her, along with a job. And thankfully the other maid, although not happy, had given her a change of clothing as well as a cloak. Her provider of goods had agreed Beth could pay her after she got her first bit of coin. She took the stairs two at a time and burst into the common room.

"Now there, Miss Beth. Where are you going in such a hurry?"

She barely broke stride as she shouted over her shoulder. "Home! Thank you for your kindness."

"But—"

Beth didn't wait for his reply, but jogged out the door, and dodging the pedestrians on the walkway, managed to reach the path to the hill, which led to the smithy. She hit the road, ignoring the splattering mud and lengthened her stride, heading uphill, grateful she was in good shape between her workouts and horseback riding, in addition to moving heavy furniture in her decorating career. Cresting the hill, she headed for the blacksmith's, following the trail through the woods.

Pulling up as she reached the building, boots, leggings, and lower dress wet and caked with mud, Beth was huffing in front of the now closed set of wide doors. When she'd left earlier this morning, she hadn't bothered to shut them. Hope surged in her. She took a breath, held it to slow its panting rhythm as well as calm her. Releasing air in a long exhale, she raised her hand and knocked. She waited. Sighing, she rapped the door harder. When no one answered, Beth's patience reached its limit.

"Answer the damn door, Remy!"

She slammed her foot, once, twice, against the door. On the third time, the door opened with her kick. Not hesitating, she entered the smithy, finding it dark and the forge cold.

"Damn it, Remy, where are you? Answer me!"

She crossed the open workspace and peered behind the room's simple wood divider. He wasn't there either. Frustrated, she spun around, and with hands on her hips, she surveyed the empty shop. *Shit*. Beth needed the cagey blacksmith. He had the answers she needed, but by the looks of the room he hadn't been back since she woke up on his cot.

Beth paced the circumference of the room and swore under her breath when she found no clues to his whereabouts. She stepped out of the shop, closing the door behind her, and then stopped and stared blankly into the woods. What the hell was she supposed to do now? She had no money, no phone, and was stuck here with no answers. She needed a plan. And food, she still hadn't eaten.

With a heavy sigh, she started to retrace her muddy steps back to Tredford, but at a much slower pace, feet dragging as she contemplated her next course of action. She'd keep checking on Remy. The innkeeper of the Boar and Rose might know how to find him. But if the blacksmith was a washout, she would definitely need a Plan B.

In order for any plan to succeed, she needed money. Hopefully running out the door of the inn with no explanation, she still had a job. She would continue to stockpile her money while waiting the stinking fortnight, which was something like two weeks, right? When the northbound coach, which she was frantically hoping was an actual bus and not something drawn by horses, arrived she'd buy her ticket and head home. With an actual plan, Beth's spirits lifted and her confidence returned.

****

Beth sat across the table in the Boar and Rose from Mr. Landon and his cook, the very rotund and cheerful Scot, Mrs. Duncan. She held her breath, waiting for the next question. The scolding about her running out on her responsibilities had gone in one ear and out the other, and now she was sitting through an interrogation. All said, she managed to be contrite and keep her job. At least she thought so.

"So you've got no family? Not even on your husband's side, to take you in?" The kindly, weathered innkeeper asked.

She supposed Grant might have ancestors alive in this century, but it would be pretty useless since Grant hadn't been born yet. In fact, Beth wasn't technically even married yet. She shook her head, confused by the time paradoxes. She really hoped she was just in a coma.

"Och, lassie," Mrs. Duncan reached across the table and grasped her hand. "Dinna ye fash. It willa be fine."

Beth hid her humor at the cook's mistake of her headshake and decided on the spot to play up for more sympathy. Any port in the storm, if she got to keep her needed job.

"I don't know how it'll be fine." Beth tried to work

up a tear. "I have no one and…I was robbed." She gave a loud sniff. "I don't even have any money."

"Oh my dear!" The cook leapt to her feet and rounded the table to envelope Beth into a bear hug, smothering her in her large bosom. She broke at the sudden unasked-for comfort and she shook, as an uneasy, unhinged laugh escaped. Mrs. Duncan, mistaking her shudders for tears, patted her back in comfort.

No matter how nice it was to held, Beth needing air, pushed herself away from the kind cook. "It was horrible. I had to walk to Tredford, and I was out later than expected. He just stepped out of the darkness." A chill chased through her, and she couldn't stop the quiver chasing through her at the thought of the masked man who both saved and robbed her. His cultured deep tones still ran through her mind, as his touch on her body seemed imprinted on her.

"He didn't hurt you, did he?" Mr. Landon looked outrage.

"No. No, he was actually sort of a gentleman, even sounded like one."

Both the innkeeper and cook gasped in unison. It was like she shocked them by saying some unexpected curse. "Is something wrong?"

"Och, my lassie!" The cook grabbed her hand again. "You are lucky to be alive!"

"Excuse me?"

"Now, Mrs. Duncan, there's no need to scare the girl. The Knightmare has never killed anyone. The stories only mention him injuring those who fought him, no deaths."

"That we know of! He's been a terror in this area

for almost a year. Who knows what evil that devil has done." Mrs. Duncan crossed herself.

Beth looked between Landon and Mrs. Duncan. Bullseye. "The Nightmare?" Beth tried not to smile at the lamest code name ever. "Is that what he's called? I thought he was joking—"

"Never! The Knightmare is almost legend in these parts." Mrs. Duncan shuddered. "Was he dressed all in black? Standing tall as a giant, with glowing eyes?" The cook asked in a breathless voice.

Well, he was certainly taller than Beth, but most men were, but a giant, naw, not so much. No glowing eyes either, though they did seem to glint and laugh at her. "He was dressed darker than night itself," she exclaimed.

"We should report this to the Magistrate, or at least to Constable Jeffries," Landon said.

"Do you really think so?" Beth asked. "I'd love my money and rings returned, but if he hasn't been caught in a year, what good will it do?" She gave another loud sniff. "I just want to put it all behind me."

"Och, lassie, you're safe now."

"Am I?"

"Aye. Isn't that correct, Richard?" The cook stared down her employer.

The innkeeper sighed. "You've the experience and we are short-handed. I'll give you the work and even let you keep the room, if you'll start immediately, and no more running away."

Score! She'd managed to keep her job and a roof over her head. Beth smiled. "Yes. Yes, of course. Thank you so much."

Mr. Landon stood. "Then it's settled. Go freshen

up and you can start tonight."

Clearly dismissed, Beth stood and nodded. She walked to the common room's stairs and started upward. If she met the roguish highwayman again, she'd have to thank him for aiding her in a roundabout way in getting her a job and a room. It seemed he'd saved her again.

Chapter Eleven

"Papa!" Anna dropped the book she was reading when she spotted Edmond standing in the doorway. When she scooted to the edge of the window seat to scramble to her feet, he held up a hand to stop her. As he crossed the room, he smiled. Today was one of Anna's good days. She was out of bed, out of her nightrail, and into a bright cheerful dress. Looking at her, he regretted he had to leave her. Her *good* days were farther between than her sick days.

Edmond's chest constricted with his heartache. Anna was his everything. He had lost so much already. Nature would not take its course. He forbid it. He took a seat beside her and gathered her into his arms as she flung herself at him.

"Oh, Papa! You are home! I have missed you so!"

He held her tight, relishing in her vigor and love. The past months had been hard. His Anna, asleep, so motionless, as if dead already. She had rarely been awake and so weak when she was. Trying to feed her to make sure her body was nourished was a challenge. It was days like today, he was grateful, once again he could hold his daughter, alive, bright-eyed, and communicating.

"My little poppy, I have been home. It is you who while away the hours asleep." He kissed the top of her head. "I have good news for you."

"No, Papa, no!" Anna pushed herself out of his arms to glare up at him. "You promised. You made a promise to me. No more!"

"Now, Anna—"

"No!" She tried to jump down and run, but Edmond caught her arm. It sadly didn't take much strength to stop her, even at her grown age of four and ten. She was unnaturally pale; her dress did not hide her weight loss and frailty. His little girl was disappearing before his eyes.

"Listen to me, Anna. I know I promised I wouldn't search out any more cures or medicines, but this time I have found the answer."

"Papa." Her eyes were filled with wisdom beyond her age. "I am dying. There is no answer."

"I will not let you die, little poppy. I am your father and will protect you," he admonished. "I must take a trip." It hurt his heart seeing her brown eyes well with tears. Edmond reached out and tucked a piece of her hair behind her ear, loose from her crooked ponytail. "It will be a short trip to York. I won't be gone long."

Anna sniffled, but her gaze never left his. "But Papa, I might be asleep when you return. We never know how long I sleep. You must stay while I'm well. Delay your trip. What happens if you leave, and I go to sleep to never wake up again?" Her mournful plea was barely a whisper. He had to lean closer to hear. The remaining pieces of his heart shattered. A breath-stealing pain burned his chest and filled the place where his heart once resided.

Edmond gathered his precious girl into his arms once again. "Then you must work hard to stay awake until I return."

"But, Papa, I'd rather spend time with you. Please don't leave."

"I must, child. All will be well. Better than well. You shall see." He kissed her honey-brown hair once more.

"Stay," she pleaded. "Every time you go away and return, you're different. Colder. I am losing you, Papa. If you go, I may not recognize you when you return."

"Hush, little poppy. I am still your papa, the same as always."

"No, no," she trembled in his arms. Anna buried her face into his chest and sobbed. "I don't want you to leave."

He stroked her hair, trying to comfort her, searching for words to ease her fears. How to convey this time, he had the answer? How to let her know, he'd gone beyond the mortal world and found a supernatural cure without scaring her?

"Sir?" Charles said from the doorway.

Edmond looked toward the open door and frowned at the interruption.

"I'm sorry to intrude, but your luggage is loaded and the carriage awaits. You requested to be notified when everything has been prepared."

"Very good. I'll be there momentarily." Anna clung to him, trying to bury herself deeper into him. Goodbyes with Anna were never an easy thing.

"I'll advise the coachman." The butler left as quietly as he arrived.

"Hush, my darling. I will return and you will be well again." He eased her away from his body, but didn't let go of her thin, delicate arms. "You must be strong, little poppy. Promise me."

"I will try, Papa."

He leaned forward and pressed a kiss to her forehead, then tapped her nose lightly with his fingertip. "That's my strong, brave girl." He stood and stared down proudly at his daughter, who had the strength and courage of ten knights. "I shall return before you know it. I love you, poppy."

"I love you too, Papa."

Edmond gave his daughter a genuine smile before turning and crossing the room. A weight lifted from his shoulders, and his steps were lighter. He would heal Anna and what was left of his small family would be whole again. Continuing down the hallway, he reached the grand stairway where the ghosts from his past lingered. He had been so helpless when Catherine and Edmond Jr. had slipped through his fingers, both passing quickly from the smallpox. His son was stricken first, then his wife, who had never left his bedside. The pox was horrible enough, but at least it was tangible, a fever to fight, an illness to combat, but Anna's wasting disease was more insidious, like a phantom your fingers always passed through, nothing solid to grasp. All the physicians and apothecaries were useless in all their knowledge, none able to help his little girl, but now he had the answer. His soul may be damned to hell for practicing dark magic, but God had abandoned him, his desperate prayers left unanswered. He would happily be consigned to the deepest pits of damnation, and worship at the feet of Satan himself if his little girl would be saved.

He owed his trusted manservant everything. It was Charles who had learned of the Viper's Eye. Edmond had been past all hope until this last chance was presented. It had to work. He couldn't lose Anna. He would not. Edmond quickened his steps and focused on his mission.

Reaching the entranceway, Charles stood holding out Edmond's greatcoat. He slipped his left arm through the sleeve while the butler stepped behind and offered the right. Next came the scarf he wrapped around his neck, stuffing the trailing ends into the front of his coat. Charles handed him a pair of soft deerskin gloves, which he put on as his butler opened and held the door.

Edmond strode down the steps and crossed the gravel drive. As he approached the coach, a nameless servant held open the carriage door. He climbed the steps and took a seat on the forward-facing plush cushioned bench. The servant removed the steps and closed the door. The tightly sprung carriage barely moved as the servant climbed onto the outside rear of the carriage. There was a slight jerk as the four horses hit the weight of their burden and began to pull it forward. In short order, they were trotting up the drive.

He settled back in his seat, getting comfortable against the over-stuffed embroidered velvet cushions. It would take most of the day to reach York, since the storm last night had left the roads rutted and muddy. Grim satisfaction filled his mind. The thief would have just as many difficulties traveling as he did.

After a night's contemplation—Edmond had been way too angry to sleep even after killing Ashton—he had come to the conclusion the Viper's Eye would be heading to York. There were two possibilities for the erstwhile thief. The first was to do nothing and hold onto the jewel. Edmond didn't think the clever highwayman would keep the jewel. The longer he held onto it, the more chance he might be caught with it. Second, he could convert his spoils now, before the heist was made public. That left two paths for the thief to take next. He could sell the jewel in either London or York. London would be the better choice, since it afforded more opportunities. However, the distance required to travel would be longer and more risky. There were many places to be ambushed along the route to London. He smiled. It would be a certain type of justice for the thief to become the victim. However, the Knightmare appeared too canny for this to happen, which left York.

Upon his arrival in York, Edmond planned to send out queries to his contacts regarding his interest in purchasing some uncommon jewels, a gift he would like to make to his nonexistent mistress. There would be no doubt when the Viper's Eye hit the market. Then it would be a simple matter to track the thief and take the jewel. The Knightmare needed to die for putting Anna's life at risk. No one crossed Edmond.

Chapter Twelve

Kit stared at the empty room. He had to pick the lock when Sophie didn't open the door. It had been almost a week since he had last seen or heard from her, although that was not particularly unusual. It was possible their normal contacts couldn't handle the gems and Sophie needed to improvise. If that were the case, she would have sent word with one of the boys they used from time to time. There had been no messages.

Another possibility—she'd run, hoping to keep the jewels or the profit for herself, which was why he was currently standing in her room. *Trust no one*. Kit strode across the floor and flung open her wardrobe. He fingered through the day dresses and evening gowns, but to his best recollection, everything was there minus a few travel dresses, which should be gone as well as…Kit squatted and tapped the wardrobe's floorboards until he found the loose one. Lifting it, the cubbyhole was empty. Sophie had taken her usual disguise as well. He closed the doors.

Next, he went to the foot of her bed and knelt. Sophie didn't realize he knew where her most prized possessions were kept, but he wouldn't be much of a thief if he couldn't puzzle out where people hid their treasures. Once again, he rapped his knuckles on the floorboards directly under the bed. On the third knock the wood gave off a dull sound, and he smiled. With his fingers, he felt around the edge of the board until he found a slight give. With a bit more leverage the wooden slat lifted away from the floor revealing a hollowed-out section between the floor and the ceiling of the room below. He reached inside and lifted a polished wooden box out of its hidden refuge.

Setting the box on the bed before him, he rose and reached inside his coat for his lock picks. It was only a moment's work to open the catch. He flipped the latch and opened the lid. Inside held Sophie's treasure—necklaces, rings, bracelets, and earbobs, all set with precious gems given by admirers, and even some from him. There were also stacks of bank notes and coins. It was more than enough capital to help set up Sophie with a new life.

Chills chased up his spine. If she'd fled, Sophie would have taken her much valued and hard-earned savings, despite the quality of jewels Kit had stolen. It appeared she hadn't double-crossed him. What had happened to her? He frowned as he closed the lid, locked the box, and replaced it in its hidden cubby.

He stood, taking a moment to study the simple room once more. There was nothing here to help him. Kit let himself out of the room, making sure the door was locked before leaving the boarding house. He may need to travel to York in order to track her.

Chapter Thirteen

The Viper's Eye sparkled like its namesake in the sunlight, shining through the window at the Royal Lion Inn. Such a beautiful gem, beautiful and deadly for those who knew its secrets.

Edmond tore his eyes away from his long-coveted treasure to glance across the room to the harlot tied and gagged on the bed, a bit battered and bruised, definitely the worse for wear. A smile turned up the corners of his mouth. Although he left the day after the jewel was taken, it had been quite an effort to find out who had his property and where they were staying. Finally, he had worked the truth from the whore. She'd been astonishingly resilient, but he had both patience and muscle, and his dedicated efforts finally broke her. He now had confirmation the Knightmare had given the jewel for her to sell. What he couldn't get was the name of the highwayman or his description. He had beaten and tortured the whore to near death, and yet she wouldn't give the man up. He'd wasted too much time trying to discover the Knightmare's identity. Anna had waited too long already. He'd find the Knightmare on his own. After all, he couldn't kill the harlot yet. He needed her alive. The Viper's Eye was now his, but Edmond needed a test run to make sure his plans ran smoothly, and there was no danger to his Anna. He would prime the jewel on the whore and use the power on himself.

Edmond wouldn't endanger his daughter's life any more than it already was. The jewel was reputed to have mystical healing powers, but at a cost. He needed to make sure the cost wasn't to his little girl. Sacrificing his own life was a gamble he was willing to take, in order to prove the gem's abilities and make sure it was safe. Hopefully he wouldn't die in the experiment. He cringed at the idea of Anna being left all on her own, but at least she would still be alive with the time allotted before her illness claimed her. Charles would care for her. Yet deep down, Edmond knew the Viper's Eye was real and would work. It was his dark faith. It was time to prove his theory.

Closing his fingers tightly around the gem, he crossed the few strides to stand beside the bed. He stared down into the face of the whore, whose eyes were dilated wide, fear etched across her face. Pathetic mewling whimpers escaped the gag, as she began to shake her head back and forth, and tug weakly at her restraints. It mattered not. His little girl would be saved and have the long life which should be granted her. This tainted woman didn't deserve to live. Her life would gain meaning in her sacrifice. This whole venture had taken too long. Almost a week had passed since he left his daughter's side. He needed to return to her quickly.

Edmond ignored the thrashing harlot and straightened his arm so it extended over the woman's chest. He turned his palm upward and uncurled his fingers so the gem rested in his hand above the woman's heart. According to the scroll, intent and the strength of his will were of the utmost importance, as well as skin contact.

He studied the jewel in the palm of his ungloved hand. It wanted him to use it. It called to him. He smiled. Soon, Anna would be whole and the little girl she was meant to be. He took a deep breath, inhaled and held it, letting the air infuse him with comfort and well-being. Slowly he released it and let his eyes close, so he could better concentrate.

"Astaroth, *ego obsident vos*, Astaroth *exaudi me*, Astaroth, I beseech you. Hear me." Edmond began the incantation, his voice pitched low, but power surged through him with each word. "*Virtute tua te invoco.* By your power, I invoke thee. *Mea voluntate ego te invitem. Potes me animam tuam.* By my will, I invite you. Your power to me, my soul to yours." The gem warmed against his skin, and his confidence grew. "Astaroth, *datis tuis libenter recipio, quod optas, gratis date.* Astaroth, what you grant, I freely accept. What you desire, I freely give."

Edmond took another deep breath. "*Infundere tua receptaculum, dona mihi tua virtute et studio.* Infuse your vessel with your power and grant me my desire." His eyes flashed open, fixated on the now glowing jewel pulsing in time with his heartbeat, rich colors of red, orange, and purple swirled within its dark translucence. He grinned. Anna would live! With his free hand, he ripped the whore's bodice open, exposing her ample breasts. The woman tried to scream, but the gag only muffled her cries. Edmond flipped his hand and pressed the Viper's Eye against the harlot's chest, directly above her heart. She let out another smothered scream.

"*Sum offeramus hostiam huius mulieris animulus.* I

offer in sacrifice this woman's heart." He pressed the jewel harder against her skin, and her back arched upward as if being drawn into the opal. When she fell back to the mattress, he lifted the jewel and quickly pressed it to her forehead as the whore violently shook and continued to scream. He pushed harder, trapping and stilling her motion. Their gazes met, and he witnessed her terror. Edmond felt nothing for her plight. She was the dirt beneath Anna's feet. Exhilaration filled him.

"*Sum offeramus hostiam huius mulieris mens*. I offer in sacrifice this woman's mind." He felt a jolt beneath his hand, and the jewel became too hot to hold, but he willed himself past the pain and pressed into the heat. The harlot went limp, and her eyes closed. He lifted the Viper's Eye, cupping it in both hands, to hold close before him.

"Astaroth, *tuum fiat voluntas tua*. Astaroth, your will be done." Without thought and holding to his deep belief, he pressed the hotly glowing jewel to his own forehead. Power jolted through him, all his muscles went ridged, stretching him taut, holding him in place. His body quivered as his muscles convulsed, but the jewel froze him in place as its power coursed through every inch of his cells. Abruptly the Viper's Eye released him. His arms weak, the jewel fell from his hand to land on the floor. His muscles turned liquid and darkness over took him as he collapsed.

****

Edmond's eyes fluttered open as he lay on the wooden floor, the Viper's Eye inches from his face. The fiery colors still danced within the dark depth, but he felt no heat radiating when he forced the overly relaxed muscles of his arm to move in order to scoop the gem into his hand.

Edmond

He clutched it tight to his chest, as he heard his name whispered in his mind. He took a moment to assess himself as he lay curled upon the floor. Had it worked? How did he feel? Relaxed. Invigorated. Renewed. A smile curled up his mouth. Slowly he straightened and rolled to a kneeling position. There was no pain. Amazed, he felt wonderful. Ever since a riding accident in his youth his knees had given him problems. With his current age, he hadn't been able to kneel comfortably in the last two years. Climbing up and down stairs also troubled him, but he knew, deep down it wouldn't be a problem anymore. He sprang to his feet and raised the jewel to his lips and gave it a reverent kiss. It was truly a miracle.

He crossed the room to the standing mirror to study himself. He edged closer to examine his face. The crow lines at the corner of his eyes were gone and replaced with smooth skin. The darkened age spots on his bald scalp, gone. Edmond leaned back. He felt stronger, leaner, and healthier. He couldn't wait to try the jewel on his Anna.

A muffled moan drew his attention away from his self-examination, and he glanced over his shoulder to the whore tied in the bed. Apparently, she still lived. He slipped the Viper's Eye safely into his vest's pocket and crossed the room back to the bedside. Yes, the whore lived, but for how long, he did not know. She appeared shrunken into herself, her full breasts withered, ribs, and shoulder bones now protruded like a gangly skeleton. He shifted his focus to her face. Reaching, he tore off her gag. Her natural ruby lips were now cracked and gray. Her cheekbones stuck out sharply as her face appeared to have fallen away. Her once silken chestnut hair lay brittle and coarse. The whore's eyes fluttered open. Edmond stumbled backward, her dark brown eyes were no more. His gaze locked on milky white orbs, staring blankly back at him.

Chapter Fourteen

Kit stepped into the road, which now consisted of frozen mud. This was the coldest January he could recall. He dodged a carriage and slipped and slid across to the far side of the street. Paralleling the buildings, his boots clapped along the wooden boardwalk while his mind was lost in thought. His breath misted into the early afternoon air on his frustrated sigh. Blast this weather and blast his uncertainty. He was a man of action. This waiting was woman's work and not for him.

He drew up short as the smell of fresh baked bread filtered past the prevalent city smells. Perhaps some food and drink would set him to rights. Decision made, he entered the Boar and Rose and took a seat at an empty table in the corner with his back to the wall. It would be warmer by the central fire, but he felt too exposed. He may be reckless, but why take the unnecessary risk? He brooded while staring into the distant fire, his instincts warning him all was not well. Saddling Dante and riding for York to search for Sophie was more than a need, almost an obsession, which wasn't good. Mistakes occurred when all thoughts fled your mind but one.

"May I get you something, sir?"

Startled, he glanced up and saw a barmaid standing next to his table looking expectantly at him. *Bloody hell*. Obsession wasn't good. He had been so lost in thought he hadn't noticed the barmaid approaching. He shouldn't have been surprised by her appearance. Disgusted with himself, he mentally slapped himself and gave the girl a winning smile.

"You're new. Are you on the menu, luv?"

The girl frowned, her blue gaze snapping at him. "No," she placed her fisted hands on her hips. "Do you want some food or drink or are you wasting my time?"

Recognition struck him. The cadence and accent, a familiar ring. It took all his hard-earned acting ability to not react. It was *her*. The woman from the woods, the one in the strange clothing he helped and then robbed. He'd recognized the look of disgust anywhere, no matter if it was dark and raining. His smile turned into a grin. He thanked the hidden spirits he'd used an upper crust accent when being the Knightmare. She shouldn't recognize his voice as he had hers.

"Ale, some bread if it's fresh and what ever stew is in the pot."

"Lamb with potatoes and vegetables."

He nodded, and the girl spun on her boots crossing the room, then entered the kitchen. Interesting and interesting. What was the girl doing working the common room of an inn? She claimed to be married. Kit highly doubted the old man running this place had landed himself the fiery female. Had she lied to him? He was pretty good at sniffing out falsehoods, but he had been distracted by her generous curves and unusual speech. He remembered her alluring scent, when he whispered in her ear, something soft and compelling, lightly floral, yet fresh. Kit also remembered the feel of her pressed against him. His hand twitched in

74

remembrance of the curve of her hip, the swell of her breast. The women in his life never left much of an impression on him; they were a romp to pass the time, but this one…she had left a mark none to date had. A fetching lass, indeed.

The bang of the kitchen door drew his attention as the barmaid backed through, displaying her lovely round rear. With deft footwork she turned, holding the laden tray up high with one hand as she marched her way across the floor to arrive at his table. She lowered and balanced the tray carefully, and with her free hand, grabbed the tanker of ale. With an economy of motion, she banged down the ale, which sloshed its liquid over the rim.

"Ale." Her voice was laced with anger or possibly sarcasm. Next, she plunked down his other requested items, each punctuated with a hardy thud and vocal identifier. "Stew. Bread."

She stood at his tableside, with both hands grasping her tray, and glared at him as if daring him to say something. He was never one to deny a lady anything.

"Are you sure you won't join me, luv?" He gave her body a full and promising perusal, lingering on her breasts before meeting her icy blue gaze. Kit raised an eyebrow in inquiry.

Her exhaled breath was a huff of disgust. "In your dreams."

Ah, there it was again. Her strange phrases. What an intriguing puzzle the lass was. "A name at least, luv? Something I can bring with me to warm me on this chilly day."

He managed to not smile or laugh at her indignant look of outrage. But then her storm cloud expression slipped away as if blown by a tantalizing summer breeze. She tossed him a saucy smile, which brightened her face as a rainbow decorates the clear skies after a storm, the same clear blue in her sparkling eyes.

"You may address me as my Lady."

With her cheeky reply, she spun and sauntered back across the floor to the bar, affording him with another lovely view. My Lady, indeed.

Chapter Fifteen

Beth shot one last glare across the room to the guy who was vigorously digging into his food, and went back to wiping the bar's countertop with a damp rag. Apparently waitresses across time, shared one thing in common—rude, asshat men. If only she was paid a dollar for each time she was hit upon or had her butt cheek pinched or slapped, she'd be well on her way to being a millionaire. Waitressing sucked. She'd gone to college and earned a degree so she'd never have to work tables ever again.

She longed for home. Beth wanted to be held in her husband's arms and comforted. She wanted Laurel to be safe. She wanted everything to return to normal. No more peeing in pots, and up before dawn. She wanted a real toothbrush, an actual bra, and modern plumbing. Remy needed to get his blacksmith's ass back here so could finally know what the hell was going on.

Slapping the rag on the bar, Beth closed her eyes and took a deep breath. She would get home. Continuing patience was a necessary fact while trying to stay optimistic, so she didn't become insane. She wasn't a quitter. There was a way out of her current situation. Finding the solution might be tricky, but she would persevere. Beth solved her own problems. No hero needed; she'd rescue herself.

She surveyed the room once more, quickly noting

no new customers, and the existing ones were fed and watered at the moment. She sighed. She really hated waitressing, her feet ached, and it was only early afternoon. Her stomach growled, reminding Beth it had been a while since breakfast. With the room attended to, she slipped around the bar and headed for the kitchen.

Pushing through the door, the aromas of surprisingly good, but simple fare caressed her nostrils, and her stomach growled again in response.

"Och, Miss Beth. Sit down. I'll fix you up a plate," the matronly cook of the Boar and Rose greeted her.

"I won't fight you on it," Beth replied, plunking down on a stool next to a raised wooden counter and wiping her forearm across her sweaty forehead.

Mrs. Duncan chuckled. "Ye say the most amazing things, lass."

Beth nodded in acknowledgement. She'd been trying to stop with the twenty-first century phrases, but old habits died hard. What a hot sweaty mess she was when it was so startling cold outside. Beth missed July, her summer in Scotland. It was so not fair to lose almost six months of her life and head straight into January with what felt like the coldest winter in history. Well, the coldest winter since 1795, if she was supposed to believe the year she was currently stranded in. How did this happen?

She glanced guiltily over her shoulder at the kitchen door. No one was covering the common room, but damn- she was tired. Once again, Mrs. Duncan read her mind.

"Never ye mind, lass." She placed a bowl of stew and bread on the counter next to Beth. "Ye're a verra hard worker. Young Claire can stand to cover for ye."

Mrs. Duncan straightened her considerable girth, and inhaled a deep breath before bellowing up the back servants' stairs. "Miss Claire, get ye down here this instant."

The command was answered with silence. Beth suppressed a grimace by stuffing a piece of piping hot fresh, bread, straight out of the oven, into her mouth. The cook was right. Claire, the Innkeeper's daughter, was a slacker, no ifs, ands, or buts about it.

"Claire! Now ye wee scunner. Nay *leisguel.*"

When Mrs. Duncan took to the Gaelic, everyone knew she meant business. Even Claire. A door slammed upstairs, followed by stomping feet. Claire appeared at the top of the stairs, but paused as she met the formidable cook's glare before trudging down the steps.

"What?" The sullen question announced by teenagers across time, was uttered by Claire the moment she entered the kitchen.

"Get ye apron, lass. It's well past time ye work the common room."

"But—" Claire shot Beth an angry glare. "She's on floor."

"Nay, lass. Ye both were to be working." Mrs. Duncan gave Claire the once-over. "Since you left her to do both jobs, ye can now trade places."

"Father—"

"Will agree with me, young miss. Now out with ye." She shooed Claire to the door while handing her an apron.

Beth watched the door close behind Claire, relieved at Mrs. Duncan's magic. She supposed the hierarchy of great chef versus lowly newly hired barmaid induced Claire to behave. No matter how Beth tried to handle the young girl, all her results led to naught. She'd finally given up and just worked, figuring Karma would catch up to Claire eventually.

"Eat up, Miss Beth. You haven't touched your stew. Is it not to ye liking?" The cook broke into Beth's internal musings.

"Of course! You're an amazing cook. My mind was only wandering." Beth quickly took a spoonful of lamb and gravy. It truly was heavenly.

"Och, ye worry too much." With a comforting pat to Beth's shoulder, Mrs. Duncan went back to her domain of kneading and pounding dough.

Beth went quietly back to eating. Hopefully, she'd earned enough money to catch the northbound coach when the fortnight was over, but what she really yearned for was the reappearance of the wily blacksmith. She wanted to interrogate him before she headed home.

The normal kitchen sounds were interrupted as Innkeeper Landon burst into the room wearing a wide grin.

"Miss Beth, there you are!" The jolly fake Santa Claus rushed over to her side. "He's back! The blacksmith is in his shop. I know you were awaiting him."

"What?" She leapt to her feet. "Now? He's there right now?"

"That he is."

"Oh my God!" Beth threw her arms around Landon in a fierce hug, before she broke away, and tore off her apron. "I gotta go." Without a backward glance, she dashed out of the kitchen door and ran.

Chapter Sixteen

Beth burst through the open smithy doors. "Where the hell have you been?" She shouted over the clang of metal on metal. Hands on hips, she glared at the blacksmith. Her foot tapped as he continued to ply his trade, ignoring her. There was no way, after waiting almost a week, she would be pushed aside and disregarded. One thing she never was—was easily ignored. She was the life of the party, the prankster, the outgoing adventurer, not some wilting wallflower passed over.

She strode into the smithy's view, dangerously close to the molten-hot glowing metal he was hammering out. He met her angry gaze with a raised eyebrow, before returning focus to his work. *Oh no he didn't.*

"No song, today? Why don't you ditch the eighties tune for something more twenty-first century? Maybe something from Taylor Swift or Imagine Dragons?" Beth took a step closer. "You can't ignore me forever, and I'm not going away until you speak to me. I want answers."

Remy slammed the hammer down on the horseshoe he was forming. He closed his eyes and sighed, hesitating. In the next instance, they snapped open, and his winter gaze locked with hers. Beth shivered at his intense crystalline blue stare.

"Are you sure? You might not like what you hear." His question was almost lost in the hiss of steam when he took up tongs and dunked the white-hot shoe into a bucket of water. He placed the cooled horseshoe back on the anvil and matched gazes with her again, waiting for her to reply.

Of course she wanted answers, but his look and the way he asked her gave her pause. Deep down, Beth knew something big had happened, and finding out the truth might change her forever, but she was practical. She'd handle whatever the universe threw at her. Roll with the punches. Beth gave him a nod and waited to see what was in store for her.

"Very well." He untied the leather apron protecting his clothes and placed it aside on a nearby stool. "There is much to be told and privacy will be needed." Remy walked to the forge and gave her a quick smile before staring into the flames.

Beth gasped as the fire quickly collapsed upon itself, shrank, and became nothing more than glowing coal embers.

"What the hell?" She froze. Did she just see him quench the forge by only looking at it? How was it even possible?

Remy chuckled. "Actually, quite the opposite." He closed the metal doors over the top of the furnace, snuffing out the rest of the heat. He crossed the room and slid one of the smithy's doors closed, and went for the next large door, and started to slide it. Looking over his shoulder, he met her gaze. "If you still want answers, follow me."

Startled into action, Beth quickly followed him out the door, which he promptly closed after she passed through. A short distance away, he led her across the road onto a path cutting deep into the forest. She was stunned into silence and needed to jog to keep up with his long-legged stride. Everything was topsy-turvy, from being shot and transported *possibly* through time, to a now magical blacksmith. When had her life become so crazy? She needed to sell the rights to her life story, because right now it would make for one hell of a fantasy film.

Beth kept silent, needing her breath in order to run in a dress and sheepskin boots. She longed for her sneakers. Another bone to pick with the frustrating smithy: she wanted her clothes back. Hell, she wanted her life back. Were they ever going to get to this *place of privacy*? Just as her patience ran out, the path opened into a peaceful clearing with the requisite babbling brook, brown frost-challenged moss, and dead leaves covering the ground. It even had a convenient low-slung, sidewise tree trunk to act as a bench. All that was needed to add to her comfort was a warm roaring fire, but she supposed it was too much to hope for. Too bad in her excitement she'd forgotten to grab her coat.

"You'll want to be seated for this." Remy gestured to the tree trunk beside the brook.

Out of breath after all the jogging, Beth sauntered over to the tree, hopped up and sat. "This is gonna be bad, I'm assuming, with the whole sitting thing." She gestured to her bark-covered chair. "And of course, I'm guessing the serene surrounding is a deliberate choice on your part...a cheery warm fire wouldn't be turned down, either." She rubbed her arms, the exercise-induced warmth was quickly fleeing. Was there a reason he had to take her deep into the woods? Maybe it wasn't the most brilliant of ideas to follow him so blindly…

Remy stood a few feet away in the center of the clearing, watching, studying her. Yup, this is not going to be good at all.

"I'll ask again, do you want the truth, or the bliss of uncertainty?"

"What? You can erase my memory or something? I'm not stupid. I know something isn't right. I've prided myself with being a realist, so go ahead and hit me with the truth. I'm tired of feeling insane."

He shook his head. "If I assured you of your sanity, would it be enough?"

Beth snorted. "In your dreams, dude."

"Very well, but first I must ask, why do you believe I hold the answers? Let alone will tell you the truth?"

Good questions, but Beth trusted her gut and her brains. She'd already figured something supernatural happened. After all, she was shot point-blank in the chest and transported hundreds of miles, if not years, away from her home. She already knew there were ghosts and supernatural objects, so the addition of time travel wasn't so far out of reality. Plus, Remy had shown most of his cards. He was either a magician or *something* else.

She gave him a smile. "I should be dead, but I'm not." She held up a single finger, shortly joined by another. "You were singing, "Don't Stop Believin'," which if I'm in the late seventeen hundreds, hasn't been written and won't be for a very long time." A third finger joined the first two. "And, like, you just put out your raging forge with a look. I'm guessing you're not what you seem."

"You would be correct." Remy continued to study her carefully, as if weighing, judging her. He closed his eyes and sighed. "The rules have been stretched so far, they might as well be broken."

"What rules?"

His eyes opened, and he smiled. "Precisely. What is one more?" Remy took two steps backward, centering himself inside the clearing. "Behold, young Beth, what few have ever witnessed."

He started to glow. Beth watched in fascination as he grew brighter and brighter, bringing tears to her eyes in her refusal to glance away or close them. Suddenly, the light exploded, almost blinding her, and she gasped.

She pushed herself off the tree, landing on her feet, blinking furiously. As her vision returned, she slapped a hand across her open mouth and stared at the figure standing before her. It was Remy, yet not.

A giant stood before her. His previously tall muscular frame of six-foot-four now stretched well past seven feet. Already chiseled features had grown sharper in contrast to his porcelain white skin, which appeared to glow. Sparkling white diamonds filled his eyes, no distinction from iris to whites, since the crystal light blue was leeched of its color, swallowing his pupils. Black hair now spilled past its normal shoulder length to fall long, hitting his waist. He stood regal, emanating a calm, which enveloped Beth, making her feel safe for the first time since MacKenzie had shot her.

She blinked again slowly and nothing changed the spectacular *other* being standing before her. Remy's mouth curled upward into a soft smile as wings of incredible cobalt blue unfurled from his back. Their wing tips almost stretched the width of the small clearing. Beth's knees buckled, dropping her to the dying moss beneath her feet.

"Oh, my God!" She stared up in wonder at the imposing and striking figure before her.

His smile grew to a grin. "No, not God, but one of his creations."

"You're a…an…angel!" Her breath became gasps, and her vision started to tunnel. "I think I'm going to faint."

In an instant, Remy was kneeling at her side, the blacksmith returned once again. He put a comforting hand to her shoulder. "Breathe. Just breathe."

Warmth flooded her, and she closed her eyes. Her racing heart slowed, and her panic gasps disappeared. Was this all in her imagination? Was she lying somewhere in a coma, dreaming incredible things? Nope. No denying her life had turned Tolkien. She bravely opened her eyes and met Remy's concerned, once again light blue gaze.

"A ghost, time travel, why not angels? Right?"

"Here." He offered her a hand and helped her up. "Sit. We need to talk."

Beth braced herself on the trunk and took a deep breath. "I suppose we do. So, you're an angel."

He sat beside her on the tree. "An Archangel, actually. One of seven. My name is Remiel."

"Wow, just wow."

"I shouldn't have revealed myself to you, but I figured you needed to know in order to trust and understand I speak the truth to you."

She snorted. "You had me at the forge trick, but there's no beating growing giant-size and unfurling wings."

"Indeed."

A comfortable silence fell between them. Beth was okay with the quiet. There was a lot to take in. But it didn't last long. Her natural curiosity reared its head, and of course, the worry for Laurel. She didn't hesitate to start her interrogation.

"Do you know if Laurel is safe? We've got to do something about MacKenzie. He shot me!"

"Alexander MacKenzie is no longer a problem." He placed a comforting hand to her shoulder. Warmth infused her, chasing away the winter cold. "He is very much dead. He was burned to death by the power Simon sent through the Orb, and if there was any doubt left, MacKenzie's corpse was crushed in the catacomb collapse. It was I who collected his soul and sent it to judgment. He can no longer endanger the mortal world."

If Beth was honest with herself, she was greatly relieved, if not content in her bloodthirstiness for what had to have been an agonizing death. Frankly, he deserved it. But regardless of MacKenzie's brutal ending, she was more concerned with Laurel.

"Please tell me, is Laurel alive?" She could endure most anything if she knew her friend had survived.

The gentle smile Remy gave her sent shivers of worry down her spine. Please God. No, she had to live.

"Yes, alive and well. In fact, she's happily married." He gave her shoulder a squeeze, before standing and turning to face her. "Laurel is a remarkable woman with an inner strength. She protected Uriel's Orb and saved Simon, at what she thought was a great cost on her part."

Great cost? Alarm trembled through Beth. Laurel would not only be shredded by Beth's apparent death she had witnessed, but giving up Simon when she'd set him free would have crushed her. Her family must have gone bonkers and circled the wagons around her. Yet Remy said she married.

"Who?" Beth asked. "Laurel's husband, who did she marry?"

Remy gave a genuine grin of happiness. "Why, Simon, of course."

"Simon? But he's a ghost. He's dead. Didn't he get to move on, you know, go into the light, once the Orb was protected?"

"He did," Remy replied. "However, he was given a rare opportunity, a choice. Simon could stay in Heaven with his departed family and friends, or he could become mortal once more, returning to Earth at the age of his death, and live out a normal mortal span."

Beth clapped and bounced a bit on her tree bench. "He returned to Laurel! Oh my God, that's so romantic." She sighed. It was right out of the romance novels she read. Content with her friend's happiness, now it was time to turn selfish and fix her own life.

"What happened to me? Do I get a choice, like Simon? I choose to go home." She smiled, waiting for Remy to do his angel magic and whisk her back home. Oh, what she'd give for indoor plumbing, hot water on demand, central heating, to see Laurel again, and be with her own husband. Man, oh man did she miss Grant. He must be so worried. She couldn't wait to surprise him and tell him of her adventure.

Wait. Why was nothing happening? Why was Remy just standing there frowning at her? She should be able to choose. If Simon could, why couldn't she?

"Remy, I want to go home."

He sighed. "It isn't so simple. Simon was never really dead, just caught in a loop because of his family's oath to the Archangel Uriel. He was a victim of his family's legacy, unaware of the reason behind his half-life. Yet, with his own personal strength, enduring many trials, he upheld his family's oath."

"But I'm not dead." Beth put her hand to her chest where she could feel her pounding heart beneath her palm. She was alive, damn it. If she wasn't dead like Simon, she should be given an option as well. Leaping to her feet, she confronted Remy. "I deserve a get out of jail free card. Please, Remiel, please take me home." Beth would get down on her knees and beg if it would get her results. Pride had no place in her ego if she could do anything or say anything to return her to normal life.

"Beth." He stood and closed the gap between them. He grasped both her hands into his. "You must understand your unique situation. Your circumstance is the direct result of your free will. You decided to help Laurel and Simon. You decided to enter Sinclair House to search for the key, and in direct result of those choices, MacKenzie shot you."

"Then why am I here and not dead? Moved on, whatever." She pulled her hands out of his gentle grasp and flung them in exclamation. "Why aren't I in Heaven or the next step in my journey? Because truthfully? My life is beginning to feel like hell. Did I take a trip downstairs instead of up?" That would be just her luck, but she didn't think she went to hell. Why would an angel, let alone an Archangel, be visiting her personal level of Dante's Inferno? Nothing was making sense. She wasn't that much of a party girl to be a condemned sinner.

"Why won't you take me home?" She met his gaze and didn't like the look in his eyes.

"Beth, you were dying…" Remy looked so sorrowful. "My brother, the Archangel Uriel, was very upset. You shouldn't have died—"

"Cool deal. Take me home—"

"But you did." He shook his head. "There wasn't anything to change it, except intervene in a different way. A way bordering in defiance of God's will. Uriel begged me a favor. He didn't want your life cut short, so he asked me to save you."

"By transporting me through time? That was helping?"

He sighed. "You were dead in your timeline. There was nothing either my brother or myself could do. Taking you *else-when* was our only option to letting your natural timeline play out."

Beth shook her head and frowned. This wasn't right.

"There's more, I'm afraid," Remy warned her. "MacKenzie wasn't the only one who died—"

"Well, duh, I was shot point blank range in my chest and you yourself said I was—"

"Beth, please." He shook his head. "You wanted answers, now you must listen, to all of it."

"Ooookay." She sat back, worried as the crawly feeling raced across her skin. Her ants were back. What could be worse than her death? Did the interfering angels rob her of options? It's all about free will, right? Beth still had that, didn't she? And her will was not to stay here. Home. Her life. But the shivers chasing through her gave proof to her unspoken doubts.

"There was much going on while you helped Simon and Laurel that you were unaware of." Remy started to pace, tracing a path in the dead moss and brown leaves before her. "Your husband, hid things from you…"

Puzzled, Beth didn't know where this was leading. She was still getting over the fact she was dead, not dead. Undead, like a vampire. Her brain was buffering on information overload. But the one thing she would always know, believe, was Grant being the best husband ever. He loved her, cherished her, and she loved him back just as strongly. It's why she didn't even bat an eye leaving her family and friends to live across an ocean in a foreign country. Grant was her everything. They kept no secrets.

"You're wrong. He'd never hold anything back."

"I'm so very sorry, Beth." He stopped pacing and stood in front of her. "This will be hard for you, and I wish to bring you no further pain."

"You're scaring me." Her words were barely a whisper, but his hand reached out to grip her shoulder, acknowledging he heard.

"Grant was working with MacKenzie to secure the Orb."

"What? No!" She wanted to bolt or fight, but Remy had her trapped by standing before her, the tree behind, his large body blocking hers; there was no escape. "No, Grant wouldn't, he couldn't…"

"He was." Remy was steadfast. "He was the one who convinced you to get Laurel to visit. MacKenzie and Grant needed her research skills to uncover the

Orb's hiding place. They both were pursuing Laurel in the catacombs after you were shot, which he still did, even knowing MacKenzie had killed you."

"No, no, no. Not true! He would never betray me like that, never!" Beth shouted her denial and started to sob. "He loved me."

Remiel gathered her up in his arms and let her cry. She buried her face into his chest while her fists pounded his shoulders. Grant loved her. He wasn't the villain in the piece. MacKenzie must have forced him, blackmailed him, or something.

It was if Remy could read her thoughts as he replied, "It was his choice, made in greed, and careless of all else, especially for your love of him. I'm so sorry, little one."

Drained, her arms fell to her sides as a fresh round of tears flowed out of her. How could she have been so wrong? How did she not know? His betrayal sliced deep and sharp, worse than a bullet to her heart. How could she so misjudge his character? She had given up so much for him. Grant still worked with MacKenzie, even knowing the bastard had killed her? How was it even possible? She didn't know Grant at all. The past year of blissful married life, a wasted lie.

Slowly anger replaced tears. No matter how much she wanted to, she couldn't hide in Remy's strong arms forever. Beth straightened and gave a slight push, which Remy answered by lowering his arms and taking a step back.

"You said he paid a price. What happened to him?"

"As I said, they were chasing Laurel in the catacombs. Part of the tunnels collapsed, trapping Grant. MacKenzie slit his throat, leaving him to die, instead of digging him out."

Okay, awful. Grant was dead. In her anger, she wished it was horrible for him, and he regretted his actions while lying there bleeding out. Yet, part of her cringed; even knowing his betrayal, she still loved him. It wasn't like she had an on/off button for her love. Too bad she wasn't lying in a coma and this was all a vivid dream. Reality sucked, but there had to be a way to turn this whole thing around.

"Anything else you want to dump on me?"

Remiel shook his head and held up his hands in supplication. "You know everything. MacKenzie, your husband's betrayal and death, Laurel's happiness."

"But why am I here? Why aren't I dead?"

"I told you—"

"You and your brother meddled. You broke God's big rule on free will." She glared up at him. "So now you're going to fix it."

"We can't change what happened. But circumstances change—"

Beth jumped on his slip. "Like Simon? Can I do some deed or service and get the chance to return home?" Hell, she wasn't afraid of some hard work. Give her a quest or something and she'd make Frodo and his ring-bearing self look like a weekend hiker.

"I can't return you to your home."

"I'm stuck here?"

"Beth—"

"No, just no!" She threw out an arm to stop him from touching her. "Why did you even bother? I'm better off dead!" She darted around him and dashed out of the clearing.

"Beth!"

She didn't stop running when the angel shouted. The tears she thought were all used up came flooding out as she sobbed and bolted. Grant's betrayal sliced at her like a knife. She was the worst kind of fool, a moron. She hated herself and the interfering angels. What did she have to look forward to? She'd already been robbed. Her life as a single woman alone and lost in time? Rape? To live another ten miserable years tops as a waitress tavern wench before dying—again—alone in this time from some completely curable disease in the future? Her life was a movie all right—a horror film. Her life was gone. She was already dead.

Chapter Seventeen

Locke gave the chestnut gelding his head, letting the reins drop from his fingers to lie against Dante's neck. "Shite, mate." He glared at the low-slung sun, fast disappearing behind the hillside, before harshly exhaling. There was no point leaving for York today. Night was fast approaching, and though he made his living in its darkened depths, starting a journey in the dead of night, with precious little preparation was tantamount to suicide, and he didn't intend to meet his end because of a careless mistake.

Dante picked his way along the path as the remaining daylight shed what little warm embrace it held during the cold day. Both he and his horse's breath puffed out in little clouds as they made their way home. He'd have a hot dinner beside a roaring fire, and a good night's sleep in his own bed before traveling the road to York and searching for Sophie. Rushing never held an advantage.

Dante jerked to a halt on the path before entering the hillside clearing, startling Kit. The gelding held himself stiff, almost quivering with tension. Copper head held high, with ears pricked forward, he snorted two sharp steamy puffs of air from flared nostrils. While Kit had been lost in thought, Dante had kept a look out, and his horse sensed something ahead. Smart boy. At least one of them was paying attention. It was probably worth a look no doubt.

Kit patted Dante's neck before slipping his feet from the stirrups and silently swinging down off the gelding. He held up a closed fist, signaling his horse to stay. With his footsteps quiet as cat's paws, Kit stepped off the path and circled the clearing, hugging the tree line. Night had truly settled, but there was a crescent moon rising on this clear frosty evening, so it made easy viewing from the deep shadows of the tree he stood next to.

He heard her first—the very disconcerting sound of a woman sobbing. He really should leave. Woman's tears held no appeal for him, but curiosity won over common sense. Why was there a woman here in the middle of nowhere? Tredford was leagues away. His home was closer, but a well-kept secret. Plus, it was blasted cold and dark, and any right-minded female would be snug away warming a man's bed or hearth, not crying alone in the darkness.

He crept closer, making sure he was still hidden in the shadows. With wide eyes, he halted at the scene before him. Bathed in the bright moonlight, stood a woman covering her face with her hands as she cried. That in itself wasn't so remarkable since he already had heard her sobs, but her state of undress was. She was barefoot and only wearing her shift. It was a frozen night, not the sort of weather to run around mostly naked. He spotted her neatly folded clothing and boots piled near the outskirt of the clearing. Even more distracting now with the moon raised, was the transparency of her chemise. Her figure was clearly outlined by the moonlight. An intriguing and most desirable form to behold indeed. Kit almost stepped forward for a closer look at the woman but stopped himself just in time.

With an anguished cry, she dropped her hands from her face. She whirled away, giving him her back before he could see her face. A chill raced down his spine, nothing to do with the bloody cold, but everything to do with trepidation. His foreboding tripled as he saw her take first one tentative step then another toward the hillside's edge. He crept from the shadows and into the clearing, stalking her on silent feet.

She reached the hill's sharp rim, and he lengthened his stride as she hesitated at the cusp. Would she jump? The fall might not kill her, but she'd lie broken in the ravine and with how little she was dressed, she wouldn't last till the morn. The moment he read the commitment in her body, Kit sprinted forward. She took a step off the ledge. He stretched out his arm and hand and managed to seize the back of her shift. He was pulled down to his knees by her momentum, falling and skidding as she screamed and dropped over the lip. The sound of tearing fabric sent him into a panic as adrenaline kicked in. He flung himself flat, his body partially hanging over open air. Kit managed to grab one of her flailing arms, just as her shift tore from his grasp. Quickly, with his suddenly free hand, he snagged her other arm, and started to pull her up as he slithered backward. When he had her on firm land, he rolled with her away from the edge, before pinning her to the ground with the full length of his body while one hand held her wrists trapped above her head.

"Bloody hell, woman. What do you think you were doing?"

She sputtered, her long curly hair tangled across

her face as she tried to toss him off. He grunted when one of her legs clocked him, but shortly had her trapped between his thighs, forcing her struggles to end.

A harsh exhale on her part cleared the hair covering her mouth. "Get off me! Why did you stop me?"

Kit eased his upper body off her and raised his free hand to brush and tuck her hair behind her ears. His eyes widened in surprise. Third time's a charm. It was the saucy barmaid and woods wanderer. Why was she trying to kill herself?

"So, luv, or should I address you as, my Lady?" He gave her a grin. "Were you trying to die a lingering death while broken at the bottom of the ravine?"

"I was hoping the fall would kill me, because freezing to death was taking too long," the barmaid huffed out. She blinked a few times before her own eyes widened. "You! You're the jerk from the tavern. Figures. Just go away." She closed her eyes and turned her face away. The tears she tried to hide glittered in the moonlight's glow.

She lay there silently beneath him, the slight quaking of her body a testament to her quiet tears and no doubt the rapidly dropping temperatures, regardless of his own body heat warming her. She's an attractive little bit, which truth be told, he had a hard time avoiding, intrigued from the first. Besides, there's a story to be had, and it would be much more comfortable by a fire and some brandy to warm them both.

"Right then." Quick as a snake, Kit rolled off her and tugged her up by the hold on her wrists. "Up you go, on your feet."

He frowned as she swayed and visibly started

shivering and if he wasn't imagining, her lips were turning blue before his eyes. Risking a chance at her dropping to the ground, he released her and quickly removed his greatcoat. Just as her knees were about to buckle, he grabbed her around the waist with one arm, and used the other to drape his coat around her shoulders. "You're rather a mess, aren't you, luv?" He *tsked* to himself when she didn't fire back a retort or even acknowledge him. Where was the saucy wench who dared to challenge him?

Like dressing a living doll, he got her arms into the sleeves and wrapped her up in the much too big coat. Hopefully it would tide her over until they reached the protection of his house. He swung her up into his arms and carried her over to the pile of discarded clothes. He crouched down and gently released her. He grabbed her boots, and got her icy feet into the wool-lined warmth before scooping up her dress and woolen stockings and then whistled for Dante. Ever the well-trained horse, the gelding trotted into the clearing and stopped beside them.

He lifted her up into the saddle and then swung up behind her. It was bloody freezing without his coat. He pulled her tighter against his chest, making sure she was secure before gathering up the reins and urging Dante into a canter.

What was he doing?

He should have let her jump and left her for dead. He didn't know her. But thoughts of Sophie kept skittering though his mind. If Sophie were in trouble, he'd hope someone would help her in turn.

The barmaid obviously needed help and maybe the Universe in turn would be kind to Sophie. The surefooted horse didn't hesitate, and by the light of the crescent moon on a crystal cold night, he set out for home.

Chapter Eighteen

Beth sat curled in the chair by the fire, knees to chest and arms wrapped around her legs—huddling inside his woolen coat. She hadn't moved since he carried her inside the small two-story cottage and dropped her into the chair without a single word. He efficiently got the fire going and with a quick admonishment to stay, like she was some sort of pet dog, he left. She stared morosely at the dancing flames, wondering how this came to pass. Everything was blurred in her mind since racing from the clearing in denial of her fate. Blind searing pain lanced through her as she ran, trying to outrace the hurt and betrayal coursing through her. She had no idea where she'd run, or how long or how far, just running until she couldn't no more.

How could she have given in to her despair? It wasn't like her to give up. She wasn't a quitter, but apparently everyone reaches their breaking point, and the news of Grant's betrayal had literally pushed her over the edge.

Blinking quickly, she banished away tears she refused to shed again, and took stock of her plight. She was trapped in the late eighteenth century. Beth could no longer convince herself she was dreaming or hallucinating. The stupid, interfering Archangel had confirmed her time travel, though truthfully, she had figured out her little trip much earlier, but just didn't want to believe it. Grant, the man she gave her heart to, wasn't the man he claimed to be—an imposter of the worst kind. Her breath hitched as her gut clenched, and she started to tremble once again. She pulled the coat tighter around her and buried her face up to her nose trying to get warm even though she was only a foot from the fire.

On the plus side, MacKenzie was dead and had died pretty horribly. Laurel was alive as well as Simon. They were happy together. Beth had been happy once. Her eyes welled up again. *Damn it, no.* She would not give up again. She was alive. Where there's life, there's hope, right?

Beth blinked when a generously poured brandy snifter appeared inches from her face, breaking her fixated gaze on the flickering flames. She raised her eyes to follow the hand holding the glass, up the arm, to his shoulder and finally his face. He wore a slight smile and a cocked eyebrow. She should have been startled by his sudden appearance, but she just couldn't work up enough emotion to care. She was numb. It was a good place to be.

"Are you going to hide inside my coat all night? Or would you like a brandy? It's French."

Well, she certainly could use a drink and her body was going numb, just like her mind, all clenched up as it was. She released her grip on her legs and with one hand, reached for the glass. Her hand met his and gave a tug when he didn't immediately release it. She popped her buried face outside the coat in order to glare at him.

He laughed, but released the glass and took a step back. "Judging by your scowl, I believe life is returning."

Smug bastard. Beth took a generous sip of the brandy as she watched him pull up another chair and sit. Handsome bastard, like a hot underwear model—all sleek and lithe muscles. He even had the same five o'clock shadow a lot of them showed off, though she'd have to guess his was less intentionally groomed. His rugged, strong face was highlighted by unruly shoulder length dark brown hair that gleamed auburn by the firelight, revealing the hidden deep red. Bright green eyes glinting like a cat's stared back at her as they traded gazes across the rim of their glasses. He had a slight build, but well proportioned. With his cravat and vest gone, his linen shirt gave testament to strong shoulders and an athletic shape. Her glance traveled downward; he certainly could fill out a pair of breeches. As she spotted the ground-in dirt from his rescue effort, she mentally acknowledged the evidence of her earlier stupidity, and then was startled by his bare feet.

"Aren't you cold?" The words escaped her mouth before she could filter her thoughts.

"She speaks," the mysterious man taunted her.

She stuck her tongue out at him and returned her interest to the brandy, surprised to find her glass empty. He clucked, drawing her attention away from the snifter.

"'Tis a sorry sight, luv." He stood and snatched the glass from her hand. "I'll fix you right up."

Her eyes were drawn to him as he crossed the room. He reminded her of a big cat at the Chicago Zoo she once watched for hours, entranced. All lean and muscled, he moved with liquid grace to the bar, his bare feet silent on the plain blue carpet covering the well-worn wood flooring. Setting both their glasses down, he removed the cut crystal stopper from the brandy decanter and poured another generous round. Collecting up the snifters, he prowled back across the room, offered her a glass, which she took and kept an eye on him when he took his seat once more.

"Do you want to talk? Or would you rather just get foxed?"

Drunk sounded good. In answer, Beth took another healthy swallow of brandy. The amber liquid traced a warm path down to her stomach, chasing away her chill and keeping her pleasantly unfeeling. If she was stuck here, she should try and make a potential ally or maybe even friend. After all, she didn't know much about this century, and if she were to survive long enough to build a life, she'd need help.

"I suppose I should thank you."

He cocked a slim eyebrow at her and raised his glass in toast before taking a sip. "It would be a shame for the world to lose a beauty such as yours, rough as it is at the moment."

She continued to study him. There was something familiar about him, but it must be from her encounter with him at the Boar and Rose.

"So, my Lady, since I so graciously saved you from a lingering, horrible death, do I at least get to know your true name?"

"Beth, Beth Mur…" Fuck it. She was not keeping Grant's last name. She was her own woman from here on out. "Leighton. Beth Leighton."

He tipped his glass. "A pleasure, luv."

It was her time to lift an eyebrow. In turn, it got her a dazzling smile followed by a throat clearing. She didn't break eye contact. She was a champion eye lock winner.

"Right. I suppose there's a certain bit of trust between us. You may call me Kit."

She almost spit out the brandy from the sip she was in the process of swallowing. Kit, really? Especially after likening him to a large jungle cat? She couldn't stop the laugh from escaping. He was so not a Kit. The man sitting next to her was anything but a kitten.

"What?" He was smiling, and his emerald eyes held a laughing glint. At least he wasn't offended by her outburst. In fact, he appeared anything but. "I'm glad I could induce you to laugh, but I'm not sure what you find so amusing?"

"I'm sorry. You don't really fit your name. Not. At. All."

"It's short for Christopher, if it helps."

"Now, Christopher I can see."

"Well, I prefer, Kit, if you please."

Maybe it was an eighteenth-century thing, or British thing, but Beth couldn't see how one got Kit from Christopher. "How about Chris?" she asked. "If I call you Kit, I'm just going to keep spontaneously laughing, and it'll make things difficult."

"You have a fine laugh, and my name is Kit."

Someone had a stubborn streak. She should know. It takes one to know one. Grant usually gave in to her because no one could outstubborn her. Grant. Her eyes welled up and before she could force them away, a tear escaped to roll down her cheek.

He was crouched in front of her before she knew it. He took her empty glass from her hand and placed it on the floor, before reaching up to brush her tear away.

"Now, luv. None of that. I miss your smiles and laughter. Why not try saying my name?"

She gave him a teary-eyed smile, but it was ruined on a choked sob, and then the dam broke.

"Ah, Christ. Don't cry, luv."

Beth shamelessly threw herself at him. Needing someone, needing comfort she so sorely searched for, she hoped he wouldn't push her away. He caught her, his arms wrapped tight around her, catching her up. She buried her face to his chest and let rein to her grief. She was so lost. She wanted her life back. If she could travel through time, why not like in *Doctor Who*, go back to the future and fix her fate so she wasn't dead in her timeline? She could stop Grant. She knew she could; he had always listened to her. The four of them could gang up on Mackenzie and save the day. All would be right in the world. She just needed a *Tardis*.

Her sobbing stopped as her courage returned. She would find a way to make things right. Beth slowly became aware she was no longer on the floor but in a chair cradled in Kit's lap. One arm around her waist and with the other hand, he slowly stroked her hair. She felt warm and protected, surprising since she was in the arms of a stranger. Maybe it was the brandy.

"Better, luv? No more tears. I'm not good with crying." He murmured close to her ear.

"I don't know." Her words muffled into his chest. She snuggled closer, enjoying his scent of winter, horse, and leather. "You're doing pretty well."

"Hmphf." His finger slipped beneath her chin and tilted her face up to look at her. "You're all blotchy and red."

"Really?" She snorted her disgust.

Giving her a smile, he replied, "Now you're angry. Much better than tears." He gripped her chin firmly with his strong long fingers. "I like it when your saucy temper comes out to play. It gives me ideas."

Her mouth dropped open in surprise, and before she could protest, his mouth covered hers. His warm lips brushed hers as his tongue slid into the apparent open invitation she unwittingly supplied. She melted. He tasted of brandy and some kind of spice. She was no cook, but didn't mind eating him up. Beth reached up to tangle her hand in his soft thick hair, while the other gripped his shoulder trying to pull him closer. Her tongue danced with his. Heat flooded her down to her toes, finally warming the cold places no external fire could reach. The man could certainly kiss. Better than Grant.

Grant. What the fuck? She was kissing a stranger. Beth tore her mouth away and with both hands planted on his chest, shoved herself off his lap, and him firmly back into the chair. Landing on her feet, she glared down at him.

"Damn you!"

Chapter Nineteen

Kit stared at the angry slip of a woman, clutching his coat around her curvy body, and glaring accusingly down at him. He was gratified at least to notice her breath was coming as short as his. Blimey, his physical reaction to her was unexpected.

"How dare you kiss me!"

"Well, luv, it takes two to dance and a mighty fine partner you were." He shifted in the chair to gain some comfort. Damn and blast the woman, his arousal would take a bit to realize the dance was over. "What exactly is your problem? You're not a prim and proper woman, as your actions declare."

"You...you...have no right...I'm married." Her eyes widened with her declaration, and she spun away, giving him her back. Her head bowed and if he wasn't mistaken, she was trembling again. Dear Lord, he hoped she wasn't crying. Again.

He stood, studying her. What he knew of her, she appeared to be a fighter. He had trouble understanding where all these waterworks were coming from. Let's see if he could get under her skin again.

"I suppose you could blame the drink on your participation. Your husband needn't know. It'll be our little secret, luv."

She whirled around Her eyes grew round as she startled at finding him standing so close. But shortly, the piercing blue gaze narrowed. Ah, target struck. He was always the accomplished marksman.

"My husband is dead."

"Ah."

"Ah, what? What is, '*ah*?'"

"Ah, as in, now I know why you were trying to end your life. You've lost your protection and felt you had nothing left."

Her mouth dropped open with a gasp, leaving her speechless for the moment. This was fun. Could he sink another arrow in the red? She was much more interesting and attractive angry instead of sobbing.

"I'm glad I saved you. Beautiful women such as yourself have more than a few options to provide for your own security. You needn't resort to death. You could find a benefactor, or in the theory of not keeping all your eggs in one basket, put yourself on the market, so to speak."

Her face flushed, and he noticed her hands fisting. Temper, temper, little vixen.

"Oh my God! You did not just suggest that!"

"Why not? It's an honorable trade. Long standing and providing a much-needed service."

Kit was ready when her arm came whipping up, so he was able to grab her wrist, stopping the stinging slap to his cheek. He had to dance quickly away, with a laugh, when she tried to stomp her booted foot to his bare one. He swung around, taking her arm with him, to twist it behind her. With his free arm, he wrapped it around her center and pulled her back snug to his front. She shouted her frustration when she realized he had her trapped.

"Let me go!"

"Will you behave?"

"Yes," she replied, too sweetly and quickly.

"Ha! You take me for a pillock?"

"What the hell is a pillock?" She blew out an exasperating breath.

He felt her relax in his hold and rested his chin on her head, giving in to a slight sigh. "All better now? No more tears?"

She snorted. "You did that on purpose."

"Aye, well, luv. You're much more fun angry than sad." He released her and took a careful step out of range, watching as she straightened, and shook out the arm he had bent, before plunging her hands into the deep pockets of his coat. Slowly she turned to face him.

"I suppose I should—" She looked down at her left hand still deep inside the pocket.

A chill chased up his spine as she slowly withdrew her hand closed in a fist. *Shite*. He watched helpless as she turned her hand and uncurled her fingers. Lying in her open palm were her wedding bands he had stolen almost a week ago. He had forgotten they were there.

She studied the rings and moved her gaze to his own. He caught the moment when her realization dawned to the only explanation of how her rings would be inside his coat pocket. *Damn*. He supposed he might try brazening his way out.

"Beauties, aren't they? I bought them the other day when they caught my eye." He reached for them, but her fingers curled around the rings in her hand.

"Oh really? You actually think I'd buy that bullshit?"

He shrugged. "I've no way to prove it. You'll believe what you will. More brandy? No, I think scotch is called for." He turned and paced to the sideboard. He needed a drink. No one had ever figured out his hidden identity. Kit wasn't sure what to do. Sophie was currently the only person who knew he was the Knightmare, when he had opened up to her in need of a set of eyes and ears. And she was presently missing. He needed to find her, not deal with this feisty, tiny, strange woman who addled him far too much already.

He let the stopper clank to the tray as he picked up the scotch decanter and poured himself a generous dram. Taking the glass, he downed the four-fingered serving in one swallow. He put the glass down and poured again. Kit turned and faced her. She stood where he left her. He raised his glass in salutation, before placing it to his lips and swallowing it down whole once again. He kept his eyes locked to hers. Damn, she was beautiful, even in her current state of dishevelment. Her blond hair fell loose in springy curls almost to her waist, tousled and unkempt, as if just having arisen from bed after a rousing bout of sex. Wide summer blue eyes and a generous mouth of plush full lips consumed her heart-shaped pixie face. He let his eyes travel downward, remembering the outline of her body revealed by moonlight in the clearing, but hidden now buried in the bulk of his dratted coat. She had curves in all the right places and when he held her in his arms, she fit him like a glove. It would be a shame to have to kill her.

Chapter Twenty

So, this was the dreaded Nightmare? Beth studied the handsome highwayman, who was currently downing scotch as if were water. A waste, really. She could see it now, the resemblance. At the very least, she should have recognized the coat, but it had been dark and raining the night they first crossed paths. His accent had fooled her. The arrogant highwayman spoke with a cultured English accent, while "Kit", the fun-loving Romeo had a lower class, Cockney-ish ring to his voice. She wondered which was the act. Did it really matter? In either of his roles, he hadn't hurt her and had in fact actually saved her life. Twice. She wasn't shot dead by a pistol or lying broken in the ravine, slowly dying. The stories about him were menacing, but he hadn't killed anyone if the rumors were true. He did steal her wedding rings, but he was a thief and anyway she had those back now. The most Beth could complain about was an unexpected grope and kiss, neither very life threatening. And the kiss, well…

She sighed. "Are you going to drink the whole bottle or will you spare some for me?" Beth affected her best Scottish accent. "A wee dram or two?"

The rogue gave her a charming smile. "I believe I can spare some, luv." He followed action to words and in no time was prowling across the room to stand once again too close, with his six-foot frame invading her personal space as he offered her the glass. An intimidation tactic she was pretty sure and one she wouldn't fall prey to.

Just like with the brandy snifter, he held on to the cut crystal tumbler when she tried to take it. This time, however, he didn't release it, but held tight. With barely the glass width between their bodies, it was easy to see the hard gleam filling his green eyes. She might be in trouble, but she wasn't going to back down or show weakness. Beth kept the grip on the scotch and brazenly met his stare. The little voice in her head reminded her he hadn't ever hurt her as he frowned down at her.

"I'm not sure what I should do."

Well, that can't be good. In his Nightmare persona, he carried two pistols, a long sword, and knives. She didn't know his proficiency with said weapons, but the stories and her gut told her he was an expert. After all he hadn't been caught. Lucky for her, he wasn't currently wearing any. He didn't even have his tie, so he couldn't try strangling her, though he could probably squeeze the life out of her with his bare hands. Truthfully, she wasn't sure what he was capable of in either identity. Stubbornly, she clung to the fact he hadn't hurt her. *Yet*.

Damn, she was going around in circles. People liked her, especially guys. She was the girl in school who had more guy friends than girlfriends. She gave him her prettiest smile. "Well, you can start by letting me have my drink."

He broke their staring contest and glanced at the scotch, as if only just now realizing his grip on the glass. Kit slowly uncurled his fingers. Beth kept a firm hold, and without moving to distance herself, raised the glass to her lips and shot-gunned the contents. The fiery alcohol smoothly crossed her tongue and warmed her all the way down its path to her stomach. Wow, the scotch was smooth. It had been a shocking waste not to savor it.

She held out her empty glass and tapped his chest with it. "Fill her back up, please."

He stood immobile.

"Look, your scotch is excellent. I should have sipped."

Kit closed his eyes and took in a deep breath, holding it. Beth held still. She knew this was probably the moment of decision for him. She hoped it didn't end in her grisly death. Especially since he saved her earlier from her own idiocy and hopelessness. It would be a shame if he killed her now.

His eyes snapped open and it was her turn to hold her breath.

"Right, luv. More drink." He spun on his bare heel and made yet another trip to the bar.

She slowly exhaled and made her way back to her chair, collapsing into the upholstered depths as relief flooded through her, turning her muscles to jelly. Nothing like a game of Russian roulette. Or was it chicken?

"We should talk." He handed her a glass, and took his seat opposite her.

This time Beth sipped at the scotch. Oh yeah, it was definitely worth the savor. "Yes, talking would be better than…you scared me there for a moment."

He met her gaze over the rims of their mutual glasses. With a shrug, he added, "I'd apologize, but I'd be lying. Certain thoughts had crossed my mind, and you had all the right to be wary, luv."

"And now?"

"Now? I have an offer to propose."

"If you think to pimp me out, I won't play whore if that's what you're thinking."

He shook his head. "You speak so strangely. I only understand half your words at times." He cocked his head. "Where are you from?"

"America."

"Ah, a Colonial. I should have known." He paused. "But at least your palate is educated enough so you can enjoy an excellent single malt. *Sláinte*." He raised his glass in toast.

"*Slàinte agad-sa*." They both sipped.

"You speak the Gaelic?"

"My husband was Scots. I learned a few phrases here and there." Her eyes suddenly filled with tears. Damn it, she was so done with crying, probably just as much as he was by his slight cringe. Of course, Kit noticed her moment of weakness.

"You must have loved him greatly. A lucky bloke." He raised his glass in toast again, but lowered it when she didn't return the same.

"I love—I mean—loved him. But he apparently didn't deserve it." She slugged back a gulp.

"Shame. You're a quality of woman to be cherished, I think."

Beth snorted. "You don't even know me. How'd you know?"

"First, it's not in my person to step out and save anyone, yet somehow I have done so for you—twice. I still don't understand why, it's uncommon and therefore interesting." Kit gave her a brief smile. "Plus, you've got a fighting spirit about you. A rare quality, one which I admire. You may be down on your luck at the moment, but you won't stay on the bottom for long. I recognize the trait."

He knew her better than most. With her short stature, curves, blue eyes and blonde hair, most thought her the stereotypical dumb blonde. Most never got past her looks to even rate her intelligence or spirit. Clearly, there was more going on behind Kit's devilish cat eyes and handsome looks as well. She supposed a thief must be able to read and assess people quickly in order to be successful. Beth had never really thought about it.

"You have no idea the bottom I've hit." It was her turn to cock her head at him. "I believe you had a proposition for me, that I rudely jumped all over. I warn you though, I won't be earning a living on my back."

"Noted." He grinned at her. "And, luv. I won't be needing to pay to have you underneath me."

"Seriously? You had to go and ruin the moment? Just when I was beginning to warm up to you and think you weren't such a jerk?"

"Jerk?"

She waved him off. "Never mind."

He shook his head. "Odd. All I'm saying. I'm having to learn a new language."

"Poor baby."

"Never fear, I'm good with languages. I'm fluent in four. Learning American can't be difficult, luv."

"You better be careful, Kit. Your Nightmare persona is beginning to show."

"It helps to understand those I rob, and my illustrious career didn't start in England."

Her curiosity got the better of her. "How on earth

did you become a highwayman? You're smart; you probably could have done or been anything. Yet, you're the Nightmare. And seriously, that was the best you could come up with, calling yourself a bad dream?"

Kit eyes widened, and then he chuckled. "An honest mistake, since you must not have seen my wanted post. Plus, I didn't name myself, my ah…donators did."

"Huh?"

"My name isn't night as in day, but Knight as in rank."

She let loose an unladylike snort. "Knightmare. Clever, a much more creative *nom de guerre*."

He inclined his head in acknowledgment. "*Vous parlez aussi le francais, ma petite fille?*"

His French was flawless and with no hint of a British accent. She assumed he asked if she spoke French. "Nope." She pointed at her chest. "Ugly American, you know. I only speak English."

Kit choked on the sip of scotch he was drinking. "Georgie would take back the colonies for how you ruin the King's English as you do, luv. And you're far from ugly."

Warmth chased across her skin. Handsome and charming, truly a rogue to be reckoned with. She needed to be careful. Men weren't high on her list at the moment. Her judgment and trust of Grant proved she really didn't know anything. She may be feeling an attraction to Kit, but he'd already lied to her and stolen from her—what else was he hiding?

"Your proposal?"

"Yes, right, down to business." He put his empty glass on the floor near his feet, beside his empty brandy

117

snifter, before leaning forward in the chair and bracing his arms on his thighs. "You know who I am."

"Hardly."

He glared at her.

"Oh, all right. Yes, at night you're the menacing Knightmare to all travelers on the road, and by day, you're an asshat to barmaids everywhere."

He laughed. "I won't ask." His eyes gleamed. Apparently asshat wasn't a time-honored word. Oh well.

"As the Knightmare, I've managed to become quite wealthy and elude the hangman's noose by being well-informed."

Beth winced inside. The thought of Kit being hung made her sick. "Why do you do it? I mean, the risk…you could be killed during a robbery or face…" She waved her hand about. "Why put your life in such danger? Especially if you don't need the money?"

Something dark flittered across his face, disappearing in a blink. He shrugged as he straightened and sat upright, stretched out his long legs, and crossed his bare feet at the ankles. "I have my reasons, none of which concern you, luv."

"Okay, got it. Stop prying."

"Information," he continued, "at times, is worth more than gold. What I propose is this. Barmaids are privy to large amounts of gossip. I would like you to be my eyes and ears. Pass on information of certain wealth traveling the lanes, or movement of the guards, of any rumors floating about me. And in exchange, you'll get a take of the profit from my hard-earned gains."

Didn't he mean *ill-gotten*? Whatever. It was certainly one way to make money. It was better than selling her body for sex. She wasn't sure of how many options there were for a single woman in this era. He wasn't really asking much. After all, if she was stuck here she'd need money, which meant a job, so she'd have to keep her work at the Boar and Rose anyway. If she still had her job. One bridge at a time. They liked her and she was a hard worker. Beth was sure she'd be able to convince them to let her keep her job. Working for both the inn and Kit was a good exchange. At least it was something to keep her occupied as she tried to figure out how to time travel, because if the angel wouldn't help, she'd find a way to help herself. She wasn't completely ready to give up on the idea of returning home. Plus, as an added bonus, Kit wasn't sore on the eyes.

"Anything more? Just information?"

"Information." He slouched deeper into the chair, his eyes glinting mischievously by the firelight. "Unless you be offering more?"

"Ha! In your dreams."

"And most pleasant dreams they'd be, luv."

She couldn't stop her smile. Rogue, with a capital 'r.' Beth placed her empty glass on the floor with the growing collection and rose to cross the scant distance to stand before his chair. She offered her hand until she realized she still gripped her wedding rings tightly. Frowning, she opened her palm and studied the symbol of her massive pain and misjudgment. They had to go and she needed money.

"Do you know where I can sell these?" She gave him a stern look. "And no, I won't let you steal them again."

"Tredford is too small. But York will do. In fact,

I'm traveling there in the morning. I could—"

"No. I'm coming with you. There's no way I trust you." She was never going to put herself in a position to rely on a man again. Her trust was fragile and belonged solely to herself right now.

"It's a long ride in bad weather. Let me help you. I'll give you my word."

Beth snorted. "Sorry. Not good enough."

Kit gave her a measured look. "I won't slow down for you. My business is urgent, and I've waited too long already."

"I'll keep up."

He shrugged. "Fine, luv. Then it's off to bed. Morning will be upon us in no time, and I mean to leave with the dawn."

She took a step back as he stood. Beth didn't know what the future might hold, but at least she had a plan. Throwing her lot in with the Knightmare may be reckless, but playing it safe wasn't an option.

Chapter Twenty-One

Edmond stomped the snow from his boots before entering through the door Charles held open. The blasted weather had turned for the worse, doubling his journey's length as he tried to return home. He pulled off his gloves and scarf, placing them within his hat, which he handed to his butler.

"How is Anna?" The retrieval of the Viper's Eye had taken longer than he had anticipated. The stubborn whore, plus the added travel from the storm had put him days behind his intended schedule. He handed Charles his coat. "Answer me. My daughter, how is she?"

"I am sorry, sir. Miss Anna is abed, unresponsive again."

Dread stretched across his shoulders. Was he too late? He couldn't be. He had her cure. "How long?"

"On the second day of your departure, sir."

Damn. He should have been faster. "She still lives?"

"Yes, sir."

Relief flooded him. She hadn't left him, he wasn't too late. His hand strayed to his waistcoat pocket and touched the bulge, reassuring himself the Viper's Eye was safe. He must act immediately.

"The upstairs maid, the one with no family, what is her name?"

"Miss Jenn, sir."

She was the one. No one would miss her. But where to use the stone? Expediency would be Anna's room, but he discarded it immediately for two thoughts. First, when he healed his daughter and she awoke, he didn't want to upset her any more than he already had, and removing the maid's body would be more noticeable from upstairs. "I want you to fetch her and bring her to my study." His study afforded him privacy and had the added benefit of being near the root cellar.

"Yes, sir."

Edmond didn't wait to see if Charles followed words with action. He trusted his butler with his life and Anna's. He strode down the hallway, and upon reaching his study, he went directly to the painting of his late wife and son hanging on the wall behind his desk. He stared at the family he had failed. How he missed them. His heart raced in fear. This must work. The jewel's power had done wonders for him and it would save his little girl. He felt better than he ever had, except for the headaches, which kept cropping up since the use of the jewel. He needed to calm himself. Edmond inhaled, holding his breath for several counts and slowly exhaled. He must be focused, push aside all his fears and worries. His intent and will had to be clear and strong.

Calmer, he sat behind his desk and waited. He needed a plan. The whore had struggled and screamed, and he was thankful he had bound and gagged her. He must do something similar with the maid. There was no need to upset the household with her screams, bringing unnecessary questions and delays. He drummed his fingers on the polished teak desktop. What was taking so long?

Finally, a light tap to the door alerted him of their presence. Charles entered, with the maid a few steps behind. It was about time.

"Please, come forward."

Jenn walked to the center of the room. "My lord, ye requested me?" Her cockney accent thick as she dropped a quick curtsey.

"Yes, my dear. I have a task of the utmost importance for you." Edmond stepped around his desk to stand before the girl. Looking past her shoulder, he directed his attention to his butler. "This requires privacy."

Charles understood him immediately, like the trusted loyal servant he was, and he quietly shut and locked the door, dropping the key into his pocket.

"Em…sir," the maid stuttered as she glanced worriedly to the closed door.

Edmond placed a comforting hand to her arm, directing her attention back to him. "I know you are confused. All will be clear shortly." He tightened his grip so she wouldn't bolt, though with the locked door, she had nowhere to go. "Charles, I'll need your help."

His butler stepped behind the girl just as she tried to twist out of his hold.

"No! Please!" Her struggles increased, but Charles grabbed the girl's arms, wrenching them behind her. He shackled both her wrists into one hand and with his free arm, slung it around the girl's neck and pulled the maid tightly to his front. Jenn opened her mouth to scream and Edmond slapped his hand over her mouth, stifling her shout. This would never do. He needed both of his hands.

"Sir, perhaps your cravat?"

Excellent. His manservant was a wealth of ideas. One-handed, he removed the diamond pin and dropped it into his pocket and then undid the knot, before wadding the soft silk into a ball. With a nod to his butler to make sure he had her secure, Edmond quickly removed his hand and stuffed the cloth into her mouth. He took a step back.

The maid continued with her struggles and muffled shouts, until Charles tightened his arm across her neck to cut off her air. Soon the poor maid went limp from lack of oxygen. Her eyes were wide with fear, and her breath pushed in and out of wide nostrils as she fought for air. Edmond saw her trembling and took pity. He placed a gentle hand against her cheek.

"I know you are frightened, but I need you. Anna needs you."

Confusion flittered through Jenn's eyes, but briefly. Fear coursed through her as her body began to shudder. She tried to shake her head no, but Charles's grip afforded her little movement.

Edmond gave her cheek a final pat. "You're about to save my child's life. I'm sure you will be blessed for your sacrifice."

He took a step back and reached into his waistcoat, withdrawing the Viper's Eye. It gleamed in the flickering light of his study. Since he used the stone, it wasn't an inert opal anymore. The translucent black gem glittered with swirling colors that once were static. Violet, orange, and red prismed and danced inside. Edmond stood transfixed; he felt a connection to the stone. It wanted him to use it. It was like it spoke to him. He could almost hear its words. The soft call of his name whispered though his mind. Yes. Yes, this was right. All for Anna.

"Hold her tight," he admonished Charles, before closing his eyes and taking a deep breath to center himself. The magic would work. Nothing less was acceptable. He had his faith, proven when he tested it on the whore; the power of the Viper's Eye was very real. He snapped open his eyes and held the jewel in his open palm before girl.

"*Ego obsident vos*, Astaroth, *exaudi me*," Edmond began the incantation. Just as before, he continued with the ritual words, and the gem grew warm in his palm. He smiled. Keeping strict focus, the Latin phrases flowed easily through him. "*Infundere tua receptaculum, dona mihi tua virtute et studio.* " He fixated on the now throbbing pulse of the shining jewel, which again was entwined, with his heartbeat.

He stepped forward and wrenched at the maid's bodice, struggling with the fabric. He cursed. Next time he would have a knife. The cloth finally tore and gave way—exposing her left breast. He didn't hesitate. Edmond pressed the Viper's Eye against the maid's heart, and just like the whore, Jenn let out a smothered scream, and her body arched backward.

Continuing in Latin, he offered the maid's heart in sacrifice and power flowed into the gem. Jenn sagged into Charles's hold, but his butler didn't falter and kept her upright. The girl's horror fed Edmond as much as the stone, the whites of her eyes rolling, sweat breaking across her skin, as a constant keening escaped around the gag.

With a grin, he pressed the Viper's Eye to the center of her forehead. The maid's shaking turned to spasms as she tried to thrash, but her actions were useless. Edmond uttered the last incantation and just as before, there was a jolt beneath his hand, and quickly the jewel turned burning hot.

He ignored the pain and heat. The maid fainted and the screaming stopped. Grabbing the gag from his chosen sacrifice, he placed the burning gem on top of the silk cravat and carefully folded the fabric over the primed jewel. He must waste no time in getting the opal to his daughter.

Crossing the room, he did pause when he reached the door, turning to Charles who had released his burden to the floor and stared at the drained woman in fascinated horror. "Charles, take the maid to the cellar. You may want to restrain her."

"Miss Jenn isn't dead, sir?"

"Not quite."

Vexed by the time it took him to give his butler orders and have him unlock the study's door, Edmond spun and jogged down the hallway. He would not waste any more time. His Anna needed him. Reaching the grand staircase, Edmond took the steps two at a time. Quickly, he reached his daughter's bedroom. With a wave of his hand, he dismissed Anna's governess.

"Close the door behind you."

With the click of the latch, he knew his order was obeyed without taking the effort to verify. All his focus was on his daughter, who lay pale and unmoving, all but swallowed up in the large bed. Edmond crossed the room and sat carefully on the edge of the mattress. His daughter's frail chest, thankfully, still rose and fell. The knot of tension inside him unraveled slightly. He wasn't too late, and now he held in his hands the artifact to cure her.

Even through the silk covering, the heat of the jewel still reached his palm. He unfolded the cravat, revealing the black glowing of the Viper's Eye, which was still strangely pulsing to the beat of his own heart. It appeared a living, breathing creature. He supposed it was, considering it held the life-force of the upstairs maid.

It was time to heal his precious Anna. He took a deep breath and focused his will.

"Astaroth, *tuum fiat voluntas tua*," Edmond incanted. *Yes, your will be done*. Holding to his belief, he pressed the hotly glowing jewel to Anna's forehead.

Chapter Twenty-Two

With a high-pitched shriek, Anna's eyes snapped open, rolling to show only their whites, while her frail body arched off the mattress. Her cry transformed into a piercing wail, the keening note of horrible pain. The Viper's Eye was burning in its intensity. Edmond panicked. The jewel wasn't healing his daughter, but stealing her life in the most horrific way. He snatched his hand away, but the jewel remained fixed to her forehead.

Shocked, he wrapped both hands around the gem, trying to lodge his fingers underneath to pry it away from her. Anna's painful cry changed to low whimpers as her body collapsed to the bed. He barely registered the door slamming open and then Charles was next to him.

"Help me. Help, the jewel!" Edmond's voice cracked in his anguish and fear. The stone was killing her.

Charles grasped Edmond's arms and together they pulled with all their strength. The Viper's Eye wrenched free, tossing both men to the ground as they fell in a heap to the floor. The jewel popped free from his grasp and flew through the air to land in the center of the room on the Aubusson rug. There it lay like a baleful eye, glaring out at the world.

Edmond.

His name whispered across his mind caused a shudder to rack through his body. He sat transfixed, unable to move with his gaze locked to the gem.

"My lord! Miss Anna…"

The name of his daughter uttered by his faithful servant broke the spell, and he leapt to his feet and reached for his girl. Charles stood beside him, tears streaking his face as he shook his head. *No! Impossible!* His Anna was only unconscious. She wasn't dead. She couldn't be dead. He gathered her up in his arms, cradling and rocking her as if she were a babe once more. He stroked her hair.

"Wake up, my little poppy, it's time to wake up. Your papa is home."

"Sir, my lord…" Charles reached out a hand to him. "She's gone."

"No, you're wrong. She lives. She must live. It cured her. She's only sleeping."

"My lord—"

"No!" He glared at Charles. About to continue his admonishment, he froze when he realized they weren't the only ones in the room. A stranger stood in the center of the rug holding the glowing Viper's Eye in his hand.

Charles half turned, his eyes drawing to the center of the room, then turning his head back to his master. "Sir, what…"

"Protect Anna." He carefully placed his daughter back onto the bed and gave her a brief kiss to her cheek. Brushing past his butler, he strode across the room to confront the stranger. How dare this man enter his home, unannounced and holding his property?

He stopped in front of the gentleman, and a gentleman he was if appearances could be judged. His black hair was neatly cut, short, and well styled. His face held an aristocratic look with all sharp angles and pale white skin, making his dark eyes appear black. Smartly dressed, his crisp white cravat was neatly folded and tied in the latest fashion, held in place with a blood-red ruby pin. The ambient light of the room made the gold and silver embroidery on his waistcoat sparkle. The rest of his elegant, expensive attire was a study in black. His fitted tight coat, breeches, and boots all dark as midnight on a moonless night. And he was tall, towering over Edmond's own short stature, easily standing several hands higher. To add to his refined facade, the stranger was well proportioned. Not hulking large for his height, but lean and muscular, like an Adonis sculpture he had once seen.

"You sir, have entered my home improperly and are holding my property."

The man smiled, showing even white teeth, and his black eyes crinkled with mirth. "Ah, but there you are mistaken, Edmond. You invited me here," his rich cultured English accent drawled.

"Who are you? How do you know my—"

"My lord?" Charles interrupted.

Frustrated, Edmond shot a glare at his butler while waving a hand to silence him. He needed all his concentration for the stranger. He turned back to confront him.

"You have me at a disadvantage, sir. You appear to know me, but I have no recollection of yourself."

"You may call me Roth." The stranger's smile grew wider.

Edmond felt the blood leech from his face. Impossible. He could not be Astaroth. There was no such being. It was a myth surrounding a gem with mystic capabilities. There was no God; he had decided a long time ago after losing his entire family except for Anna. If there was no God, then there was no heaven with angels or demons in hell. He didn't know what game this man was playing, but Roth would not win. The Viper's Eye was Edmond's.

He held out his hand. "The gem, sir. It's mine and I want it back."

"In good time," Roth replied. The man glanced to the bed, drawing Edmond's attention with him, to where Charles sat beside Anna, holding her hand and weeping.

As if he felt their eyes, Charles looked up and met Edmond's gaze. His butler's eyes were filled with grief and confusion. "My lord—"

"There's still a way to save Anna," Roth interrupted, drawing Edmond's attention away from his manservant.

"Of course, there is. My daughter will live."

"Everyone will not see things your way. You must protect her. They will try to steal her away." He thrust a chin at Charles. "Send him away. He would deny you your little girl. He plans to take her away."

"Never!" Edmond whirled and charged the bed. He flung an arm out—pointing his finger at his butler. "Leave! Now! Get out! Get away from her."

Charles held up two hands in protest. "My lord, please—"

Edmond grabbed his butler's arm and yanked him off the bed. "You will not touch her. You will not take her from me."

He dragged his manservant around the bed and

pulled him across the room, all the while Charles was stammering out protests and questions. His words fell on deaf ears, as a rage fired and consumed Edmond. No one would take his Anna from him. No one. He shoved the servant from him and out into the hallway. Snatching the door, he slammed it shut, and threw the lock. Anna would be safe. He would protect her at all costs. Do anything, use anyone, even a man who thought he was a demon, if it would heal his daughter.

He whirled and marched to the stranger. If he had the answers, Edmond wanted them and he would get them.

Roth *tsked* at him while shaking a finger. "Your disrespect and disbelief are unacceptable. Kneel before your better."

The command lanced through Edmond, tearing a cry from his lips as he resisted.

"Kneel, human." Roth's face grew dark in anger. "You have given me dominion over you. Kneel!"

Edmond's legs collapsed from underneath him, and he fell to the rug, landing on his hands and knees. His breath came out in bellows as deep sharp pain racked his body. His vision tunneled, and he gagged on the bile rising up his throat.

"Enough! You are no use to me like this."

His pain abruptly stopped, and like a puppet master pulling strings, he was raised up off his hands and found himself kneeling with his head bowed before Astaroth.

"Better. Look at me."

On his command, Edmond lifted his eyes to stare at the demon before him. He tried to speak, but found he could not make his mouth form any words. Instead of fear, he felt his defiance grow. No one controlled him. The demon would pay.

Roth laughed. "You would defy me? I, who have given you renewed strength and vigor, added years to your life? I, who would offer you even more? Grant you your deepest desire?" The demon reached out with his free hand and patted Edmond's cheek. "You are a strong one, aren't you? I like that. It's been a while since a man with such character and strength of will was holder of my jewel."

The demon walked a circle around him, and all Edmond could do was stare straight ahead, until Roth stopped once again in front of him. He held the Viper's Eye out on his open palm. "Do you know what this jewel truly is? It is the most wondrous creation I have ever made! As well you know, it holds the stolen life of the sacrifice."

He crouched down and drew eye level. "The life-force isn't the important bit. Well, it is to its bonded wielder; the power of life is what keeps you younger, healthy, immortal."

Edmond's eyes widened at this information. Immortality?

"Ah, I see you did not know. But that is of no importance, just a gift from me to my, say, employee. For you see, the most magically incredible power of the stone is its harvest of souls." Roth straightened to stand tall before Edmond. His smile grew wide as he stared and marveled at the gem in his hands. "No longer do I have to tempt, torment, or trick a mortal into his fall. I can simply take the soul directly, skipping over all the balderdash of free will. And with you, my dear Edmond," the demon tore his gaze from the stone to stare directly into Edmond's eyes, "I will rise faster and farther than I ever have before. High enough to challenge the Prince of Darkness himself, if I so choose."

Edmond could feel the power flowing out of the demon before him. How did he ever mistake him for just a man? Here was the true power of the jewel. Standing before him was the answer to all the prayers he had sent heavenward but were ignored. His pulse raced in excitement as he knelt before his salvation.

The demon gifted him with a gentle smile. "What do you truly wish for, Edmond?"

He found he could speak and bowed his head in reverent gratitude. "To live in peace with my Anna, to be a whole family again, her illness gone. That is all I ever needed, all I want."

"Then you shall have it." The demon placed a hand to his bowed head. "But it shall not be easy."

Edmond looked up, eagerly. "Anything," he vowed. "What would you have me do, Astaroth?"

"Use the jewel, Edmond. Harvest me souls and keep yourself strong."

He nodded his agreement. It would be so.

"Know this: it will take great power to be with your Anna. Many souls you must sacrifice. Young, old, innocent, kind, I would have them all. And when you have gathered enough, I will return to you and you will be united with your little girl."

Edmond felt relief flood him. This he could, would achieve. No lives were more important to him than Anna's.

The demon grew stern, his eyes narrowing, and his lips thinning. "Protect your daughter if you wish to be with her. Many will try and steal her away. But you must keep her safe as you do my will."

"I promise. No one will harm my daughter."

Astaroth nodded. "You must be strong. Use my jewel as intended and you will become invincible."

With those final words, Astaroth thrust his hand out pressing the Viper's Eye against Edmond's forehead. The burning gem's power coursed through him and just as before in the boarding house in York, he lost consciousness.

****

Edmond slowly became aware of the banging on the locked door matching the throbbing of his head. "Cease your incessant pounding!" He clutched at his head. The pain was near unbearable. He took several deep breaths. "I'll be out in a moment." His order was obeyed, and with the noise lessened, he was able to relax and uncurl himself from his prone position on the rug.

He scooped up the jewel as he rose to his feet with renewed vigor, though his head still lanced with spikes of fire. He rubbed his temple and studied the black opal. The deep colors continued to swirl, but it no longer pulsed and was cold in his hand.

There was a spring to his steps as he crossed the room to sit on the mattress beside his sleeping Anna. He had work to do, but he could spare a moment for his little poppy. He brushed a hand across her pale cheek and shuddered at the iciness of her skin. She was cold, her skin dry and icy. He quickly pulled up the warm woolen blanket at the foot of her bed and tucked it tightly around her. He didn't want her to catch ill after all he was about to do for her.

Edmond sighed as he gazed down at his beloved daughter. All would be right soon. He needed a plan. All souls could not be equal. For instance, the whore he first sacrificed must be worth less then the upstairs maid. Would quality trump quantity? Would youth be worth more than the elderly? Edmond would need to reach his quota quickly. He didn't want Anna to suffer anymore than she had already.

There was only one way to find out. He would harvest the most innocent, pure, and the youngest sacrifices he could find and hope the quality of his choices would speed him on his way. With a final tender kiss on Anna's cool cheek, Edmond rose and crossed the room. He unlocked the door to find his distraught butler ringing his hands in worry in the hallway.

"Charles, I'm glad you're here."

"My lord, Anna—"

"Will be fine," he admonished. "I want a guard placed on her door. No one is to enter. She will be protected at all times. Do you understand?"

"Of course, my lord, but she—"

"Enough! Do my bidding." Edmond pushed past Charles as he entered the hall. He paused and turned back to his butler. "We have a stable boy?"

"Yes, my lord. Several."

"Who is the youngest?"

"His name is Matthew."

Edmond gave a wave of his hand. "His age?"

Charles cringed, but answered in a whisper. "Eight, my lord."

"Excellent," he smiled. The boy would do. "Fetch him and bring him to my study."

Chapter Twenty-Three

The wind picked up, blowing sleet in Beth's face. She tugged her scarf higher. Frozen to the bone, she was happy when they had ridden through the Micklegate Bar and entered the city of York. But instead of turning and finding lodging, as any sane person would do in the middle of a storm, Kit kept them riding steadily deeper into the city.

Drat the man! All she wanted was to be warm, dry, and out of this saddle. She was used to riding, but not the hours they'd put in since leaving Tredford and hitting the road. The dawn had broken crisp and cold, but the sky had darkened, and a light snow began to fall, soon after their leaving, which gradually changed to sleet with gusting winds. She really didn't want to think what the temperature was. Frozen wet ass cold, is what it felt like. She should be grateful Kit had clothing to outfit her for the journey. She didn't want to think where he had gotten woman's clothing from, but she was grateful for the warm dress and leggings, oh, and the cloak she was currently wearing. The clothes had even fit her reasonably well. Though the draft from riding astride was held a bit at bay from the warmth of her borrowed mount, she couldn't and most definitely didn't want to ride sidesaddle. Lucky for her, Kit didn't have one of those saddles in his possession.

Beth glared at the greatcoat, hat wearing, man

riding ahead of her on his flashy chestnut. He'd traded in his iconic tricorne highwayman hat for a gentleman's beaver hat, and she wasn't sure how it stayed on in this wind. It didn't matter; he still looked strong and sure somehow. Even in this nasty weather, he oozed masculinity. It wasn't fair. Both he and his mount looked fresh as daisies. How was that possible in this weather, let alone the miles they had ridden? Kit still sat tall in the saddle regardless of the blowing frozen rain, and Dante still had a spring in his hooves.

How had she not recognized his horse? She was a horse lover. There's no way she wouldn't have remembered the large shiny chestnut with four matching socks and a big white blaze. Kit must have done something to disguise Dante, or all the gelding's white markings would stick out, and practically glow in the moonlight. Even disguised, she should have known the horse by his athletic flashy movement. Dante was a fancy horse.

She slouched lower in the saddle and gave a pat to her plain bay gelding named Root. He was the exact opposite of his stable mate. Sturdy, brown, and a bit rotund, but she believed he could plod on for miles, days even. And sensible. No spooking or gallivanting about like Dante had done for the first miles of their trip. Thank God for the blessing. She had woken up drunk, since she'd only had a few hours of sleep before their departure, and now she was tired and greatly hungover. She'd kill for some aspirin and a quiet bed.

They picked their way over the bridge spanning the river Ouse, and Kit finally turned, leading them off the main road. Oh please, God. Let their destination be near. Beth had lost all feeling in her feet, and her fingers were frozen inside her gloves. A sudden gust of wind caught her hood, tearing it off her head. *Shit.* She wrestled with the heavy woolen material and managed to cover her head once more, but not before she got soaked. *Damn this weather.*

They rode a sharp left between two buildings, narrow and barely wide enough for their mounts, but emerged into a small courtyard. A stable boy ran out just as Kit dismounted. She couldn't hear his instructions, but she saw the boy pocket coins. They must have arrived at their destination. With an inward sigh, she wondered if she'd be able to dismount. She might be stuck up here.

Kit unbuckled his saddlebag and turned to gaze up at her. Okay, she could do this. Beth wasn't about to embarrass herself. She may have complained internally the entire trip, mentally ranted actually, but she hadn't verbalized her discomfort, nor hindered their journey in any way. She'd kept up with the pace he'd set as promised, and never faltered even as the weather grew horrible. She was no wilting pansy. Keeping up with Kit had been a challenge, but she had vowed she'd do it or die trying. Since she was presumably alive, though it was up for debate at this very moment, she'd get off this horse on her own.

Beth kicked her feet out of the stirrups and swung her right leg over and slid off the gelding. When her feet hit the icy cobblestones, they slid out from under her, and she crashed to the ground, landing on her ass in a chilly puddle. *Great. Just great.*

A brown glove-clad hand appeared in front of her face. Blowing out a disgusted snort, Beth clasped his arm with her hand and held tight as he tugged her upright. She swayed as she got her feet under her. Luckily, he didn't let go until she was steady. He turned to Root and removed the second saddlebag, flinging it over his shoulder to join where the other one rested. Kit started for a door in the rear of the building opposite of the stable. She took a stride to follow, but her foot slipped on the icy stones, almost sending her crashing back down, except Kit managed to grab her arm and kept her from falling. Beth felt heat flush her face. Well, at least her face was warm now.

Without a word and keeping a hold of her arm, Kit guided them to the door, and they entered a bustling dining room. Crossing the room, he led them into a lobby and stopped in front of a roaring fireplace.

"You're bluer than your cloak, and soggier than bran mash. Stay here, thaw out. I'll arrange for our rooms."

Beth wouldn't argue. It's not like she had any money, anyway. She nodded and turned her full attention to the lovely blaze next to her. Her teeth began to chatter as she held out her hands to warm. A hot shower. Thermal underwear. Central heating. She really missed the twenty-first century.

Wanting to distract herself from her depressing thoughts, she looked for Kit while soaking up the heat from the flames. Crowded up to the bell desk, holding his beaver hat under his arm, saddlebags slung over his shoulders, hair and coat dripping wet, he didn't appear much better off than she did. Except, somehow his skin wasn't the same lovely shade of blue. Men and their internal heaters. She'd loved snuggling with Grant on a cold Scottish winter night. He had kept her so warm. Her eyes welled up. *Damn.* She really needed to stop thinking about him. He was a traitor. A liar. He wasn't worth her tears.

Beth blinked them back as Kit crossed the room. She would not cry in front him ever again, so help her God. She gave him a tired smile and rubbed her temple where her head still throbbed. Mentally she added OTC medicines to her list of things from home she missed.

"Right, luv. Follow me." Kit turned and went to the stairs off the lobby. They climbed the first, turned on the landing, and started up the second.

Beth looked up. How many more flights? Her legs were beginning to wobble. She was an accomplished rider, competing in jumpers and events, but her specialty wasn't in endurance riding. Since she'd married Grant and helped run Cleitmuir as a hotel, she'd been lucky to make an hour in the saddle a few times a week. The trek across land to York had been a test in her will power. Thank God she didn't have a watch; she didn't want to know how long the ride had taken. But by the numbness of her butt and the tiredness of her legs, it had been hours. If they went to the top floor, she may well slit her wrists now. She doubted she'd be able to climb the stairs, up or down, with sore legs tomorrow.

A groan escaped her when Kit started up the third flight. He chuckled, the bastard.

"Not much farther, luv. We're on this floor."

Good to know. She followed him blindly, one foot in front of the other, almost colliding into him when he stopped before a closed door. He turned the knob and flung the door open.

"Here we go. Ladies, first." He gestured with a sweeping arm. She didn't care, as long as there would be a fire and some sort of bed to crash on. Beth stumbled in and let out a string of curses when she saw no hearth. She wanted to break down and cry no matter her earlier vow. A fire was all she asked for, how hard was that? She was stuck with only a stand of coals like in her room at the Boar and Rose. Central heat was only in her far away dreams.

With a laugh, Kit closed the door and let the saddlebags slide to the floor. He dropped his hat onto the small wooden table, and then removed his coat and draped it on the back of a chair.

"Not much of a lady with those words, luv. Can you get the coals going?"

"I could, if every joint and limb weren't frozen solid. And it's not that." She rubbed her temple again and sniffled from the cold. "I was just really looking forward to a fire in an actual fireplace." She waved her hand over at the brazier. "Not some lump of rocks."

"Here, then, let me at it."

She stepped to the side, while Kit crouched beside the coal stand and grabbed the tinder and flint. Brisk and efficient, he set out the tinder on top of the coals and then, taking flint to steel with a firm strike, the tinder ignited. Beth wondered when matches were invented, apparently not in 1795. They were so much more convenient than flint. It was like living in the dark or cold ages.

As her mind wandered, Kit added a few more pieces of tinder, and in no time, the coals began to redden. She shivered. It wasn't soon enough.

He straightened and reached for her water-laden cloak. "Off it goes." Untying the garment, he hung it on the freestanding rack placed near the brazier. "You did well today. I was expecting to have to stop and hole up some place before York."

"You mean that was an option?" She huddled closer to the coals, extending her hands over the heat. Surprisingly, there was a fair amount of warmth.

He ignored her and strode to the door where he left the saddlebags. He snatched them off the floor. "You should change garments. You need to get dry." He tossed a bag in her direction, which she barely caught. Beth stood staring as he walked to the table and placed the other bag on its surface. Opening the flap, he pulled out some tidily rolled clothes. He reached up and tugged at his drooping cravat, working at the soggy knot.

"What are you doing?"

He faced her while pulling the linen away from around his neck. "It should be apparent. I'm getting out of this foul attire and into something more comfortable and dry, as you should be doing."

Beth's mouth dropped open. She quickly snapped it shut and glanced around the room. Nope, the only door was the one they entered. There was only one small bed, a table, and a single chair. One room. Not even a room divider.

"Wait. I thought you said *rooms*, as in more than one?"

Kit slipped out of his jacket, followed quickly by his vest. He was tugging his shirttails out of his breeches when he replied. "Plans change and one must adapt. A lesson I learned a long time ago. The boarding house was out of rooms due to the storm." He caught her gaze. "We're sharing." He grabbed the back of his shirt and pulled it over his head.

Seriously? He expected them to stay in the same room? Sleep in the same room? Was he really undressing in front of her? Did he assume she would in turn? "No. Absolutely not. Get out!" She was so done with men and their promises; there was no trusting them. It wasn't really his fault. Stupid weather. But Beth was tired and cranky and wanted to find some peace and quiet, not be trapped in a small room with a man who was too self-assured for his own good.

Like the feline his name implied, he prowled across the room to stand before her. Her gaze dropped to his bare chest before she could stop herself, noticing various scars, small puckered ones, along with various slashes decorating his well-defined muscles and the light smattering of reddish-brown hair. Her eyes lowered to his six-pack and followed the hairline which narrowed and arrowed below his waist. Beth jerked her gaze up and stared into his green eyes, which were glinting like a cat's in the lamplight.

"You have two options, luv," his voice was low and soft. "This is my room, paid by my coin. I'm happy to share. Or..." He gestured toward the door without breaking eye contact. "You're welcome to leave and take your chances. After all, you're the one who insisted on coming along."

Eyes wide, her mind a jumble of thoughts, Beth knew her options were few to none.

"But—"

He gripped her chin with strong fingers. "You're safe. I give you my word, for what it's worth." Kit gave her a roguish grin. "I'll not be doing anything you don't want." He dropped his hand and crossed the small space and plunked himself into the chair next to his saddlebag. He pulled off his boots and stood. The ass looked up when he reached for the buttons on the flaps of his breeches. Grinning, he spoke, "You're welcome to watch, but know this, I'll have my turn as well."

Beth spun and gave him her back. She heard him chuckle, the jerk, and assumed he resumed changing clothes. He made little noise, while she continued to stare at the wood paneling before her, making sure she remained in the heated area of the coals. Her wet clothes began to steam and smell, reminding her of a wet dog. She wished he'd hurry; she'd love to be out of her soggy clothes. Of course, she didn't believe for one moment he'd keep his eyes to himself. He wasn't that type of man.

She leapt upward and squealed at the same time when his hand suddenly landed on her shoulder.

"A bit jumpy, are we?"

She spun and glared at him. "You did that on purpose! You could have just told me you were done."

"Where's the fun to be had?"

"It's all about fun and thrills for you, isn't it?" Beth shook her head.

A dark look crossed his face but disappeared in a blink when he smiled. "If you can't enjoy yourself, what's the point of living?"

There was no changing the man. Or any man in fact. And she certainly didn't want a man to try and change her. Fine. He could remain Peter Pan if he wanted to and never act the grown-up. She'd take the higher road. "Turn around." She made a twirling motion with a finger. He didn't budge, and even raised an eyebrow at her. "Turn. Around," she demanded. "I didn't watch you."

"Your loss." He grinned.

Beth juggled the saddlebag to free up a hand, which she raised, ready to smack him across the face. Kit took a few steps backward and held up his hands in surrender.

"Easy, luv," he admonished. "I was only teasing."

She dropped her hand and swore. How did he manage to do that? Get under her skin? It's as if he enjoyed getting her angry. *Hmmpf.* So be it. She had to stop walking into his traps. "You're still looking."

"And so I am." He gave her a sweeping, elegant bow, bending full at the waist with a slight dip to his knee. The other leg extended behind as he waved and twirled one arm down to the ground. He straightened and gave her his best smile. "I'll be going down to the dining room and securing us a table. No doubt you must be starved."

As if on cue, her stomach let out a large growl, which turned his smile into a grin. "Change quickly," he admonished. "Or there might not be enough food left." He got to the door and paused in the opening. "Unless you need some help with your laces?"

"Out!" Beth pointed a finger to the hallway. "I'll manage just fine on my own."

"No doubt." With those words, he slipped through and closed the door behind him.

Beth stared at the empty space, while the silence closed in around her.

Chapter Twenty-Four

Kit stood and pulled out a chair, admiring Beth as she approached. The new fancier dress suited her more than barmaid's clothes. The day dress, though a simple cut, clung to her curves in a flattering lavender, to swish enticingly around her ankles. My lady, indeed. She looked much better, with roses back on her cheeks and purpose in her stride. He hadn't lied when he complimented her endurance throughout their journey. He'd been greatly surprised when she had kept pace and never complained, not once. It had been impressive.

She quirked an eyebrow when she reached his side, so he gestured to the chair. She sat, and he pushed her closer to the table before taking his seat. He reached for the plainly folded cloth napkin and picked it up. With a flourish, he placed it onto his lap. Looking up, he noticed Beth's smile.

"You're such a puzzle of contradictions," she stated.

"Am I?" Kit poured her some wine and gestured to her full plate of simple fare. "I could say the same. You are obviously hungry, yet you haven't set to."

"Actually, I'm afraid of embarrassing myself. I think I might be able to inhale all this food in one fell swoop."

"Worry not, my lady. I'll not judge. Please, eat. I

know you're hungry."

She ducked her head at his comment, and he smiled. He relaxed when she picked up her fork and started eating. Returning to his own plate, he could only imagine how starved she was, since he was famished himself, not even waiting for her arrival to rectify his hunger. It hadn't been his intent to ride straight through with Beth accompanying him, but with the turn of weather and his worry for Sophie, he had forgotten his manners and had ridden in single-minded pursuit of his goal. He'd felt the cad when he saw how cold and miserable Beth was at the end.

Which he shouldn't have. There was no place for caring in his life; he looked out only for himself. It shouldn't have mattered. She was the one who insisted on riding with him. He had been set to leave her behind if she hadn't been able to keep up. Yet she had and he did feel guilty. What was it about this woman?

"So." Beth placed her fork down and took up her cup and sipped at her wine. "What's your story? How can you be both gentleman and rogue?"

If only she knew, but he shared his life with no one, and he would keep it such. She certainly didn't need to know the dark history he kept locked away. He was a danger to her and everyone around him. The less she knew the better.

"I am no gentleman."

"Well, you could have fooled me. Quite the impressive bow upstairs, and I wasn't the one flinging a napkin around as if it were a fabulous cloak. Plus, didn't you say you speak four different languages? That takes education. I'm just saying…" She shrugged and sipped more wine.

Kit stilled. He'd have to keep in mind she wasn't the pretty flower she appeared. The chit had a brain and a memory. He needed to keep her at a distance.

"Think of it as set dressing."

"Like in the theater?"

"Exactly. Like the pretty props hiding the dirt and wear of the backstage." Kit took a sip of his wine to hide his own discomfort.

She shook her head. "I'm not really buying it, but whatever, I get it. You don't want to talk about it." She picked up her fork and idly pushed a lone potato around her empty plate. She lowered her voice. "Have you killed anyone in your...you know..." she waved her fork in the air, as she checked out the room to make sure no one was paying attention to them. "In your line of work?"

He sighed. He should say yes, make himself the blackguard most thought him to be and yet... "No."

"Well that's something, I suppose."

He gave her his menacing highwayman stare from across the table. "It doesn't mean I'm not dangerous. My reputation precedes me; therefore, I have only had to wound to get my point across."

She snorted, and he found himself smiling at her disdain. He didn't think she'd ever take him seriously, which was a difficulty and a reward at the same time. He liked her. His growing admiration was a problem, but bloody hell, her resilience and beauty was a drawing combination. He froze. What was he thinking? In a sudden revelation, he realized his proposition of her being his eyes and ears was detrimental. It was a mistake and one he would rectify.

"So, you never did tell me why you needed to get

to York?" Beth interrupted his thoughts. He raised a brow, and she smiled in return. "Yeah, I get it, too much prying, but still, come on, tell me."

Kit mentally sighed. He supposed it didn't really matter. "I'm here looking for a friend. She was to return to Tredford by now and hasn't."

"She? Perhaps a partner of yours?"

Too quick by far. This time he didn't hide his sigh. "Sophie came to York to sell certain…items of mine. I'm concerned something may have happened."

Beth's blue eyes sparkled. "I could help you."

"No."

"Come on, let me. Think of it as repayment for saving me. Seriously, I'd like to help."

"Repayment isn't necessary, and I don't need your help."

"Kit—"

"It's getting late." He interrupted and held up a hand to stop her when Beth shook her head and was about to argue even more.

"Fine. Have it your way for now." She smiled. "I'll change your mind later."

Kit highly doubted it. "If you are finished, we should retire. I want an early start." He stood and before he could reach her chair, Beth stood as well.

He offered his arm, which she took, laughing.

"No gentleman, right."

Kit led her from the room. After he helped her sell her rings, he would abandon her in York, and she'd soon see the truth. Kit wasn't a gentleman, not even a man, but a monster. Beth was best left far and away from him.

Chapter Twenty-Five

Kit slowly awoke from a deep sleep. He was warm, rested, and currently wrapped around a soft curvaceous body. He smiled to himself as he tugged Beth tighter against his chest. It had taken some convincing on his part to get her to share the small bed. It helped he refused to sleep either on the chair or floor, which had caused quite the tantrum. The reminder of shared warmth, especially as the coals burnt down and the temperature lowered, finally had her acceding. Their argument amused him. He hadn't had so much fun in a while.

She fit him well, he thought, as he tucked his chin upon the soft hair on top her head. Pretty hair, like spun yellow gold. Pretty all over, truth be told. He didn't know what attracted him to her. He'd had his share of beautiful woman, she was just another among them. He wished he could treat Beth as he did Sophie. No attachments, two consenting adults with the fun they shared, yet he couldn't find the distance he had with Sophie. Somehow Beth was different. He inhaled. She smelled good, like a spring morning, surprising since neither had an opportunity for a bath. What was it about this woman? At times she acted oddly, like she was privileged, and her speech, so different from what was usually spoken. Was it because of her feistiness? He appreciated smart and brave women, ones who didn't back down when confronted. She stood up for herself.

Once to bed, it hadn't taken Beth long to find her sleep. Although, once asleep, it hadn't been restful and damn him, she had even cried, lightly, but still cried. He hated woman's tears. It always made him feel helpless. Kit preferred action, let him shoot someone, stab, rob, or woo. A hard man with little cares, softness was burned out of him. He did what he wanted, when he wanted, and assumed he would hang when his card came up. And he was fine with his fate. He deserved his fate. Until then, he'd live life to the fullest and have as much fun as possible, since he didn't have a choice, all due to a promise.

He let out a soft breath and placed a hand on her rounded hip. Slowly, he stroked his hand down to her thigh and up again. What was it about her that started changing him so? Making him want more than he should? Reviving dreams of love and family, he'd denied himself. Sophie had never affected him this way. No woman had. Beth was trouble. He needed to set her aside, before she weakened him further. Too many times he'd gone against his nature already. It worried him.

He wasn't concerned with her knowing his secret. After getting to know her somewhat—she was as closemouthed about her past as he was, and he couldn't fault her secrets since he held so many of his own. She seemed honorable, and she knew she owed him, and in doing so, would not expose him. At least that's what his gut told him, and he always tried to listen to his instincts. That same gut told him to run far and wide from her. She'd make her way. York was a large town, filled with opportunities for an intelligent and beautiful woman. He had no doubt she'd survive.

One partner was enough. He had Sophie. A missing Sophie. Worry coursed through him, cutting sharp like the sword he wore when robbing. What was happening to him? When had he started to care? Sophie and he had a comfortable relationship with no strings attached. He needed to keep it that way or cut ties. No entanglements, it's how he liked his life. There was danger in relationships, a weakness, one he vowed to never involve himself in again. Sophie's fate was a direct result of him putting the jewels in her hands, he was responsible. Once settled, he was done, a man alone and beholden to none. It was time to move on, a change in scenery would be good, perhaps somewhere closer to London, or return to the Continent.

His fingers curled into Beth's hip, through the fabric of her dress to press into her flesh. She stirred. Their peaceful time was coming to end. A shame, but for the best. He stopped the sigh before it escaped him. His lips curled upward. Time for a bit of fun, a bit of play. He couldn't pass up the opportunity. Just a small taste before they parted ways. He wondered how far he'd get before she came to her senses.

Kit brushed Beth's hair aside to reveal the long slender column of her neck. He bent closer, inhaling the spring day reminding him of better times. His lips pressed to the hollow behind her ear. So satiny, like the softest rose petal. He indulged himself, deepening his kiss as his tongue darted out to sample. Her skin tasted like molten honey, an addictive flavor. Beth stirred against him, and her lips parted on a gentle sigh. Encouraged, Kit decided to explore. He dropped kisses down her neck, and upon reaching her pulse, he paused and gave a hard suck. With a low moan, she pressed her backside against him. He continued downward with his kisses until reaching the next intriguing feminine hollow, below the shoulder but above the collarbone. His hand at her hip bunched the fabric of her dress, exposing her woolen clad legs. He moved his hand to her thigh once more, stroking and caressing.

Beth's movements became restless against him. Stopping his kisses, Kit propped himself on his elbow to study her. Her breaths came faster, and her cheeks were flushed. She turned toward him, which he aided by pulling her leg over his own. He ached to move his hand off the back of her thigh to grasp her bottom, but denied himself. She would be angry enough with him when she awoke and realized just what they were doing. No matter how tempted he was, he wouldn't cross the line unless she was fully awake and consenting.

Her mouth sought out his, on her own unwitting volition. Happy to oblige, their kiss turned heated when she slipped her tongue into his mouth. His tangled with hers, causing a moan to escape him as she pressed her heated center against his arousal. When she started to languidly move, stroking herself against his hardness, he lost the battle, and his hand moved to grip her lovely round butt cheek, keeping her firmly pressed against him. He'd had hints at her hidden sensuality, and in her sleep her mental blocks and restrictions were gone. The woman was molten fire in his hands. He tried to roll onto his back, but crashed into the wall. Damn. He wished the bed were larger. Their movements hindered in the small space, yet it didn't appear to matter to Beth, who moved more urgently against him as she made cute mewling sounds into their kiss. She was hot and wanton, and she was driving him crazy. He wanted to touch her, taste her all over. He wanted their clothing to vanish so flesh touched flesh. He'd had many pleasures in his life, fine brandy, good food, a nice horse, a reckless profession—and sex was one of his favorites. He was always up for a good time. Kit groaned. He wanted to sink himself deep inside her and hear her shout his name.

"Kit! What the hell?"

Not exactly as he had imagined, but probably for the best.

Beth placed both her small hands against his chest and pushed. His back slammed against the wall again, as she rolled backward off the bed, crashing to the floor. He peered over the edge of the bed, and found her floundering and sputtering on the ground. Right then, she appeared uninjured. He hoped he'd remain the same as well.

Resigned to his fate, he sat up and swung his legs off the bed, cringing at the discomfort his hard erection earned him in moving. He held a hand down to Beth in aid, but she slapped it away and promptly shot to her feet.

"You promised! You're such a bastard." She fisted her hands as if about to punch something. Probably him.

"If I were a gentleman, I'd take all the blame, but since I most obviously am not, I will point out you were kissing me. I was just holding on and enjoying the ride."

He was ready for her predictable slap and caught her wrist and tugged her closer. "I'm a man of my word," he stated, to slice the knife deeper into their soon separation. "I promised not to do anything you didn't wish, and I do believe you wished."

She yanked her arm from his hold and spun, practically running across the small room to the table, where she gripped the back of the chair hard enough to turn her knuckles white. She stood there shaking, head bowed, breathing hard. He did nothing but sit and watch, waiting for her next move. Kit expected her to whirl around and hurl accusations and toss him out of the room, vowing she'd wish to never see him again. Perfect really. She'd make him leave, doing all the work. He really was a bastard, in so many ways.

Her grip loosened, and she slowly turned to face him. Her face still flushed a bright red, her blue eyes were wide, and her tongue darted out to moisten her lips, causing him to ache where he was still hard, remembering her taste. He was doomed. Kit silently willed her to start shouting and tell him to get out. He needed to leave before he did something stupid. He looked away, trying to erase the temptation she represented standing tousled and flushed before him.

"I'm sorry." Her voice came out breathy and hushed.

Kit's head whipped around to stare at the tiny woman standing across the room. He hadn't expected her apology. After all, he was the one who started it, without her permission, taking entire advantage of her, but apparently she didn't know or remember.

"You're right. I can't blame you for my actions. I was the one on top of you..." she waved her hand about. "Kissing you. I don't believe there is a man alive who wouldn't accept what was being offered." Her cheeks now blazed a brighter impossible red. "I can only blame myself. My only excuse was I don't think I was really awake…"

Plan *A* it was, because *B* went to hell on the gallop. His depressing thoughts deflated part of his problem, so the ability to stand was a function he could partake now. Putting action to thoughts, once on his feet, Kit stalked across the room to stand in front of Beth. He picked up one of her hands and raised it to his lips, placing a kiss, probably his last, on her silken skin.

"Apology accepted." He let her hand drop and then couldn't help the mischievous grin curling up his mouth as he leaned into her. He heard her gasp, and she tried to step back, but the table hindered her. He reached around her, brushing her arm as he snatched his saddlebag from the table and straightened, holding up his prize for examination. She blushed prettily again, as she realized her mistake of his intentions.

"We should finish dressing and break our fast, there's much to do today."

"Right, dress." Beth skirted around him and went to the brazier where her bag lay on the floor next to it.

"I've booked the room for another day," he said as he tied yesterday's cravat around his neck with the precision of a peer of the realm. "I'm not sure how easy it will be to locate Sophie."

"Do you have any idea where to look?"

"A few." He slipped into his waistcoat, then shrugged into his fitted dark blue jacket. "But first I'll take you to the jewelers. There's no need for you to wait around all day and certainly no need for you to traipse around York helping me search."

"I want to help, as I said last night."

Not good for Plan *A*. He stomped his foot to settle it into his tall Hessian boot. "Are you familiar with York? Know how to get about? Know where a working woman would stay? Know where stolen gems could be sold?"

"No, but—"

"I don't need your help. You'd only slow me down." He deliberately made his voice harsh as he grabbed his greatcoat and hat and strode to the door and opened it. "Come down when you're ready."

Without waiting for her reply, he crossed the threshold and shut the door. He was better off on his own. It was for the best. He'd have no one to care for but himself, a difficult enough job on the best of days.

Chapter Twenty-Six

Beth was grateful for Kit's arm, which she tried not to clutch, but just rested her hand on, for the boardwalk was still icy from yesterday's storm. How in the world was he not slipping? She should be grateful at least one of them could keep their balance. Surely rock salt was discovered, invented, whatever, by now? Couldn't they do something in this century to make the simple act of walking not be a death-defying experience? She was so tired of feeling out of place. But since returning home was off the menu for now, she'd grin and bare it, face the elements, do whatever, in order to survive. Her new normal was figuring out how to recreate a life for herself.

Kit led her into the shop. The bells above the door jingled, announcing their arrival to the jeweler. He'd told her this store would have the means to buy her rings outright, plus it was one of the jewelers Sophie would try to hock Kit's ill-gotten gains. At least she wasn't hindering Kit's search for the missing woman. He needed to stop here anyway.

"Greetings, I'm Mister Feinstein. How may I be of service?" The middle-aged man, standing behind a wooden counter, greeted them. The shelving behind him contained ornate boxes, all closed and apparently locked, if the keyholes held true to their purpose.

Kit gave the shopkeeper his best smile and affected

his upper-class accent, or as Beth liked to think, his debonair highwayman speech. "Most definitely. Mrs. Leighton," he inclined his head toward her, "is in need of your appraisal services."

He had warned her previously he'd do all the talking, since the shopkeeper wouldn't work with her. Evidently women merely stood around and looked pretty in this century. Men did business, not women. God forbid a woman had a brain and the independence to use it. How in the world was Sophie supposed to sell the gems, being a woman and all? It made no sense.

"Yes, by all my means." Feinstein reached under the counter and withdrew a velvet pad. "Please, if you do not mind, place your items here."

Beth looked to Kit and waited for his nod, before opening her small purse and removing her wedding rings. After all, men did all the thinking, and of course she'd need his permission. Her hand fisted around her engagement and wedding ring. She figured one day she'd marry, but Grant had taken her by surprise. It had been a whirlwind courtship; he'd swept her off her feet. Remembering his proposal, she teared up. The restaurant had been elegant, the food amazing, and when her favorite dessert was placed in front of her, there had been a small blue box on the plate. She had forgotten how to breathe. Her hand shook when she opened the box and saw the engagement ring, a simple but elegant oval cut one-carat diamond on a white gold band. She'd been touched by his thoughtfulness. Beth rarely wore rings, as they got in the way with her decorating career. It was a ring she knew she'd wear and never take off. When Grant slipped from his chair, and got on bended knee, and gathered up her hands, his simple, "Will you marry me, lass?" had her wilting. There was never any doubt in her mind of answering anything other than yes.

"Madam?"

Kit touched her arm, startling her out of her memories. "You need not go through with this. Keep them, if it is so troubling."

It was then she realized she gripped her rings tightly in her fist. She blinked back her tears, ones she refused to shed, and tossed her shoulders back, and turned her attention to the shopkeeper.

"No. I'm good. I don't need these anymore." She opened her hand and dropped the rings onto the soft pad. It was all too true. Grant was dead. The rings were simply a reminder of his lies. She'd have a fresh start and make better choices, but in order to do so, she needed money to survive. Good riddance.

Feinstein raise his jeweler's mono glass to his eye as he cleared his throat. "Let's take a look." First, he raised the wedding band, a simple white gold ring with a series of five chip diamonds inlaid. He started humming to himself as he twisted her ring this way and that, examining from all directions. He placed it back down on the mat and quickly glanced at her. "I need more light."

With his announcement, he spun around and reached for a lit candle, which he picked up and carried to place next to the velvet pad containing her rings. Once again, he picked up the wedding ring, but this time he held it closer to the light, leaning in with his mono glass taking a much closer look.

Crap! Chills sliced through her as she realized her mistake. Her rings were from the future. What if he could tell? Sweat broke out across her brow, and she clasped her hands together. *Wait, don't panic.* There was no reason for him to think the rings were anything but what they were. Why was he looking at them so closely?

"Is there something wrong?" Beth had to know what was going through the jeweler's mind. It didn't look like a simple appraisal inspection. He was way too intent.

Feinstein looked up, monocle still attached. "Quite the contrary." He didn't elaborate further. Instead, he placed her wedding ring down and picked up her engagement ring with the one-carat diamond. The shopkeeper started humming to himself once more during his concentrated scrutiny. After a while, he placed the ring back on the velvet, removed his eyepiece and stared directly at her. A shiver of warning crawled up her spine, worry coursed through her again. Something was up.

"Madam, these rings are yours?"

Oh my, God. Did he think she stole them? How dare he! "Yes, I've had them over a year."

"Your husband, he does not mind?"

He did not just go there. Beth felt sorry for the women of this century. "My husband is dead. His opinion no longer matters." *Even if it ever had...*

"Ah, my condolences, Madam."

"Is there a problem?" She shouldn't be pushing, but Beth couldn't stand the suspense. She really needed the money.

"Again, no," Feinstein replied. "Your rings are magnificent."

Relief coursed through her. Oh, thank the beautiful

baby Jesus.

"I have never seen their likes before. The precision and clarity of the cut, from such a small carat is truly unique. Do you know the artist who crafted such work?"

She was pretty sure the store in which Grant had bought her rings hadn't made them, it probably didn't matter since it was about a hundred years before their doors would open. Beth stifled a laugh. "Um, Hamilton and Inches, they're...um...up in Edinburgh."

"I have not heard of them. Perhaps I should take a trip. Their work is exquisite."

Well maybe in the next seventy-one years, he could. She gave him a sweet smile, practically batting her eyelashes. Being underestimated as a dumb blonde came in handy at times. "Can you tell me what they're worth?"

Feinstein made a mistake with his enthusiasm. She knew he coveted her rings and as planned, Kit would make him pay. Pay well above the appraisal value. She knew what her rings were worth in the modern times, but there was no way she'd be able to haggle in this current market. She was pretty sure the jeweler would start with a low-ball offer, so he could put one over on her and make a huge profit on resale. But he didn't know he was dealing with a master thief. Kit wasn't a novice when it came to gems and jewelry and he knew their prices. He needed to, in order to know if an item was worth the time and trouble to steal. Beth was more than happy to hand the job over to Kit. An expert, after all, is an expert.

When the jeweler's assessment came in low, Kit's smile turned predatory. Let the games begin.

Kit countered. "You are not purposely underestimating the rings' values, are you?" Kit eyed the man with a speculative look, before turning to her. "Mrs. Leighton, retrieve your rings and we will go to a more honest shop."

Beth smiled, more than willing to play her role, and reached for her rings. But before she could touch them Mr. Feinstein waved her off and started apologizing. The true art of the haggle started. With each new estimate, Kit would point out the clarity or cut or their pure color, and the price continued to climb.

"I truly can go no higher, sir. You have heard my final offer."

He must not have been lying, because Kit held out his hand and closed the deal on a shake. He'd just earned Beth a hefty payday, she would be well set for a while.

"Mrs. Leighton, I should have the funds arranged for you by opening, tomorrow."

She graciously inclined her head to the jeweler, who smiled and reached for a contract to fill out. As he wrote, Kit leaned casually against the countertop.

"Now that Mrs. Leighton's business is finished, I was wondering if you would be able to help me?"

Feinstein glanced up with a smile. "Most certainly, sir. How can I be of service?"

"I am a bit of a gem enthusiast." Beth had to smother a laugh. She supposed that was one way to look at it.

The man nodded. "You appear well-educated."

It was Kit's turn to incline his head. "I am a collector of the rare and unique. I heard of a gem coming on the market I am most eager to obtain. You may have heard of or even seen it," Kit paused. "It is large, polished gemstone; it would be about palm size. Unusual coloring. The rarest of black opals, with the vaunted striations of red, orange, and violet.

The jeweler straightened. "You wouldn't be the first gentleman to make such inquiries. A Lord Renweard questioned me earlier in the week, about the exact gem. He was most adamant in locating it." Feinstein shook his head. "A most unpleasant man. I will tell you what I told him. I saw the jewel. A young man brought it in just the day before Lord Renweard queried. He's brought me items before, but I deal with stones I know I can make a profit on. It was too rare for me. Had I known there would be such interest, I wouldn't have turned him away."

Ah, mystery solved. Sophie disguised herself as a man. Maybe she should try it. Women didn't have many rights in this century.

"Do you know where he went? Did you recommend another shop?"

"I recommended Rare and Unique Antiquities, a block away. I advised him, Geoffrey, the owner might be interested." Feinstein turned to Beth, spinning the contract on the countertop and handing her a quill. "Please sign both copies."

She did as requested and accepted her copy when the shopkeeper handed it over. "It was my most honored pleasure to do business with you, Mrs. Leighton. I will see you tomorrow."

"Thank you for your time, sir." Beth gave him a glowing smile. When Kit offered his arm, she placed her hand on his coat sleeve. They then exited the store.

Outside, the cold air hit her, and she shivered. She

tugged her cloak tighter with her free hand.

"Will you be able to find your way back to our room?"

Startled, she jerked to a halt, nearly slipping, but Kit steadied her. "What? Yes, of course." She stared up at him. "But I thought I'd go with you to the store. I want to help." She'd made a great teammate, helping Laurel and Simon, well at least until MacKenzie shot her, blasting her into the past. She could be of use to Kit. It would keep her occupied and not so fearful of her future. Besides, she wanted to meet Sophie, the prostitute with the heart of gold. It sounded like she could give Julia Roberts a run for her money.

"I appreciate the offer." He held up a hand to forestall her interruption. "I'm not sure what I'll find, and I don't want to put you at risk. There's this Lord Renweard to be concerned about. Sophie is missing. I have no idea what might have happened to her. I'd be most remiss if you were hurt in anyway, luv."

"I can take care of myself." She knew some self-defense. True, she wasn't a black belt or anything, but she could protect herself. "Let me help you." Then she remembered being shot, and her chest ached with the memory. On second thought, how capable was she against pistols and knives, or a sword? Plus, self-defense in a dress, and oh yeah, she couldn't even walk without falling on her ass without his steadying arm. He might have a point.

"Beth, luv." He took her hand. "Please, return to our room. I'm not used to looking out for anyone but myself. You'll be a distraction. One I can't afford."

She pursed her lips into a frown. "How do I know *you'll* be okay?" It's not like cell phones had been invented yet so he could check in with her. What if he disappeared like Sophie? "Promise me you'll be back."

He blinked and stilled, but then a slight smile turned up his lips. "I'm always well, luv." He bussed a kiss to her cheek. "Off with you now." His order was followed with a slap to her butt.

"Fine." With a glare and a shake of her head, she left him standing there as she strode down the boardwalk, hoping she wouldn't fall. When she reached the intersection, she glanced over her shoulder and spied Kit still standing there watching her. She turned left to escape his gaze. The man unnerved her. She was so drawn to him, but he was everything in a man she didn't want. Too arrogant, too egotistical, and too handsome for his own good. Yet...her body betrayed her. This morning... She wanted him, felt safe with him, rogue and all. How could she trust her instincts? She had loved Grant and look how that turned out. She was better off with men out of her life. But why, with the thought of never seeing Christopher Locke again, did the tiny ants start crawling all over her skin?

Chapter Twenty-Seven

"I told the gentleman who inquired about the gemstone to return the next day," Geoffrey, the proprietor of Rare and Unique Antiquities explained. "I would have it in my possession by then. Or at least I thought I would. I had sent the lad on his way and told him I'd get word to him at the inn where he was staying, if I decided to purchase the stone. Once I knew there was an interested party, I quickly sent the note over. He never returned, nor in fact, did the gentleman. It could be he found the young man and made a deal directly."

"Did you tell this Lord Renweard where the boy was staying?" Kit asked.

"Of course not!" The shopkeeper waved his hand in the air, gesturing his frustration. "I knew I could make a profit. I wasn't about to cut myself out of any deals to be made."

"Would you be willing to tell me? The young man, Stephan, hasn't returned. I'm afraid something foul has befallen him. I came to York to trace his steps. Any information would be greatly appreciated." Kit jingled the coins in his pocket.

Geoffrey held up a hand in protest. "If the lad is in some trouble, I'm more than happy to help. The goods I've purchased from Stephan have given me solid profits. I'm always happy to see him enter my shop and would hate to lose his business. He said he was staying at the Slaughtered Lamb on Birkstrum Street. But I have no way to verify it. Perhaps he lied? After all, he never responded to my note, nor showed in person."

"Thank you, sir." Kit placed a gold coin on the countertop. "For your time."

Geoffrey inclined his head in thanks, and Kit turned, leaving the shop more puzzled than ever. Sophie had the sale; why hadn't she returned? Was it as the shopkeeper surmised? Lord Renweard had found her and to what purpose? Worry crawled across Kit's mind. If this Renweard had taken the stone instead of buying it, he very well might have tidied up loose ends.

A gust of wind nearly blew his hat off his head, catching it just in time. He glanced up and saw the dark clouds rolling in. The weather was deteriorating rapidly. Closing his coat to cut the wind's chill, Kit's pace increased. Darting into an alley, he hoped to shave off some time, at least to arrive at the Slaughtered Lamb before the weather hit. Popping out of the alley, he crossed the street and dove into a close. In short order, he arrived on Birkstrum Street, and Kit started searching for the inn. His keen eyes caught the sign bearing a sheep strung up by his back legs. Finally.

Kit darted inside the inn just as the first fat drops of freezing rain started to fall. He stopped within the doorway, taking a moment for his eyes to adjust to the dark room. The Slaughtered Lamb wasn't in the best area of York, and it showed. Wondering why Sophie chose this place instead of somewhere nicer, he made his way across the common room to the bar. He ordered a pint and contemplated his next move. Would Sophie be Sophie or Stephan? Glancing around the dank and ill-reputed tavern, he had his answer—Stephan. This was no place for an unescorted woman.

He waved the barkeep back to him and placed several coins on the bar, pushing them toward the burly man.

"What can I get you? Another pint?"

"No, sir. I'm looking for someone. I was told he was staying here. A young man by the name of Stephan Medcalf." He made sure his lower-class accent was on full display.

The tavern owner gave him a fixed gaze. "I'm not sure. There's plenty of men who rent rooms from me."

Kit fished out and pushed more coins to the owner. "He arrived about a week ago? Short." He raised his hand to Sophie's height. "A bit round with brown hair. Do you remember him?"

The man pointedly looked down at the growing pile of coins in front of him, causing Kit to sigh as he added more to the pile.

"Ah, right. Stephan Medcalf. Nice young man, better than our usual sort, if you know what I mean."

"Is he still here?"

The barkeep shook his head. "He's gone. Just up and left. He even abandoned his belongings."

Kit's spine stiffened. He knew Sophie would never desert her belongings, unless she had an excellent reason, or was forced to. "Do you still have them? May I see them?"

The owner gazed steadily back at him, not saying a word. His sigh was internal this time as Kit added a gold coin to the pile. "Please?"

The barkeep gathered up the coins. "Since you asked so nicely, follow me." He gestured to Kit while pushing through the door behind the bar leading into the kitchen. Kit stalked behind, close on his heels.

"Now mind you," the man said, while taking him to a storage room beneath the back stairs. "I'm planning on selling everything since it's abandoned, and I've claimed the boy's property. He glanced over his shoulder. "Unless you'd like to buy it all?"

"Let me take a look."

"Here you go." The tavern owner pulled out a small crate and handed it to Kit, who in turn placed it on a nearby table. He pried the lid off and rummaged through the contents.

Male clothing and a calling card from Rare and Unique Antiquities. So, Sophie did receive Geoffrey's request to return, but never made it back to the store. Kit looked up and met the tavern owner's gaze. "You're welcome to these," he gestured to the crate. "This is everything? You're not holding anything back?"

"No, sir. This was everything left in the room."

Sophie's female clothes were gone. She left her room as a woman. "Has there been anyone else inquiring for Mr. Medcalf?"

"You've been the only one."

With a nod, Kit excused himself and entered the common room, crossed the floor, and went out the door. He cursed and stood under the building's overhang. The storm was out in full force. The downpour looked more like sleet every second the deluge pounded from the sky. What to do now? He had no more leads. Where could she have gone? Did she meet with Renweard or flee from him? If she had fled, why hadn't she contacted him, or returned to Tredford? He brooded into the ugly night, realizing the rest of this evening was a loss. The day spent hunting for Sophie had taken longer than expected. He needed to regroup. He was tired and frustrated. Tomorrow he'd try and track Renweard down. It was the only option he had left since Sophie's trail went cold.

He decided to return to his room. There was nothing left to do for tonight, and he would need to reclaim his own clothes, and of course Dante, before relocating to another part of town. He wasn't sure if he'd leave Root for Beth. It might be best if she couldn't follow so easily. He hoped to slip away when she went to retrieve her money from Feinstein. Kit would stay one more day at the most in York, less, if Renweard turned out to be a false lead.

He stared out into the storm. Too bad the ugly weather wouldn't dry up like his clues had. There was no hope for it; he was going to get soaked. He glared into the frozen night. Why wasn't he home, warm by the fire with drink in hand? Instead, he was about to get drenched and miserable because he was a man who paid his debts. Once he did all he could do for Sophie, he was severing ties. It had taken her disappearance and Beth's arrival into his life to realize he'd slipped back into dangerous territory—starting to build friendships instead of safe acquaintances. It was time to become a man solely beholden unto himself. Lonely, to be sure, but safer. Kit stepped into the night and into the storm.

Chapter Twenty-Eight

Beth savored her last sip of coffee, grateful the hot savory hit of caffeine was available in this century. There were times for a good cup of tea, but this morning wasn't one of them. She eyed Kit seated across the table from her in the main dining room. He was uncharacteristically quiet. None of his witty barbs or roguish innuendos greeted her this morning during breakfast, instead she received grunts and one-word answers. Though he hadn't come out and said it, she surmised Kit was worried about Sophie. He'd told her last night of the discovery of Sophie's abandoned room, and the only trail left to follow was the mysterious Lord Renweard. Kit may act selfish, pretending not to care about anyone but himself, yet his actions proved otherwise. She knew he must be upset at the possibility his theft might have caused Sophie harm.

Kit had saved Beth twice, a complete stranger. So, she wasn't surprised when he set out for York in miserable weather to search for his partner in crime. Not being able to find her was probably eating him alive. She decided to try one more time.

Placing her empty cup down, she cleared her throat. "Getting my money shouldn't take long. I'll be back before you know it. Why don't you wait for me? I can help you track down this Renweard dude. Or come with me and we can start right from the store. Feinstein might have more information."

He shook his head. Taking the linen napkin from his lap, he placed it on the table. No dramatic flourish this time. "No, for the same reasons I've already told you yesterday. Nothing has changed since then." He glared at her. "Except for the weather. There's no reason for both of us to be miserable."

He abruptly stood up from their table and strode across the common room, retreating without another word. Beth scrambled to her feet and gave chase. She caught up to him as he entered their room and prepared to argue.

"But I'll be already wet and cold from going outside to get my money—"

"Then you can return here, to dry out and warm up." He grabbed the folded one sheet which passed for a newspaper in this time from the table, and plopped himself into the chair. In short order, the paper was expanded to its full length, and blocked him from her sight as he read.

"What are you doing? You're just going to sit there reading? What about Sophie?"

She heard his sigh before he lowered the paper to glower over the top of the page at her. "Aren't you supposed to be on your way?"

"You're dodging my question." Beth placed both fisted hands to her hips and glared right back at him. Somebody was a bit grumpy this morning.

"I'm not really used to explaining myself to others, but if it gets you on your way and out of my hair, I will. I'm looking for any possible leads."

"Oh, yeah, right, that's good. I would never have thought to search a newspaper. I would have just

Googled or surfed the web. But when in Rome..." Kit frowned at her, and she realized her mistake, so she waved him off and turned to fetch her cloak to hide her flub about the future. Best to change the topic. Especially back to one she knew irritated him. "My offer still stands to help."

"It's unnecessary and not needed." Kit replied from behind the paper.

Bingo. The exact reaction she needed. Beth wrapped her scarf around her neck and left the room, shutting the door quietly behind her. She probably had worried for nothing; after all, he would chalk it up to her *foreign* American language. Until she found her way in this century, she needed to be careful. Beth didn't want to sound crazy and be locked up in some loony bin. If she remembered her history well enough, mental health care was still in the dark ages, possibly using bloodletting and weird torture to drive the demons out. Note to self: think before you speak. Ha! That's a good one. She was infamous for doing the exact opposite. She also should have paid more attention in her history classes. It would have been helpful to know what the hell was going on or even going to happen while stuck here. If wishes were fishes, she'd never starve.

Exiting the boarding house, she ground to a halt in dismay. As she hugged the inn's wall, she mentally tried to psych herself up for the dash to the store. It was sleeting once again. Seriously? Couldn't it be actual snow or at least plain old rain? Kit was right about one thing; today was not the day to be outside. With weather like this, even the brazier of coals in their room seemed an inviting way to spend the day.

The sooner gone, the sooner returned. She pushed herself off the wall and strode purposely on the boardwalk. The instant she stepped out, the pelting hard frozen rain pounded at her, and she was soaked before she covered ten feet. Though only a few streets away, the shop was going to feel like miles and miles instead. Lengthening her stride and saying a silent prayer her feet wouldn't slip out from underneath her, she plowed onward, with her head bowed and one hand grasping the hood to keep it from blowing off her head. Her other hand clutched at the front of her cloak, trying in vain to keep her body heat inside its woolen depths. Soon her feet were squishing inside her boots. Miserable and wet, she searched for the store's sign once she turned right onto the last street. Half way up, there it was.

Beth grabbed the doorknob and flung the door open, bells jingling madly as she dashed out of the sleet and into the store. She took one step to the side and stood by the door. Pushing her dripping hood off, she searched the small store for Mr. Feinstein and found him directly, standing behind the counter.

She gave him a smile. "Pardon me for not venturing farther into your store, I'm afraid I might submerge us both. I'm a bit water logged."

He returned her smile. "Have no fear, Mrs. Leighton. My shop can withstand you. Please," he gestured for her to approach. "There are receipts to be signed and money to give. Plus, it's warmer here by the coals."

Sold! Beth crossed the room and was before him in an instant. She pulled off her gloves and shoved them into a pocket, before reaching out her blue hands toward the burning coals.

"May I offer you tea, to warm your insides as well, Madam?"

"Thank you. Tea sounds heavenly."

"If you'll excuse me, I'll return in but a moment."

She inclined her head, and Feinstein disappeared into the back room. True to his word, he returned shortly, carrying a tray with two cups, a teapot, and the obligatory cream and sugar. He set down the tray and lifted the teapot, pouring out a cup.

"Cream? Sugar?"

"Just a splash and no sugar."

He followed her requests and handed her the cup, which she enveloped in her palms, cherishing the warmth of the hot liquid released through the porcelain. Soon her numb hands thawed.

"Thank you so much, Mr. Feinstein. This is exactly what I needed."

"You're very welcome, Madam." He took a sip from his own cup. "This has been the coldest January I can recall. We are either being pounded with frozen rain or buried under drifts of snow. It feels like winter will never end."

"It is extraordinarily miserable, sir."

They sipped quietly at their cups. Perhaps this was an opening to help both Kit and Sophie. Feinstein might have more information on this Lord Renweard guy, or at least a description. It certainly would help to know what the man looked like when they searched for him.

"May I ask you a question?"

He inclined his head in permission.

"Mr. Locke followed your advice and located the establishment where Sop...err, Stephan was staying."

She cursed herself mentally. What kind of detective would she make if she couldn't even stick to the facts? Think before speaking. Think before speaking. She mantra'd to herself, hoping it would stick. "The problem at the moment, Stephan seems to have disappeared. His belongings were still there, but he wasn't."

He frowned. "I have always enjoyed doing business with Mr. Medcalf. I hope the young man hasn't succumbed to a bad end."

"As do we." Beth met his worried gaze straight on. "Since Mr. Medcalf left no further clues, Mr. Locke was hoping to find Lord Renweard and err…query him. I was wondering if you could give me any more information besides his name? Anything would be helpful, even just his appearance…" She shrugged.

"Certainly. Anything to help the young man. I've already mentioned Renweard wasn't a pleasant person. He was the type of lord who believed he was entitled, and everyone else was below him, as servants."

Beth nodded her understanding and encouraged him to continue.

"Though he chose not to remove his hat when he entered, I could tell he was bald or balding, and yet he didn't affect a wig. He isn't as tall as Mr. Locke, closer to Mr. Medcalf's height, yet for his statue he was very robust—large in a strong way. But what I noticed most were his eyes. I don't know their actual color, but they appeared very dark, almost as if they were black. I know this sounds strange, but when meeting his gaze, I was uncomfortable." Feinstein looked down into his teacup before placing it onto the tray. "I hope this helps."

"I appreciate the information. At least we know what he looks like while searching for him."

Feinstein frowned. "You must be careful, Mrs. Leighton. Stay away from Lord Renweard. Let Mr. Locke deal with him. I would not be at all surprised to find out Renweard was involved in the young man's disappearance. I'm very worried for Mr. Medcalf."

"Yes." Beth placed her own empty cup onto the tray. "Thank you for the tea and allowing me to thaw out, and especially for your information on Lord Renweard."

"You're very welcome, my dear." He slid the tea tray aside and pulled two identical receipts out, placing them before her on the counter. "Now, let us get down to business, so you can be on your way. I'm sure dry clothes and a warm hearth is the best way to spend the rest of your day." Next, he pulled a large metal box from underneath the counter. He withdrew a long antique-looking key from his coat pocket and unlocked the box. Lifting the lid, Mr. Feinstein extracted a pile of banknotes and placed them on the counter alongside the receipts. "The agreed amount. Please feel free to verify if you'd like, Mrs. Leighton."

She smiled. It was a large pile, enough to survive on for a while. "There's no need."

Mr. Feinstein inclined his head and returned her smile. "If you would please sign both receipts acknowledging payment for your rings, you'll be free to leave."

Beth picked up the quill and quickly signed, and then scooped up her money and stuffed it inside her purse, which she now knew people called a reticule. Feinstein handed her one copy of the receipts and smiled.

"It was my pleasure doing business with you. Please take care of yourself." He lifted her hand up and bowed briefly before releasing her.

"Thank you, Mr. Feinstein. You made this exchange extremely easy."

"Now off with you. Be careful, I wish you had an escort. The weather will make travel difficult. Perhaps I can hail a hackney for you?"

"No. No thank you. Don't bother. I'm already a mess and the inn is just around the corner. Please stay and keep yourself dry. I'll be fine." She gave him a smile and a little wave as she crossed the room and opened the doors. The merry jingles of bells were a sharp contrast to the ugliness outside the shop. If possible, the sleet had worsened since the short time she was in the store. Perhaps she should have taken him up on his offer, but she needed to be frugal with her money, and a little freezing rain wouldn't kill her. Taking a good hold on her cloak and hood, Beth plunged back into the storm.

Relief flooded her when she entered the Blue Ox and headed directly for the stairs. She couldn't wait to get warm and dry. The streets had emptied out on her return journey. Most sane individuals who had no important or demanding business took the sensible route and stayed indoors as the strength of the storm kept growing in its intensity.

She worried for Kit. Maybe he'd postponed his search for Renweard and was safely holed up in their room. She couldn't imagine him out in the storm making any progress. Reaching said room, Beth unlocked the door, entered, and closed it firmly behind her. Grateful the brazier was still lit, she crossed the room to hover near its warmth. She yanked and pulled at the sodden leather gloves, peeling them off her frozen fingers to let them drop to the floor. She held her hands out to the warmth and sighed. She really had hoped he would still be in the room, but obviously he stuck to his plans because there certainly was no place to hide in the tiny space.

Beth froze, her gaze scanning the room, a chill dread filling her as her mind caught up with what her eyes already processed. Her spare clothing lay on the bed and both saddlebags were gone. *What the hell?* Where were Kit's belongings?

"He did not!" Beth spun, water spraying off her cloak in her need to reach the door, which she flung open and slammed behind her as she dashed for the stairs. She bolted down two steps at a time, hitting the lobby, she ran through the dining room, ignoring the looks the customers threw at her. She didn't care. She had to reach the stables.

Beth ran into the courtyard, completely unfazed as the hard-driving frozen rain hit her uncovered head, soaking her more. Her hair became drenched and water leeched underneath her clothing. She burst into the stable, startling the stable boys from their makeshift poker game. Frantically, she searched the stalls for Dante and Root. Not finding them, she turned on the boys.

"Where are they?"

"Who, Madam?" The largest of the boys, more like a teenager, asked.

"The flashy large chestnut and the plain bay that came in with him?"

"I know." The smallest boy spoke up. "The man took both out earlier. About an hour or so."

Of course he did. The timing too coincidental not to be on purpose. He must have left their room only seconds after she had gone to get the money. He'd had it all planned out, especially with the way he just sat there casually reading the damn newspaper. She had fallen completely for it. Had he even really searched for Sophie yesterday? She could have sworn he cared. Apparently not.

"Did he mention when he'd be returning?" Beth asked the question her gut and mind already knew the answer too.

"He's not, Madam. I inquired since the stalls are full. He told me his mounts wouldn't be returning."

Damn. A chill chased through her that had nothing to do with the weather. She took a deep breath, pushing her fear aside, and let her anger build as she walked to the stable's entrance, and peered out into the dark storm. The bastard had abandoned her in York.

Chapter Twenty-Nine

Kit was done. He wanted out of this miserable weather, back in his new room, warm and dry. After leaving Beth and checking into the Yorkbridge Inn, he'd ventured into the city looking for Sophie or Renweard. He had spent what was left of the morning and all of the afternoon on the streets, only stopping once to lunch so he could thaw and dry out a bit. There was simply no trace of either of them. With hopefully better weather tomorrow, he'd head back to Tredford, and perhaps Sophie would have returned.

The already dark day was losing what little light it contained as the evening encroached. Looking around, Kit realized he was farther from his room than he thought. *Blast.* It was going to take him longer to return than he had anticipated, but if he left the boardwalks and cut through the alleys taking a more direct route, he'd shave off at least another twenty minutes. Granted, stepping off the boardwalks posed a risk of mud and thieves, but Kit smiled for the first time today. He didn't mind a little dirt and he was, after all, one of the thieves. Not hesitating, he left the walkway and took to the more hidden and dangerous back ways of York.

Kit was well into his return journey, boots mud splattered and drenched, but it had stopped sleeting and even the rain had finally quit. The night air was brisk and sharp, his face numb, and his sodden coat was

183

turning crunchy with ice. An unpleasant evening to be out, but with the improved conditions he was able to pick up his pace, making better time.

A woman's scream froze Kit in place. The scream was echoed by more women, and the harsh voices of men followed. He ran, closing in on the public ruckus until he darted out of the alley and found a crowd surrounding the entrance to a more upscale boarding house than the one he had taken Beth to, and much more high class than the tavern he was currently staying. He crept closer and eavesdropped.

"It was only a woman."

"No, it was horrible."

Kit began to weave through the crowd, catching more comments, as he tried to gain entrance to the building.

"…old woman, pretty nimble for the number of wrinkles."

"A monster!"

"Move along," a Watchman ordered. "There's nothing to see. Everything is fine."

Kit slipped into the Royal Lion Inn and worked his way to stand outside the office behind the bell desk. He stayed off to the side after peering into the room, finding a distraught maid, the Inn's owner, and two of the city's Watch.

"The gentleman left strict instructions to leave his room undisturbed," the owner explained. "He paid in advance for a week. I don't know when he left; it could have been at any time."

"So why wasn't the room opened until now?" The Watchman asked.

"The room was paid through this morning. The

maid," he gestured to the girl quietly sobbing on a chair, "only went to attend the room just now. We've been quite busy due to the storm."

"And when she opened the door she quote, found a living mummy, unquote inside." The Constable's disbelief was evident in his voice. "Did you see this *mummy*?"

"I did not. But Miss Catherine is one of my best maids. She saw something, which scared her greatly, before it fled past her and out of my establishment. Others saw it as well, I might add."

"Yes, I have the Watch interviewing other witnesses as we speak."

"Aren't you going to hunt down this creature?"

"If it *is* a creature, when we establish what we're looking for, I'll have my men out tracking it. My best theory: your *monster* was only a traumatized woman, held prisoner." The Constable sighed. "Can you give me the name of the gentleman who let your room?"

"Certainly." Papers were turned in a thick black ledger. "Renweard, Lord Edmond Renweard."

Kit stiffened at the familiar name, and dread coursed through him as he assumed the *monster* must be Sophie.

"Did he say where he was from or where he was going?"

"He did not. As I said, he paid in advance and was left to himself."

Kit was already out the door and into the departing crowd. He had to find Sophie. There were still men milling about an alley entrance, so he approached and was rewarded with a direction to head.

"...through here, sir. Everyone was too stunned to

give chase, especially with all the women screaming. No one really knew what was happening."

Kit walked past the crowd, and continued down the boardwalk until he found another alley entrance and slipped inside. He now paralleled the path Sophie had run. He had to find a way over; with the rain stopped and the paths muddied, he might be able to track her through her footprints. Starting to run, he darted in and out until he was back to the alley Sophie had originally fled. He slowed and crouched at the first possible intersection to study the ground. *Bloody hell*. It was dark; how was he supposed to find tracks without light? He stayed low, examining the ground, and then he found it. A small barefoot print in the adjoining alley. It appeared close to her size. This neighborhood was too upscale for street urchins. Hoping he wasn't wrong, Kit followed the trail.

Sophie's path wove through the back ways and into the shambles, until he reached an inner courtyard in the meat market district. There was movement inside. Kit stepped cautiously into the dead end, keeping his back to the opening.

In a low, quiet voice, he called out. "Sophie? Is it you? Are you all right? Sophie?" He took a few more steps into the courtyard. A breeze stirred the night, and moonlight began to fill the yard, as the clouds parted to highlight a woman he at once recognized, though her back was to him.

"Sophie." He closed the distance and was about to reach out to touch her shoulder, when she turned. Kit froze.

What had Renweard done? He took two steps back before he could stop himself. The moonlight highlighted her appearance, giving Kit a perfect view, reminding him this was Sophie, or at least it had been once. The beautiful woman was no more. Her skin was desiccated and shrunken, her face and arms looked like a skeleton wrapped in puckered gray leather. Her exposed breasts, no longer ripe and full, but limp husks of their former selves. Her ruby lips were cracked, and the same gray as her skin, giving an eerie appearance of a boney skull. He forced himself to meet her gaze and stumbled back another step. Her rich chocolate brown eyes were gone—replaced with solid milky white orbs.

"Oh, Sophie." His voice cracked, as he stared at the horror before him. She never deserved this; no one did. The Viper's Eye was rumored to have mystical powers, but Kit had dismissed it as legend when she had told him. The bearer of the stone was to gain great youth and health, a form of immortality. It must gain its power by stealing the health of others. He had chalked it up to tales of cursed stones; all large unique gems had some sort of story surrounding them. The myths increased their value. He never once thought the tale Sophie spoke about the Viper's Eye had any bit of reality to it. Kit should have believed her. Guilt sliced at him. He had scoffed and laughed it off, and Sophie paid the price.

She reached out her boney hands to him as a mewling hiss escaped her mouth. Kit held his ground but shuddered when her fingers pressed on his chest. Grateful for the protection of his greatcoat, he could only imagine how her fingers would feel on bare skin. This close, he could smell her. Her scent was of the grave, decomposing and foul. Like the Egyptian legend unwrapped, she was a dried-out husk. Her fingers trailed upward as she continued to mew. When they reached above his cravat and touched his neck, he couldn't help his tremor as he slipped to the side, away from her hand. She turned and tried to reach him, but Kit continued moving and stepped up behind her.

He could not leave her like this. He wished for any of his weapons, but the small dagger in his boot would not do. Would she even bleed? Quickly he reached up and grabbed her neck and the side of her head. With a powerful twist, Kit broke her neck.

She collapsed instantly and Kit followed her down, cradling her in his lap on the damp cobblestones where he sat. He'd killed Sophie. She lay unmoving, not breathing. Reaching out with a gentle touch of his fingertips, he closed her once beautiful eyes, covering the milky dead stare. It shouldn't bother him. When he found her in this courtyard, she was already dead; there was nothing of *Sophie* left, what made her, *her*. He just helped her physical body join her spirit. Lifting his hand, he realized it was shaking. He clenched it into a fist and hit his thigh. His killing her meant nothing; he refused to allow it any meaning. He. Would. Not. But it was already too late. His physical self trumped his mental denial. The shaking consumed the rest of his body, setting it trembling and shudders racked through him. He grew nauseous and curled over Sophie's remains, gagging as his breath left him in gasps all the while he shook. Kit grew both hot and cold. He was tired of killing people he cared for.

Chapter Thirty

Beth sat on the bed, warm, dry, and wrapped in a blanket as she stared blindly, trying to figure out what to do next. She had money and could buy transportation, but where should she go? Up to Cleitmuir Manor in Scotland? It existed, but it was the wrong time. All the money in the world wouldn't get her to her real home. She was stuck here. She could stay in York. It was a large city compared to Tredford, and she could get a job easily here, maybe even in decorating. She hadn't really thought about it, but she was sure stylists were around during this century. She could return to the Boar and Rose where she still had work, or at least she thought she did. With the length of her disappearing act, she wasn't so sure they'd give her a second chance. Or was it already a third chance? She'd lost track. Beth knew she could probably talk her way back in if she had to. People liked her. Getting her job back might be better than trying to start a business from the ground up. Were women allowed to be their own boss? Sadly, it didn't really matter which path she chose. Neither got her what she wanted most.

"Beth."

She screamed and jumped, her back hitting the wall at the unexpected sound of her name while alone in the room.

"My apologies, I hadn't meant to scare you."

Heart racing a million miles per hour, Beth gaped at the man who startled her by literally popping into her room. Remiel. The blasted Archangel who could bop about space and time without a *Tardis*. The angel who refused to return her home.

"Are you trying to kill me now?" She accused. "What? It wasn't enough to ruin my life and drop me into the past? If you can go anywhere in time, how come you didn't take me to the far future. At least then I'd have indoor plumbing." She blew out a huff of air. "Try knocking on the door next time. You practically gave me a heart attack."

"I did apologize." Remy frowned, making her realize just whom she had been taunting. Goosebumps rose on her arms, and she shivered. Think before speaking, she reminded herself. How hard was that to remember?

"We must talk. It is important. May, I?" He gestured to the chair.

"Please." Beth scrunched tighter under the blanket, tucking her knees to her chest as she wrapped her arms around her legs. Her curiosity took over as she watched the angel in human form take a seat. He said it was important. Did he figure a way to take her back home? Hope surged through her.

"I need your help," Remy stated. Once settled, his light-blue gaze studied her from across the small room.

An Archangel from Heaven needed *her* help. Finally. She now had a bargaining tool. A smile curled up her mouth. "I'm listening."

He tilted his head, appraising her. Oops. Could he read minds? She thought back hard at him. *Too bad, angel boy, I've got leverage now.*

He smiled. Yes, definitely can read minds, she added to her mental list of information on angels.

"There is a rare artifact, a demon artifact, actually—"

"Wait, there are demons? I knew about ghosts, but what about vampires? Are they real? Werewolves, werecreatures?"

He sighed. "Yes, demons are very much real. Just as there is a Heaven, so there is a Hell." Remy waved her off when she was about to follow up with more questions. "If you keep interrupting, we will never get to your bargaining and time is important right now."

"Maybe if it matters so much, you should have popped in sooner—"

"Hush."

Beth shut her mouth. Think. Before. You. Speak. Really, how hard was that? Did she also need to add the mental mantra of "don't antagonize the angel?"

"Yes, that would be splendid."

Oops. Busted. "Sorry, please continue. I'll try and keep my questions for the end."

"Have you heard the concept of free will? At least how it applies to Heaven?"

"Sure. You guys upstairs aren't allowed to interfere with our human choices because it voids the whole free will thing."

"Indeed. Uriel and I have already *bent* this rule by saving your life. Because my brother was unable to interfere with Simon's plight, you became an innocent victim to the circumstance." He spread his palms wide in supplication. "I am in a similar situation, but worse."

"What's going on, Remy?"

"I am not competing on a level playing field." He

bowed his head, blew out a breath before meeting her gaze. "And I am tired of my opposition ignoring all rules of play."

"You're talking about a demon, aren't you?"

"Yes. His name is Astaroth and he has created and set loose on humanity an artifact so tainted it is an abomination." Remiel shook his head, looking both sad and angry at the same time. "It's been hidden for centuries, until now." Beth's goosebumps returned. This wasn't going to be good. Not at all.

"It is a jewel."

"Like Uriel's Orb?"

He shook his head. "No, Uriel's Orb was as unique as it was large, its purpose was to help mankind. Astaroth's stone is an atrocity of creation. A black opal large enough to fill the palm of your hand."

"Wait, a black opal?" How many could there be? Kit said they were rare and she wasn't one to believe in coincidence. Beth swallowed her shock. "You're talking about the Viper's Eye, aren't you?"

"Yes. The stone itself is harmless until it's imbued with power, then it is extremely dangerous. Once the bearer chooses to use it, the opal has the ability to steal souls."

"The bearer? So, anyone who touches it can steal souls? And what does that even mean?" Was Sophie using the stone? Is that why she disappeared in York? She somehow activated it? Or maybe Renweard has it and is using it?

Remiel sighed. "No. The wielder of the opal isn't simply the person holding it. The true bearer must use a special incantation to activate the demonic properties in order to rip out the soul of their victim. The bearer uses the soul as a sacrifice to honor the demon."

Beth narrowed her eyes at the angel, but he ignored her and continued on. "Astaroth circumnavigates the rule concerning free will because the stone must be wielded by a human and he must give his consent, unlike the victim."

"What happens to a body once the soul has been stolen? Can you use the stone in reverse to put it back?"

He shook his head and frowned. "Without a soul, a body is just an empty vessel. Death isn't mercifully swift, it's long and lingering, but just as sure."

"But who would do such a thing? That's terrible!"

"The naïve, the power hungry, some are simply evil. Astaroth fools them into thinking they can wield the power of the souls stored inside the stone, but the bearer pays an ultimate price just like their victims. Perhaps it is why my Father allows its existence; I do not know. By taking up the stone, the person becomes vigorous, healthy, stronger, and practically immortal. Yet, with most things demonic, there is always a hidden price."

Beth was riveted in "an accident along the highway" kind of fixation. She couldn't understand how someone could choose to brutally kill innocent people just to gain power, but then again people did it all the time without the help of a demonic stone.

"The more you use the stone, the more addicted the user becomes, forcing him to use it over and over again. However, with each use, a bit of the victim is left behind, inside the mind of the wielder, driving him insane."

"You said practically immortal and now insane?" Beth bit her tongue, about to say *that's like being a little bit pregnant*, before she remembered her mantra about not antagonizing the angel.

"The wielder dies eventually, either by his own hand or others," Remiel answered her unasked question. "Damned to Hell for all eternity. There is no salvation, no redemption for those humans who choose to use the stone. Their souls were lost the instant they picked up the Viper's Eye and used it."

Beth wondered if the person using the demonic artifact knew what was going to happen to them. Would they have ever used it if they knew the results? What could drive someone to kill others, go insane, and lose their own soul?

"What happens to the souls trapped in the stone?" She had a sinking feeling she didn't really want to hear the answer.

Remiel sighed once more. "If the stone is full, when the wielder succumbs, the innocent souls are delivered to Astaroth in hell, gaining him great power."

"But is there a way to stop this?"

"By removing the opal before it reaches capacity, thus freeing the souls to their correct destination."

"I'm going to jump out on a limb here and say you need me to get the Viper's Eye for you." Beth said carefully, the pieces starting to fall into place.

"Correct."

"Because you can't personally retrieve it and take it out of play on account of the whole free will thingy. Just like the demon dude, you need a human intermediary."

"Correct, again."

"But aren't you breaking the rules by telling me all of this?"

"Perhaps. More like bending."

Thoughts tumbled in Beth's head. The stone had caused enough problems already. She feared for the missing Sophie. Retrieving the stone wouldn't be easy; in fact, it would be downright dangerous, especially if the gem's user was collecting souls. It could mean he was already going nuts.

"If I do this…"

Remiel kept his gaze steady. "You'll receive your heart's desire."

And there it was. Her leverage to have him return her home. She'd finally go home, but only if she managed to recover the jewel and didn't die trying. Was it worth the risk? She didn't have or know any other way to return to her time. Grant was dead, but she still had family and friends who grieved for her. Beth missed them. She missed her life. Explaining how she returned from the dead would be tricky, but if a body was never found, she at least had an advantage. Home. Her heart's desire.

"Count me in. I'll do it." Besides, innocent souls were at stake, and she couldn't stand aside condemning people to hell if she could make a difference.

Remy nodded. "Thank you."

"Do you know where the Viper's Eye is right now? Is it still in York?"

"No. It's near Tredford, you'll need to return—"

"Wait," Beth began to see a pattern and she wasn't happy with it. "You had this planned all along, didn't you? Why else drop me in this time and place? You're using me!"

Remiel sighed. "Perhaps. Uriel didn't want you to die, and I needed an intermediary. A win-win for us."

He shrugged. "It's not like you won't benefit from this. You have your life, and you'll be generously compensated for your efforts." He stared her down.

He did have a point, but she still felt used. "Fine," she huffed out. "I'm not happy with the games you angels are playing with my life, but if it means I get a chance to go home, I'll hunt the jewel for you. I guess I need to go buy a horse or something…" Remy raised his hand to stop her planning.

"There is something you must do first before returning to Tredford, and we have wasted enough time already." He stood and strode over to her. "You must go to Christopher Locke."

"What?" Beth jumped to her feet and flung the blanket to the bed, glaring at the angel. "You're kidding me, right? The man is an asshat. He abandoned me. Good riddance to bad rubbish."

"Beth, please think for a moment. You need him. He's a thief and there's a jewel to be stolen. Locke has already proven he can do it."

"This Renweard guy has the opal, doesn't he?"

"He's the other reason I would have Locke with you. It would be safer. I wouldn't want you harmed."

The angel had a point. It would be good to have back up when tracking an insane person, and then she was struck by a thought. "Why not use Kit directly. Why me?"

"Perhaps I could have, but I've bent the rules almost to the breaking when I revealed my true self to you. I can do no more. However, I would like you to be as protected as you can be, and Locke is an effective solution."

Kit wasn't the worst partner she could have. In

fact, she was willing to call him a friend until he left her stranded, without a single hint or word. She'd give him hell when she caught up to him. "Okay, fine."

"A final word of caution, do not touch the stone directly. The opal has been empowered and has already eaten souls. I don't know what might happen if someone other than the wielder should touch the gem."

"Right, got it. No handling the demonic soul-stealing artifact, directly. Seems kind of like common sense."

Remiel nodded. "Get your cloak. I'll take you to Locke."

She crossed the room to the coat rack and wrapped herself into its depths. When she reached for the door, Remiel stopped her.

"No. It will take too long."

She turned with a frown and faced the angel. Just how did he expect them to go to him? Air Angel?

The Archangel smiled at her. "Air Angel, indeed. Take my hand."

Beth grasped his outstretched hand, and Remiel pulled her up against him. He released her hand and wrapped his around her waist, holding her in a tight hug. She peered around him when the rustle of feathers drew her attention. Giant wings of bright blue appeared from nowhere to spread wide and then fold over her, encasing her. Instantly she felt warm and comforted, protected, at peace, for the first time in a long time. Beth didn't want to leave his heavenly embrace. But she had no choice when he withdrew his wings, which vanished, back to wherever they had appeared from and stepped away from her. The night's cold air slammed into her, jolting her back to reality. She clasped her cloak tighter.

"One last thing," Remiel said.

Of course, there's always one more thing. Everyone always saves the best for last. "Let me have it."

"You cannot tell Locke about me or the demon. Share nothing about Heaven or Hell. It would bend the rules too far."

"But—"

"He is already aware of the jewel's claim to supernatural properties, but nothing of the souls. He knows enough to be cautious." Remy gestured past her farther into the alley. She turned and looked into the dark path. "Locke is nearby, in the courtyard. Go to him."

When Beth turned to say goodbye, the sneaky Archangel was gone. Great. Another disappearing act. He could have at least left her with a light. It was pitch-black. Suddenly the wind picked up, and the clouds drifted away, causing moonlight to streak down. Right. Ask and you shall receive.

Now she could see where she was walking, Beth headed into the alley. In a few yards, she reached the courtyard and jolted to a halt. Revealed by the moonlight, Kit sat on the damp cobblestones, holding a woman in his arms. He was bent over her, covering her.

"Kit?" Beth walked slowly over to him. "Kit?"

When he didn't respond, she squatted down and reached out to touch his shoulder. He was trembling, actually shuddering. What was going on? She firmed her grip and gave him a shake. "Christopher."

He looked up, and Beth gasped when she was able to see the body he cradled. It was a dried-out husk, barely identifiable as female except for her ripped clothing. She looked like what she'd imagine an unwrapped mummy would appear. Stunned, Beth turned her gaze to Kit and was shocked again by the utter anguish in his face.

Beth gripped his shoulder firmer, as he continued to quake under her touch. "Kit, what happened? Who is this?"

He stared at her; his mouth opened and closed as he tried to speak, yet nothing came out.

"It's okay," she coaxed quietly, trying to comfort him. "You can tell me."

"I killed her," Kit choked out. His voice was low and cracked. "I killed, Sophie."

Dear God. The mummy was actually her? Kit couldn't have killed her; the woman looked like she had been dead for years, yet Beth couldn't deny his anguish. He must feel responsible. "It's not your fault, Kit."

"Yes, it is." His eyes were glazed and dead, while his body continued to shake under her hold.

"No. It's Renweard."

"You don't understand…"

"Kit—"

He shoved her away, dropping Sophie's body, and lurched to his feet as Beth fell on her ass. His face filled with rage, nostrils flaring, eyes wide, as he loomed over her with clenched fists. "She was alive! She was here, alive and walking when I found her. I…" He shuddered and turned, looking down at Sophie.

Beth gasped, as she sat sprawled on the ground. Before their gazes, Sophie was disintegrating, breaking apart and turning to papery ash. The wind whirled into the courtyard, it lifted the remains and blew them apart, spinning them in all directions. Beth covered her mouth and fought back the bile creeping up her throat. In less than a heartbeat, all that was Sophie was gone.

Beth jumped to her feet and grabbed Kit around his waist when he started to collapse. "Hey there, easy." She managed to prop her shoulder under his arm to brace him. Dear God, Sophie had been alive in the husk of her body? Is this what Remiel meant by a slow death as an empty husk? Had she been aware? It was something out of a horror film. *The Walking Dead* transformed from zombies to mummies? Kit must have given her a mercy killing. Beth shuddered at the thought he might have killed her in self-defense. Neither scenario was good. Oh God in Heaven, the stone! Renweard used the stone on her. She had to get the opal and release Sophie's soul.

Beth reached up her hand and placed it against his cold cheek. She pressed, turning his face toward her. "Kit?" His eyes were glassy, he was still shaking and cold to the touch. He was in shock. "Come on, we're going home."

Chapter Thirty-One

Edmond clutched at his head as the tormented voices within his mind clamored, overlapping, calling for his attention. Bits and pieces, flotsam and jetsam, shouted and swirled in currents of ever increasing waves. A jumble of distraction he could barely separate from himself. The inner voices lancing like knives through his consciousness, the pain never ending. He knew he lost time in his misery, sometimes just a few blinks, other times longer, even hours. All precious time taken away from his beloved little Anna.

It was a test. Edmond forced himself to concentrate, willing himself free as he pushed the voices into the background. Astaroth was making sure Edmond's will was strong. Why else did the voices exist except to distract him and prove him unworthy? Surely, he was close to his goal? The cellar was nearly filled with the dried-out husks of his sacrifices. There was no one left on his estate except for his trusted butler Charles, and his sleeping daughter. He had done everything Astaroth wanted and more.

Edmond anticipated the purer the soul, the more valuable. He was determined to reach his quota in the most expedient manner. Starting with the stable boy, the stone consumed the remaining five children on his estate, but still the demon hadn't shown. Next, he worked his way through more of his staff until he dismissed the rest, before they realized what he had been doing.

More!

The need sliced through all the voices he had thrust aside. He pressed his fingers to the bridge of his nose as a throb built behind his eyes. The varied voices screamed in protest. His hands clamped over his ears. He trembled. Pain carved through his brain, and a moan escaped him. His trembling turned to shudders. Edmond knew what was to come as the periods between respites grew shorter and shorter.

The voices shouted and screamed from their cage but it didn't matter, they were just as powerless against the Viper's Eye as he was. The stone was stronger than its victims. Stronger than Edmond, though he fought. It mattered not. The opal wished to be fed, and with no sacrifice close at hand, punishment was swift and torturous.

A shaft of lightning pierced his head and shot downward through his body. His back arched, and he screamed. The pain voided everything. The non-stop voices silenced, even the jewel's whispering demands disappeared. There was only pain, a reminder of the demon's will.

Edmond's cries filled his ears. Lancing pain was all he knew. His vision tunneled until there was only darkness and agony as time stopped, trapped in the prison of the stone's devising.

"Sir? Sir?"

Edmond's awareness slowly returned as a gentle hand on his shoulder carefully rocked him. His eyelids fluttered open, and he found himself curled upon himself on the floor, with Charles crouched next to him.

"How," his voice croaked off. His throat and mouth like dry parchment trapped his words, until he swallowed several times and then licked his lips. "How long?"

"Moments, my lord. Not long," his butler reassured him. "Let me help you."

Weakened as he was, Charles needed to leverage him up in order to get Edmond in the chair he had fallen from. His strength returned quickly. It always did. The jewel made sure of it. He had never been healthier. Edmond needed to find another sacrifice and quickly. The stone was all too happy to crack its whip when its needs hadn't been met.

"Charles."

"Yes, sir?"

"We'll need to clear the cellar; there must be a way to rid ourselves of these human shells. I can't just release them to wander the grounds and countryside." He required privacy. His actions to save Anna must remain secret, lest the town form a lynch mob and go after him. After all, they were his prey. He would not be theirs.

"Of course, sir."

"And Charles, ready the horses. A trip to town is necessary, I believe."

"Yes, my lord. It will be as you wish."

Edmond sprung to his feet, invigorated. It always helped to have a plan. "I'll be upstairs with Anna when you're ready." Without waiting for reply, he left Charles in the study and went to his daughter.

He paused in the doorway, studying his sleeping girl. She looked so peaceful, comfortably tucked into the bed. He closed the door quietly, shutting himself inside alone with her. Feeding the opal's appetite took most of his time now, leaving little for Anna.

He crossed the room and sat gently on the mattress. Edmond was sure his little poppy would forgive him the missed time; after all he was doing everything for her.

Breathing in deeply, his nose scrunched at a foul stench, which coated the air. A shudder racked him, and he blinked to find a horror before his eyes.

His beloved Anna, lay dead before him, her little body both wasted and bloated as she rotted on the bed. Her face was shrunken away, showing the outline of her skull. Nothing remained of his beautiful little girl.

"No!"

He flung his arms out in denial, trying to hide the hideous sight before him. Edmond squeezed his eyes shut. "No, no, no, no!" His heart shattered; how had this happened?

Head bowed, he lowered his hands to his lap. Taking a deep breath, he forced himself to open his eyes and raise his head only to gasp.

Anna lay peacefully, pristinely asleep. Her rotting corpse replaced with his whole little girl. Relief washed through him, his limbs shaking with the adrenaline release. His little poppy lay asleep, not dead. Astaroth's promise still held.

Was the foul vision a warning? Was his time running out? Edmond took Anna's small hand into his. "Soon, my dear. You will be healthy and whole. I will not fail you." He leaned forward and pressed a kiss to her forehead. "Sleep well, until you wake once more."

He stood and crossed the room to open the door, pausing once to look back to his daughter. Damn the thieving highwayman. This was his entire fault. Edmond had lost precious time when the Knightmare stole the Viper's Eye. He owed the man retribution. Edmond stalked down the hall while fingering the cool jewel within his vest pocket and made a vow. He would find the Knightmare and his life was forfeit.

Chapter Thirty-Two

Beth stared morosely into the flames. How was she to garner Locke's help, the help the Archangel implied she needed, if he insisted on drinking himself to death? The merrily burning fire in the hearth kept its answer to itself. She hugged her legs tighter to her chest and laid her cheek on her knee, as she sat curled in the same chair Kit had dropped her into after saving her life. A day eons ago.

The ride from York had been a tedious torture of freezing wet cold weather, and trying to engage Kit to draw him out from his self-imposed prison. For all her efforts, she was occasionally granted with one-word answers or graced at times with grunts. No amount of coaxing changed his demeanor. It tore her apart to watch him punish himself for things not in his control. But as the miles trudged on, her desire to help him pummel himself grew.

She was shocked when they'd arrived at his home. For he leapt off Dante to stumble into the house, abandoning his beloved horse, who she knew he considered his only true friend.

After taking care of both Root and Dante, and feeling chilled to the bone, sodden and miserable, Beth entered the house and went directly to the cottage's main room. There she found Kit sprawled in a chair with an empty decanter at his side and a glass in hand.

At least he had started the fire.

Her temper snapped. She crossed the room and snatched the glass out of his hand, shouting at him she'd had enough.

He slowly stood, standing way too close as he replied, "Then leave." He shoved her, and she lost her balance, tripping backward to land in the chair where she had been sitting previously. Kit crossed the room, none too agile, his smooth cat-like grace gone in his drunkenness, and grabbed a full decanter. He tore off the stopper and threw it across the room, where it dented the woodwork, and fell to the floor. Deliberately meeting her glare, he tipped back the full decanter to his mouth and took a heavy gulp. He lowered the bottle, carelessly holding the heavy crystal with a few long fingers.

"You're not needed or wanted. Be gone!" With those ominous words, he'd spun, stumbled, and weaved his way out of the room. She wondered if he'd make it upstairs to reach his bedroom, and found she didn't really care.

Well screw him! She wasn't leaving. Kit would have to sober himself up and physically throw her out if he wanted her gone. She wasn't going to give up. He was her chance to go home and also to save a bunch of innocent souls. Besides, Beth couldn't abandon him when he was hurting this much. What kind of person would she be leaving him in his current state? Though at this moment, she'd love to smack him upside the head, but you shouldn't beat a man when he's down.

She needed a plan. The angel was right about Kit's help. But how was she going to get it when he was drunk and wanted nothing to do with her? Why did everything have to be so hard? Just once, couldn't all the pieces fall into place? Kit steals the demon gem with no harm, gives it to her, and in turn she hands it to Remiel, who saves the souls and returns her home. She sighed. She missed her old life, feeling so lost it was a physical ache. Her eyes slid shut. Finally getting warm, exhaustion claimed her, and her mind drifted.

Beth jolted awake, heart pounding as she blinked her gritty eyes. Startled, but still half asleep, she scanned the room trying to ascertain what woke her. The room glittered in near darkness from the dying embers in the fireplace. Silence greeted her in the empty room. Her heart rate slowed, as she realized she was alone and not in imminent danger.

Yawning, she stretched in the chair, and with another glance at the glowing embers, decided it was time to find a bed. Uncurling from her seat, her muscles protested after their long-cramped position. She stood and stretched again, unlocking the last of her kinks. Beth padded lightly over to the fireplace, and grabbed the iron poker to stab at the low burning wood until it broke apart, dropping the room into darkness. She blinked as her eyes adjusted.

"Stop!"

The iron poker dropped from her hand and crashed to the hearth's stone floor with a clang. Beth spun, heart racing, and stared across the large room into the darkened hallway.

"Nooooo!"

Kit! Beth raced from the room, darted down the hallway, and flew up the stairs, taking three at a time.

****

"Run!"

"We can't leave him!"

"He's dead, Christopher, and so will we be if we don't go. Now!"

Julian grabbed his arm, and as Christopher was spun around he had his last glimpse of Adisson's broken and bleeding body. He swallowed the bile rising up his throat. The shot from the Brown Bess had rung out of nowhere, the long range ball bursting through the back of Adisson's skull, dropping him in his tracks, brain matter and blood spraying the ground. Alive one moment, dead the next. Shock warred with adrenalin as he shook free of Julian's grip and ran under his own power instead of being dragged. They were almost to the woods. Was the shooter taking a bead on them now?

They plunged into the tree line, dodging English oaks and alders, grateful for the cover, but it slowed their outright bolt. How many were chasing them? How had he made such an enormous mistake? They should be heroes, not running for their lives. He shied left, but not fast enough as a branch clawed his face leaving a bloody furrow on his cheek.

The gap widened between Julian and himself as Julian hit a small clearing. Julian looked over his shoulder checking on him, and didn't see the bandit step out of the woods in front of him.

"Julian!"

He was too late. Julian turned and was impaled on the brigand's out thrust sword. A primal scream wrenched from Christopher's throat. He saw his brother fall to the ground as the swordsman withdrew his weapon. Christopher charged, his own blade in hand. He crossed the clearing in three strides, leapt the body of his brother and swung his sword like a bludgeon, all finesse and skill gone, years of tutelage gone, as blind rage took over.

The blades clashed, metal ringing as they fought. It was no polite duel, but a brawl of muscles, dirty fighting and grunts. Christopher whirled beneath the bastard's guard and managed a blow with his fist to the bandit's chin, but little good it did to the large brute, who barely rocked back. Christopher paid the price for getting too close, when in the brigand's off hand, a dagger slashed out, scoring a deep gash to his sword arm.

He leapt backward and tightened his grip on the pommel as blood sluiced down his arm, coating his hand. He got his guard up in time to block the follow through sword thrust. The man was bigger and stronger, but Christopher knew he was faster. Spinning, he lashed out with his leg, his boot connected solidly to the bandit's knee, crashing him to the ground. Christopher lunged, his rage strengthening the thrust. The blade pierced through the weathered leather vest, punching through the thief's chest straight through the heart and out his back, to impale his sword point into the forest's ground. He gave the sword a twist.

The man thrashed once, before his eyes lost focus, and stared blindly at the tree-shrouded sky. Christopher took a moment to kick both the villain's sword and dagger from the dead man's hands, before wheeling and dropping to Julian's side.

"No, no, no, no," the words tumbled out of him as he reached for his brother, whose gut was laid open and blood oozed between Julian's fingers, which were covering the wound. Christopher pulled him up into his

embrace, cradling him in his arms.

Julian groaned and lifted a hand away from his stomach to grip Christopher's shoulder.

"Chris...pher."

"I'm here, Jul." He latched on to the hand, squeezing.

"Go," Julian gasped, choked and coughed up blood. He spat, clearing his mouth. "You need...run."

"I'm not leaving you."

Julian chuckled, which led to another bloody coughing fit. "Of...course...are." His breaths came out in pants. Slipping his hand out beneath Christopher's, he dropped it to his side. Fumbling one-handed, he withdrew first one pistol and then his second, before dropping them beside to the ground. "Take."

"No."

"Yes." He stared directly into Christopher's eyes— the Windmere glare their house was infamous for. "I'm dead. We...know...get out. Survive."

"No, I'm not leaving you."

"You will." Julian smiled. He fumbled once more at his side and withdrew a dagger and held it hilt first to Christopher.

Christopher shook his head. No. Absolutely no. He wouldn't do what his brother silently asked.

Julian pleaded with his dark brown eyes, the same eyes as the Duke's. "Pistol...loud...give...position." He coughed and spat again. "Don't...want...linger."

Christ above. He couldn't. Christopher shook his head in denial as tears coursed down his face.

"Do it. Now."

A groan escaped Christopher's mouth as he reached with a shaking hand and grasped the dagger.

Julian gave him a small smile as his hand dropped away.

"Don't...bastards...get you. Promise to...live."
Julian waited for his nod before he closed his eyes and turned his head, baring his neck.

Christopher didn't let himself think, only react. He struck out and slit his brother's throat. Choking on a scream, he forced himself to swallow. He dropped the bloody knife. Gathering up the pistols, he stood, taking a few stumbling steps, before reaching his stride, just as shouts of pursuit closed in. He never looked back.

****

Beth stood frozen in the doorframe as she watched Kit thrash on his bed. Between his sleep-laden moans, tears coursed down his face. She could only image what nightmare clutched him. Was he dreaming of the courtyard and Sophie? Should she wake him? Asleep, even though obviously troubled as it was, he allowed himself to mourn what he wouldn't even acknowledge while awake.

Quietly, she crossed the room and reached his bedside. On the floor, lying on its side was a half empty decanter; obviously, it had fallen when he passed out. Dressed only in his breeches, his bare chest and arms with their outward scars were a testament to his hard life, but she worried more for his hidden scars. His tears stopped, and his moans turned into short panting breaths, legs and arms thrashing around. He was going to hurt himself if he kept this up.

"Kit! Wake up. You're having a bad dream."

He continued to twist, a grunt of effort escaped, followed by a cry of pain.

"Kit!" She reached out, careful of his whipping

arms, and touched his shoulder. In a flash, Beth was grabbed and flung onto the bed. Before she could even react, he threw a leg over her hip, straddling her; leaning forward, he grabbed her throat with both hands in a crushing hold. When he started to squeeze, panic set in. Beth bucked her hips off the feather-ticked mattress, trying to throw him off, but she couldn't get much leverage. She slipped both her arms between his to try and break his hold. It wasn't working. Her lungs screamed for air as she pummeled him with her fists— striking blows to his shoulders and chest, but it was too hard to concentrate. Her limbs felt like wet noodles. Her hits became frantic pats. She had to wake him. With the last of her failing strength she managed to claw at his face.

Chapter Thirty-Three

Astaroth lounged in the blacksmith's doorway, shoulder propped on the frame, ankles crossed, and his thumbs tucked into his jeans pockets as he watched Remiel hammering out whatever tool he was currently working on. Wasn't the *Smith* supposed to be the devil? At least in the fairytales he was. Remiel should have picked a different cover. Or was it foreshadowing? He smiled.

Remiel tossed his hammer down and spun to face him. "Are you just going to lurk there and stare, or are you coming in?"

Straightening, his smile grew to a grin. "I didn't want to interrupt."

"Since when did you develop manners, demon?"

"I'm crushed." He clasped his hands to his heart covering the Las Vegas devil logo on his T-shirt. "I always strive to be a gentleman."

"I think hell just froze over."

Astaroth *tsked* and sauntered into the smithy. He circled the angel and ambled over to the workbench. Picking up a bottle of scotch, he tilted his head. "May I?"

Remiel sighed. "Suit yourself; you will anyway."

With a smile still curling up his mouth, Astaroth pulled over a clay mug and poured himself a stiff four finger amount. He paused. He might as well play nice;

after all, he was finally going to win after so many centuries. And if he read Remiel right, the Archangel was frustrated, and possibly ready to cross the line and ignore his boss's will. He pulled a second mug over, and poured another generous amount before placing the bottle down. It would be quite the angelic feather in his cap if he could get his time-honored enemy to fall. Ah, what a plunge that would be.

He gathered up both mugs and walked to Remiel, offering him one. The stubborn angel pursed his lips and glared. Astaroth smothered another smile.

"You expect me to drink with you?"

"Why not?" He kept the drink thrust at him. "We've known each other for centuries. True, we're dyed in the wool enemies, but I like to think of us more as *frenemies*."

Remiel snatched the cup from his hand. "In your dreams, demon."

"So, no toast?" Roth quirked an eyebrow.

Remiel took a healthy shallow. "What do you want, Ass...ta-roth?"

He ignored the taunt. "So many things. World domination, a lifetime of souls, or maybe I'll settle for watching the latest *Star Wars* movie." He sipped the whiskey, noting it was smooth as silk. "But mostly, I wanted to take this opportunity to face you this one last time."

"Why? Are you planning to die?"

"Cute, Remy. Happily, no."

"There goes that dream."

Astaroth sipped more scotch. He almost felt sad their rivalry was coming to an end. Across time, his opal had been empowered by one wielder after another, and yet each time, his canny feathered nemesis somehow thwarted him. The souls stolen back, released to their appropriate destinations and not into Roth's hellish account. As a Grand Duke in the underworld, very few would challenge him, or even match him. Remiel was a worthy opponent. He had lost several battles to this Archangel, but now he was primed to win the war. It was worth the wait. This time there was nothing the angel could do.

The Viper's Eye was packed with innocent souls with a few more to come. Edmond was everything he hoped for and more, so meticulous and ruthless in his goal, a simple matter of the right leverage. Soon the harvested souls would be his, once the chosen wielder imploded after filling the stone, and Roth would be elevated to a rank others in hell only dreamed of. Remiel was too late this time.

"I have to give you a compliment, Remiel," he offered. "The last hiding place for my opal was quite clever. I thought perhaps it was lost for all time." He shrugged. "Tragic, really, since the Viper's Eye is one of my finer works."

"Your *jewel* is a travesty to humanity."

"Demon." Astaroth pointed to his chest. "It's my job."

"You need a new career."

His smile returned. "What I will get is a promotion. I'll be Lucifer's right hand, with all the benefits and glory such a position holds. I'll be well rewarded for stealing all those lovely virtuous souls from your dear old dad." He would keep refilling the stone and be a threat to Heaven; even Lucifer himself would envy. "Sorry old bird, but you've lost. I hope your boss doesn't lose his shit on you."

Remiel placed his empty cup on his anvil. "You haven't won yet, Roth."

"Ever, the dreamer, Remy. I like that about you." Astaroth placed his empty cup next to Remiel's. He met the angel's icy-blue eyes. "You're in a tight spot. I don't envy you. You'll have to handle this quite differently than in the past. Your old tactics won't work, no nearby volcanoes or convenient glaciers. You'll have to step outside your box." Roth's blood pumped with happiness. "Be careful; the first step might be a long drop, my friend." He could only wish. Remiel's fall would be an event to behold.

Without another glance, Astaroth spun on his sneakers and strode from the smithy. He paused outside the open doors, out of sight, curious as to Remiel's reaction. He cocked his head, and frowned when he heard Remy's strong baritone sing the opening lyrics to a Journey's power ballad. Remiel's belief would be shattered. No small-town girl or city boy would stop Astaroth now.

Chapter Thirty-Four

Kit's eyes snapped open. "Shite!" He flung himself backward, falling off the bed to land next to the decanter on the floor. The shallow furrows Beth scratched on his face burned, but his guilty flush soon overpowered the hurt. Her coughs and gasps reached him from his prone position. What had he done? He could have killed her in his sleep. Shaking from both the shock of his vivid nightmare and the reality of his actions, his hands clenched and unclenched. It wasn't safe to be around him. He needed her gone. There would be no more deaths by his hands. He was meant to be alone.

He grabbed the brandy carafe and staggered to his feet. Taking a healthy swallow, he studied Beth, who lay curled on the bed with her hand protectively around her throat, still trying to recover her breath. Christ, they were both lucky. He needed to make this convincing. If she ended up hating him, it was for the best.

"What the hell?" Kit deliberately slurred his words; after his nightmare, he was icily sober. Too bad. Hell, why fake it when there was an obvious solution to the problem. He took another gulp, then gestured with the bottle toward Beth. "Bugger off. Git out." He thickened his lower-class accent.

Beth sat up on the mattress, eyes wide, her mouth open in shock.

"Do I need ta throw ya out?"

Her mouth flapped a few times before closing into a firm slim line as her sky-blue eyes snapped in anger. She leapt off the bed and snatched the brandy straight out of his hand before he could react. Her face flushed red with anger, Beth hurled the bottle out the door, where it crashed into the wall and shattered onto the floor.

"You asshole!" Her voice a hoarse rasping. "You tried to kill me and *you're* angry?" She closed the distance between them, getting in his face. "What the hell is wrong with you? You want me gone? Good luck."

Kit dropped his gaze. It wasn't working. He knew the stubborn look she was shooting him. His frustration fled in his desperation. A hollowness filled his chest, and he became aware of his fatigue. Aches and pains made his muscles tremble, and he gave up the fight; slumping to the floor, he came to rest on the rug with his back leaning against the side of the bed. He closed his eyes and bowed his head. So tired. He sat there, shaking. This particularly horrific dream hadn't visited him in years, but this night it had returned with a vengeance.

The nightmare, so real, had broken open long-suffering wounds. He'd buried the hideous day in a mental box so well, he hadn't thought of Julian or Adisson since the lurid dream had left him. Sophie. Her death brought back all his ghosts. He wished they would stop haunting him. There was no fight left in him, and if he couldn't figure out a way to drive Beth away, sooner or later she would be added to his collection of gruesome specters.

He didn't registered Beth joining him on the floor until she nudged his shoulder with her own as she mimicked his pose next to him.

"What's going on, Kit? Talk to me."

With an inward wince at her still gravelly voice, he shook his head. "If I beg and say please," he whispered. "Would you leave me?"

"Nope. It's not going to be that easy."

Though his head felt like it weighed a ton, Kit managed to lift his gaze to hers. "And if your death was a certainty, likely by my own hands, would you then go?"

She met his stare, her eyes widening as his words sank in. "We've been through a lot. You saved my life. I don't think you'll murder me now, so stop with the threats."

He sighed, turned his head to stare blankly into the hallway, and stretched out his legs. "You don't understand." Kit closed his eyes. Weary to the bone, he longed for sleep but worried what might be waiting for him if he did.

"Then help me." She placed a comforting hand on his arm. "What aren't you saying?"

"It's a long story."

"I'm not going anywhere." Beth slid closer to him so their bodies were touching from thighs, hips, and chest. She tilted her head so it rested upon his shoulder. "Go on. Spill it."

"I'm a bastard."

She snorted. "I already knew that."

He released another sigh before a slight smile curved up his lips. "I'm illegitimate."

"Ah, that kind of bastard."

Was he really doing this? No one knew his whole story, not even Sophie. Maybe if he laid himself bare, Beth would see the logic in abandoning him and if he purged himself, perhaps he'd be able to lock away his nightmares again. It was worth the try.

He picked up her hand and laced his fingers through hers, resting their clasped palms on his thigh. "My ma was a famous London actress, Charlotte Locke, a rare talent and even rarer beauty, with fiery red hair, and dancing emerald green eyes. As you can imagine, tickets to her performances were highly sought after as much as her favors." Kit loved his mother and cherished the time he had with her growing up backstage. How different things might have been if she had lived. "For a time, she favored his Grace, the Duke of Windmere. Their relationship was discontinued when he left for the country to attend his pregnant wife."

"You're kidding, right?" She lifted her head off his shoulder to stare in disbelief at him. "You're the son of a Duke?"

"No, a bastard from a Duke, quite the great distinction, believe me. My father, his wife, the *Ton*, made sure I knew the difference every day of my life." He reached with his free hand to coax Beth's head back to her earlier resting place. For some reason, it gave him the illusion of comfort.

"So you lived in his household? And by the way," her hoarse voice laced with sarcasm. "Nice of him to cheat on his wife with your mom."

His shrug lifted her head slightly. "It's common enough among the aristocracy."

"Remind me never to get involved with a peer of

the realm." A comforting silence filled the space before she added, "So, go on, tell me the rest."

"My ma discovered her own pregnancy shortly after he left. She notified him, and when she gave birth to me, he actually sent a monthly stipend to her."

"Oh, how generous." The sarcasm was back. Strangely, her unguarded support calmed him, easing tightly clenched muscles. Without thought, she sided with him, and he wondered at her uncommon generosity.

"I was raised in the theater, backstage, everyone in the troop taking a hand in my education and care." A genuine smile crossed his face. "Though young, I still remember the time. It was probably the happiest moments of my life."

"It explains so much," she commented. "Since you're not strutting the boards and using your talents for good, I suppose this tale turns to woe?"

"She developed a cough."

"Oh, God. Of course she did."

"I was just eight when she died." Beth squeezed his hand. "I was lucky, I suppose. He was notified and Windmere sent for me. He could have washed his hands and left me to make my own way in the world—"

"Oh, sure, leave an eeight-year-old to fend for himself. People would do that?"

"All the time." It was his turn to squeeze her hand. "I was raised at Langston Place alongside his heir, Julian, who was only three months older than I. I was given the same education and training. Learned to ride, use of the sword, taught to shoot, schooled in languages, everything a duke's son would be expected to know."

"I can see where your many contrary talents stem from." Beth pursed her lips. "I'm assuming they never let you forget your status though, right? What about Julian? Did you have only a cold antiseptic upbringing, or was there a silver lining to your storm clouds?"

"Antiseptic?" She was always saying such odd things. He needed to study how to speak colonial, or he'll always feel out of step with her. He liked languages and had a knack for them; what's one more for his collection?

"Sterile? Nope, not that either. Um, did you find any warmth in the rest of your childhood?"

"Julian and Adisson, a neighboring Baron's third son, were my saving grace, I suppose. The three of us were best friends."

"I'm glad."

"I'm not." His heart started pounding, and he squeezed his eyes shut, fighting off the panic at just thinking of what he had done.

"You're shaking again." Beth released his hand to turn into his side and wrap her arm around his waist, tucking her head under his chin and resting on his bare chest. "It can't be that horrible."

It was. His most regrettable mistake. *Mistake*, such an inadequate word. How had he lived, when they had not? It wasn't right. Kit fought for control, all the while Beth held him, quietly giving her support.

"It was all my idea," he choked out. "A grand scheme, before I was kicked out of the estate on my eighteenth birthday."

So, he told her. In starts and stutters, how there was a band of brigands, well-armed highwaymen, tormenting an area north of them. The three of them were to hunt the villains and return as heroes, but the table was turned, and they had become the hunted, Adisson shot dead, with his brains blown out, the mercy killing of Julian by his own hand. The whole sordid, unforgiveable tale spilled out of him. Almost fifteen years ago and the day was still etched vividly in his mind.

"I couldn't return, not after what happened. I took only the clothes on my back, my sword, and the pistols Julian gave me."

"What did you do?" Her whispered question tore at him.

"A bit of everything. I had the skills to blend in with both the upper and lower classes. I eventually ended up a mercenary. I was very good at fighting, my weapons skill unmatched."

"So how did you end up here?"

"I was tired of fighting someone else's battles. Hated the politics of it all and decided I needed to be on my own." A tired, sad chuckle escaped him. "I decided to let Fate take a hand. An inspired choice really. Take the line of work that changed my life and that of my friends, forever."

Beth sighed and held him tighter. "So," she drew out the word. "You're trying to kill yourself, aren't you? A robbery gone bad, or caught by the Watch?"

"Actually no." He rested his chin on top of her head. "I made a promise to Julian. He told me I had to survive, to live. If I wanted to die, there are certainly easier ways to go about it then as a highwayman."

He wouldn't break his promise to his half-brother. But after all the shameful years, perhaps he decided to cheat a little. Truly, what better choice than to become a highwayman? The thing he despised the most? He had killed his closest friends. The guilt would never be washed from his soul, so Fate could have the final say. Her judgment would let him live or die, and his word wouldn't be broken. Kit was surprised he was still alive. He knew his days were numbered. Death would embrace him, and he would finally pay for his sins.

Chapter Thirty-Five

Beth's heart broke. His life so disparate from anything she'd known. He really needed to stop blaming himself for those deaths. And now, Sophie. No wonder he had a nightmare. In context, her life was a piece of cake. Well, except for her death and traveling back in time. In the scheme of things, it wasn't so bad. Sure, she missed her friends and family, but she'd encountered some marvelous people in this century. Mr. Landon and Mrs. Duncan were solids, but no one had touched her as much as Kit.

She held him tight, her head resting on his chest. The light dusting of hair made a soft cushion against his solid muscles. He smelled good, when he had absolutely no right to, a bit of wood smoke, leather, and something purely male. Beth had missed the unique manly aroma. She snuggled in closer, and Kit wrapped his arm around her.

This was no way to live his life. Torturing himself over deaths he had no control over, then gambling with his own life everyday. Kit had so many options, but throwing his life away shouldn't be one of them. Beth had many of her choices ripped away from her, but she was never one to give up. Life was always worth living. She may have forgotten this once, but it was time to live and introduce the concept to Kit.

There was something she could do for him, well,

for both of them. Mourning her life of should-haves and could-haves wasn't getting her anywhere. She was weary of feeling so lost, and guessed Kit was as well. This was her choice and there was really nothing holding her back. Everyone she had known hadn't even been born yet. Grant was dead, either way. She was her own woman again, at least until she returned home. It was time to start having fun. And if she was being truthful with herself, this moment had been building ever since she met the dashing highwayman.

Beth twisted and swung a leg over Kit's thighs straddling him, her skirt hiking up past her knees. Her hands gripped his shoulders as she met his startled cat's gaze. She hid her smile. It was awesome to finally catch him by surprise after all the times he had her off balance.

"I believe we both could use a distraction."

His reply was a quirked eyebrow. Ha. Two can play this game. She looked pointedly down, paused, then looked up to meet his slatted gaze.

"Unless you're not *up* for it?"

She was happy to see his mouth twitch as he almost smiled. Even happier when both his arms reached around her, and his hands gripped her ass, tugging her forward so she sat on the most encouraging hardness growing beneath her. She squirmed to settle herself where she most wanted to be. His hands clenched tighter with the added friction. Definitely not so immune.

"I told you I wouldn't have to force you."

"Hush, stop trying to ruin it."

Beth slid her hands gently across his shoulders to caress softly up his neck. She paused, and squeezed, in retaliation to her earlier choking by Kit—earning her a snort.

"I understand the revenge," he said as one of his hands left her ass to rise up and stroke the side of her tender neck. "But I'm sure I can earn your forgiveness, in a much less violent endeavor."

"You think? Perhaps I might want to be the one driving the bus."

"Bus?"

"Quiet." She held his face, gently yet firm, and kissed him. Her first thought was his lips were surprisingly soft, before they parted for her. She slipped her tongue in and gave his mouth a slow sensual caress. He tasted of brandy. Yum. And then he took control. He sucked on her tongue, which she felt all the way down to her core. Oh yeah.

His right hand gripped her butt tighter, and his left rose to cup the back of her head, before his fingers plowed through her hair, holding her tight, pressing her to him.

The kiss changed as she struggled to take charge, but lost. His tongue battled hers and all thought fled at his dominance. She moaned, her hands dropped to his shoulders to grip tightly as sensation flooded her, and she kissed him back.

Kit's lower hand went wandering. It stroked past her hip and down her thigh to grip the edge of her dress, and with a tug, the skirt climbed higher as his hand found skin. His touch trailed across the bare skin of her thigh causing her to shiver. Heat flooded her, and Beth rubbed herself against his hardness, as a hungry ache consumed her.

She moaned into his mouth, his grip tightening in

her hair. His other hand clenched her thigh, so close to where she wanted him to stroke her, but he broke their kiss, his hand releasing his grip on her head. Each of them breathing heavily, so close, their noses touching, before he leaned to rest his forehead against hers.

He stayed motionless. When she went to kiss him again, his hands, one on her hip, the other still on her thigh, tightened, halting her. She wasn't sure what was happening, but didn't mind waiting him out. It was nice being held so close and a bit desperately. Beth hadn't realized how much she missed intimate contact since her travels. Their breaths slowed, and a hush descended.

A quiet sigh passed Kit's lips. "I'm not sure this is a good idea." His soft, lilting words broke through the silence.

Was he kidding? He had physically hit on her more than once. He was a guy! How in the hell was he turning her down? This was a first for her. Her lips pursed in a moue of discontentment. She needed this, wanted it. Stopping was not an option.

"Well I do." Her hands dropped from his shoulders to reach between them. In a flash, before he could react, his breeches were unfastened, and she filled her hands with his hot hard flesh. Kit's head bowed back against the bed as a groan wrenched out of him. With one hand gripping the root of his shaft, her other started to stroke.

In the next instance, Beth found herself flat on her back with her wrists shackled in iron grips on either side of her head. How had he turned the tables so quickly? His nimble strength startled her. Straddling her, Kit leaned down across her, pressing her into the rug. He was breathing hard and glaring at her.

"Seriously?" She huffed. "We're just going to stop?"

"You misunderstand."

Beth twisted, trying to break his hold, but to no avail. Though she did manage to illicit a hiss from him, when her gyrations ground against his erection. She smirked, which earned her more of his weight as he settled lower, trapping her securely with his body.

"Be still," he admonished. "You're not helping matters."

"I believe I am. We'll have to agree to disagree."

"Hoyden," he chastised, before closing his eyes on a sigh. With a slight shake to his head, his eyes snapped open, and she was caught in his green gaze.

"I want you." His words, low and throaty, sent heat rushing through her. "I just…" He took a deep breath. "I can't…" He kept his gaze locked to hers. His eyes glittered with need and steel.

"I believe you can." She pressed her hips upward into his as much as his weight would allow, earning her a frustrated growl.

"Woman, be still!"

She laughed up at him as he continued to glare at her. "What exactly is your problem? Spit it out, *man*."

"I'm a bit…raw, desperate." Kit looked chagrinned, yet somehow still hurting. "My repertoire is a tad bare…"

Her mouth dropped open. Was he worried about hurting her? "Kit—"

"I—"

She lifted her head and placed a quick kiss to his chin. "You can be gentle and slow next time." His eyes widened at her words. "Fast and dirty has its bennies.

I'm game. Go for it."

His slow smile lit his face as an eyebrow quirked. "Bennies?"

"Benefits."

"Ah," he lowered and kissed her slow and deep. "Are you truly sure?" He asked, his accent thick and his voice husky.

"Yes."

"Well, then…" He was giving her yet another out. So not going to happen. She nodded her approval.

Kit released her wrists and with his graceful speed, had her skirt yanked upward with one hand while he grasped himself with the other. He wedged her thighs wide with his body, and in one smooth move, thrust inside, rooting himself deep.

Beth cried out as she arched upward. He was hard, hot, and deep, stretching her to her limits and flooding her with sensation. Before she could acclimate, he was pulling out. She clenched to hold him, but once again he proved himself stronger. An emptiness filled her core as he withdrew completely. A protest crossed her lips, but she shouldn't have worried. He filled her again and set a punishing pace, which left her mind reeling. She curled her legs around his waist, digging her heels into his lower back, and grabbed his biceps to hold on. She couldn't breathe; her world spun as her body tightened and spiraled higher with each of his vigorous thrusts. He was hitting all the right spots.

"Kit!" Her back bowed upward as her orgasm slammed into her, hard, and fast. He joined her shortly with a shout of his own, his muscles failing him as all his weight dropped on her. So limp and relaxed, Beth didn't mind at all.

A few heartbeats later, Kit rose up and braced his weight on his forearms. His color looked better, much less pale, and the smile curving his lips was a sight to warm her heart. "Well, my sly minx, that was over way too soon."

"Agreed." She smiled up at him. "Plus, way too much clothing."

"My thoughts exactly, luv." He agilely pushed up to his feet and offered his hand. She grasped it and he pulled her up. He gave her a slight smirk, and in one swift motion, peeled off his unfettered breeches and tossed them aside to stand before her in all the glory God had granted him. It was well worth the view. Definitely hotter than any male underwear model. With his dark auburn hair and his athletic dancer's body, lean-muscled and strong, he would look amazing in briefs on a billboard. Though nude wasn't bad and apparently, he was now quite happy to see her. His erection grew as she studied him. Oh boy.

"I believe it's your turn." His comment lifted her gaze to his smiling eyes. "Do you need any assistance?"

"Just admiring the view."

"Do you approve?"

Absolutely no shame. "Well…" She drew out the word and mock outrage crossed his face. Kit began to stalk toward her. Beth backed up and turned, skipping to place the large bed between them. He paced gracefully, moving cat-like once again in his relaxation and sobriety. She held up a hand to stop his stalking, which he did with a questioning gaze.

She lifted her hand and tugged at the strings of her bodice, never glancing away from him.

"I can help you with that, luv," he offered, while

staring at her chest.

"No, no. I'm good."

"Are you sure?"

"Yup." The laces dropped to the floor, and she pulled off the stiff cotton vest. Next, she wiggled, and pushed her skirt past her hips, where it slid to puddle on the floor. She stood in her gauzy shirt covering her down to mid-thigh, thankful she forgot to wear her chemise. Kit's attention was glued to her. It was her turn for a sly smile. She undid a few of the small tiny buttons from her neckline, causing the shirt to gap wide. Ever so slowly, she trailed her hand down, brushing past her breast, lightly skipping across her stomach, and was gratified with another strangled hiss from him, when her hand reached the juncture of her thighs and let her fingers grasp the cottony fabric. Kit was riveted.

The time for teasing was over. Beth tugged her shirt over her head and tossed it to the floor. She studied him as he studied her. His stare was currently locked on the neat blond curls at her heated juncture, and ever so slowly, he raised his gaze until they paused at her chest, taking in her breasts as her nipples tightened with his attention. He smiled and then looked her in the eyes.

"You're gorgeous, luv."

She felt herself flush with his praise, momentarily mute. Kit took advantage and prowled around the bed to reach her side. "So lovely." He raised his hand to gently stroke her face. "I'll enjoy taking my time."

"Will you?"

"Indeed." He stepped forward and gathered her into his embrace. His mouth settled on her lips, and she opened for him on a groan. With a slight chuckle, he slipped his tongue inside for a languid dance. Without breaking his slow and sensual kiss, he pushed her backward, and they collapsed on the bed.

Chapter Thirty-Six

Kit woke from a dreamless sleep, thankful the night of sport kept his terrors at bay. Beth was still asleep, draped over him as another blanket, a soft silken one. He raised his hand, and lifted one of her long golden curls and stroked it between his fingers. The thick wavy tresses splayed about in lovely disarray, her glossy hair shone in the creeping morning light, revealing layers of colors from white to a deep burnished gold, a pretty sparkling treasure indeed. As was their night together. He'd started out desperate, anything to chase away his demons and lose himself. He was surprised by her acceptance, how game she was to take his coarseness and match him.

But something shifted, his normal, impersonal bed play changed. He found himself aching for intimacy, for connection, to be part of a whole, instead of always so alone. And again, Beth followed where he led, with no hesitation, questions or doubts. She was unlike anyone he knew—a puzzle of contrary pieces. His life, never dull already, would be challenged with her around. A smile crept over him, as he toyed with her hair, twining the lock through his fingers. He would enjoy the distraction of Beth.

She stirred in her sleep, her breath huffing over his chest, warming his skin. Maybe he could keep her? Her hair slipped through his fingers, and he stroked his hand down her head, trailing fingers down her spine, to rest his hand on one lovely, firm round cheek. He wouldn't mind spending his days sparring with her and the nights with her warming his bed.

The smile fled his face. It was a nice dream, one he might conjure in his darker moments, but she could never be his. All he brought to those he cared for was death. Beth was so filled with life, it truly would be a crime to see her taken from this earth. Even a thief such as he couldn't do it. But it had been nice to warm himself in her glow, even for a brief time. *Damn*. When had he grown so attached, developed intimate feelings for her? It was another complication he didn't need.

"Such a serious expression first thing in the morning." Her sleep-laden voice startled him out of his reverie. "You're not having second thoughts? Isn't that the woman's job?" She propped herself up on her elbow. A cold chill caressed his chest with her warmth removed. At least she left her leg slung over his thighs. She reached out and smoothed his hair off his forehead, then trailed her fingers down his cheek over the raised welts she had given him breaking him out of his nightmare, before leaning forward and placing a quick chaste kiss to the scratches. She pulled back and met his gaze.

He studied her sexy and sleep tousled self and drank in her beauty, but mostly, it was the honest, caring blue gaze that struck him the most. He'd miss her unconditional support. Why she did so, he had no clue. He certainly didn't deserve it.

"Cat got your tongue?" She smiled at him.

"No, luv." He smacked her bottom, causing Beth to squeal and leap away from him, giving him the much-needed distance.

"What was that for?" She rubbed her arse, easing the sting from his sharp slap, the action causing an enticing movement to her breasts. Perhaps he could have her one last time?

"It's getting long in the day, luv, and you're trying to sleep it away."

She glared at him. "It's not like I have anywhere I need to be."

"Have you not?" Her brow crinkled in puzzlement. "I believe you're forgetting our agreement."

"What are you talking about?"

"The Boar and Rose? A job you need to insure you keep…"

"Oh, that." She lifted the sheet to cover herself. He supposed the room did have a certain chill with the fire out, but he missed the lovely view already. "Look, something else has come up."

Kit quirked a brow. Beth's eye was drawn to the tented blanket covering him. "Ha! No, not that. Though…no." She shook her head. "Stick to the plan," she muttered to herself.

"Plan?" He laced his arms beneath his head. "Exactly. You're supposed to return to the inn and be my eyes and ears."

"No, no, not that plan, a new one."

"I wasn't aware there was a change?"

"Yes, well, I've been thinking—"

"A dangerous pastime to be sure."

Beth smacked him on his chest. "Quit that, beast! I'm trying to be serious."

"Very well." He sat up from his prone position and settled himself up against the headboard, the blanket pooling in his lap. "So what new scheme have you devised?"

"This Lord Renweard…we should steal back the stone."

He blinked, not sure what he heard. "Why would we do such a thing?"

"Well…Sophie. We need to avenge Sophie."

"You don't even know her."

"Yes, but you do. We can't let Renweard get away with it."

Beth wasn't making any sense. What wasn't she telling him? Besides, there was no way he would let her anywhere near the Viper's Eye, it was too dangerous. The jewel held supernatural abilities, all proven too true with the state he had found Sophie in. Guilt lanced through him; if he had only believed Sophie when she told him the opal's story. It was best to let the stone be lost and nowhere near either of them. He was cursed enough without it already.

"No." He leveled his gaze at the petite beauty in his bed. She wasn't getting anywhere close to the accursed gem.

"What? What do you mean, no?"

"Exactly that."

"You're just going to let a treasure like it go? And what about Sophie's death?"

The jewel was no treasure and it was a shame about Sophie. Her death he would carry alongside Julian and Adisson's, with him for the rest of his days, but he wasn't about to get involved with something so dangerous and unprofitable. He certainly wouldn't let Beth either and he knew exactly how to push her. "She was just a whore."

"Oh my God, you didn't just say that!" She jumped out of the bed and snatched up her shirt, drawing it on, covering her nakedness. "She was your partner! How can you be such an asshat?" Target in the red, his marksmanship proven again. A pity she was covering herself though. He'd much prefer her arguing in the nude; it was such a lovely view, but what did he expect? It was for the best.

Beth was huffing and puffing as she struggled with the laces of her bodice, then she flung the tangled strings down, and raised her chin to glare at him across the bed. She took one deep breath and slowly exhaled the air out.

"You said that on purpose."

"Well, Sophie was a whore."

"Stop it!" Her lips pursed in displeasure. "You are purposefully making me angry and distracting me off the topic. Fool me once, jerk."

Shite. He had remarked on her intelligence. It was time to be blunt. "Leave Renweard and the stone alone. I won't help you kill yourself."

She braced her fisted hands on her hips. "I'm not planning on dying."

"You will if you go after the gem."

"I need…" She looked down, breaking eye contact.

"Beth." He slid across the bed and stood naked in front of her. He placed a finger under her chin, tilting her face up so he could read the emotion in her summer gaze. "Luv, what aren't you telling me?"

"Nothing, it's nothing."

The lie was easy to read across her face. "Leave the Viper's Eye alone."

"I can't." Her voice was low and soft.

239

"Why?"

She just shook her head. "Can't you just trust me?" Her gaze implored him. He steeled himself against her. It was pure foolishness. Too dangerous. Why would she want the blasted jewel after seeing Sophie with her own eyes? He would protect her against herself. Without his help, he doubted she'd have any luck.

"Is it money? I have funds enough to help you."

She stood mutely before him. Kit sighed internally.

"I should go." Beth finished dressing and turned to leave. When she reached the bedroom door, he knew he needed to try one last time.

"Beth, don't do it," he pleaded with her. "I've stayed alive this long by instinct and it is screaming at me. The opal will bring you nothing but pain and most likely end your life. I wouldn't see you dead, luv."

She stopped in the doorway, with her back to him. "Then help me."

"No."

"I guess I'm on my own."

Beth walked out, leaving him standing naked and alone. It shouldn't have hurt, but the ache in his chest said otherwise.

Chapter Thirty-Seven

"The Knightmare has been a menace to West Yorkshire for far too long." The Tredford Constable flung a frustrated hand in the air.

"And who's at fault? You haven't done your job and brought the bastard down," Edmond spat.

"My lord—"

"Enough!" Edmond slammed his fist on the table. The Constable and his thief-takers, the privately hired individuals, all took a step back. "No more excuses. This man, and he *is* only a man, will be captured and hung."

"But, sir, um, my lord, surely the Knightmare has help—"

"Which I'm counting on." Edmond glared at the brown-haired thief-taker on his right. "When the scoundrel robbed my courier, there were only a handful of people who knew of the true contents. This will work for us."

The five thief-takers Edmond hired to aid in his revenge, and the Constable closed ranks around the table, to gather and stare at the map unrolled on its surface, held in place with various objects at hand—a book, a candle, an inkwell. The map and occupants of the room swam before Edmond's eyes as a sweat broke across his brow. *Not now!* His vision tunneled, and a pressure built behind his eyes. The Viper's Eye wasn't pleased with this side trip. There had been only one sacrifice since he and Charles left the manor. He pinched the bridge of his nose, willing the pain and voices back. He wanted to save his Anna, but almost of equal measure, he would see the death of the highwayman who put him in this circumstance to begin with. Had the jewel been delivered on schedule, Anna wouldn't be lying asleep now. She'd be whole and shining. The man would pay with his life.

"My lord, are you all right?"

Edmond waved off Constable Jeffries's query as he willed himself to focus. He punched a finger to the map. "Here. This is where we lay our trap. It offers plenty of cover for our men and meets the conditions the Knightmare favors to stop a coach."

It was a shame he couldn't be there personally to witness the highwayman's downfall, but Edmond needed to be with his daughter, care for her, and feed the stone. How many more souls could it possibly want? Edmond must be near his goal. Yet, even if the gem clamored and punished him, he would not miss the lynching. A smile curled up his mouth.

"We have the bait of treasure, the gold and jewels I'm supplying, and now gentlemen, it is up to you to spread the word about its worth and its travel." He met the gazes of the men surrounding the map. "Tell your whores, have loose lips in your taverns, spread your gossip to the shopkeepers. Just one," Edmond held up a single finger to their riveted attention. "The information in the right ear, to the right person, and our trap will be laid. You have your incentive. The treasure will be yours to split if you're successful. A bonus for your efforts."

The Constable and thief-takers grinned, several nodded in agreement.

"In five nights' hence, the new moon will rise, his favorite hunting time. The tables will turn, and the Knightmare will be ours!"

Chapter Thirty-Eight

Beth stifled a frustrated sigh as she closed the door to her room and scurried down the inn's back stairs to enter the kitchen of the Boar and Rose. Five days since she forced herself to walk out on Kit and five days of aggravating failure. It took her no time locating Lord Renweard's house, a large sprawling manor located just south of Tredford. Beth even had the awesome idea of getting a position in the home, but trying to get an *in* with the servants of the household was the most frustrating part. She strangely couldn't find any of them. It was a large house; there should be plenty of people working there. She even managed to find the time to visit in person, but oddly, the house appeared empty, even though everyone she spoke with assured her Renweard was in residence. At the end of her rope, Beth didn't know what else to do, except perhaps break in and search for the jewel. Not her forte, since the last burgling job ended with her shot and shoved into the past. It really appeared she needed Kit's help, but the man hadn't spoken or visited since she left.

She nodded a hello to Mrs. Duncan as she snatched her apron from the hook and quickly tied it on. Beth was at loose ends. With the money from her rings, she didn't really need to work the tavern floor, but it was at least familiar and gave her a place to stay while she searched for the stupid opal. It had taken tons of sweet-talking, but she managed to keep her position at the Boar and Rose. She kind of hoped Kit would seek her out, since it was where he expected her to be. Yet the stubborn fool never appeared. But he was right about one thing, there was plenty of gossip among the customers, and she had her fingers crossed that either word of Renweard or the Viper's Eye would find its way to her, if not the frustrating highwayman.

"Evenin' to ye, Miss Beth," the cook greeted. "Ye know the menu for tonight?"

Beth smiled. "I do, since I sampled it earlier. Delicious as usual." She was rewarded with a smile and a nod.

"Ye best hurry. It's a full room and then some."

"Terrific," Beth mumbled, as she pushed her way through the door and stared at the sight before her eyes. The tavern was certainly bustling tonight. All the tables and benches occupied, and there were even people standing, since no seats were available. She paused, not looking forward to all the ass slaps and pinches. She didn't mind the rude proposals, but the fondling she could do without. She'd be black and blue tomorrow. Best get it over with.

Beth sauntered up to a table crowded with eight men. "What can I get you tonight?" Immune to the ribald suggestions and talk, she managed to memorize their orders and veer out of the way, just missing the butt slap as she left. The rest of the night was rinse and repeat.

It was nearing midnight as she trudged to the bar. Dropping her tray to the counter, she snatched up a rag and wiped the sweat from her face. The room had been stifling hot all night with the number of bodies stuffed inside, great for business, but terrible for oxygen. It was easy to forget it was below freezing outside. With the approaching witching hour, the tavern had emptied somewhat, and she'd be happy when they closed. Hopefully soon. The Boar and Rose didn't really have a set closing time; only when there weren't paying customers did Landon close his doors. Currently they were down to two tables, six men total. It couldn't end soon enough.

She braced her hip against the bar and kept the two tables in view, which was easy, since they shared the corner by the glass paned window, with only an empty table separating them. The table of four gestured to her. Please God, don't let it be another round. No need for her tray either way. She straightened and crossed the room. Plastering on a smile, which didn't reach her gritty eyes, she stopped at the table.

"Gentlemen?"

Her query earned her a round of laughs. These men had been a bane to her existence for the last three hours and apparently, they knew it.

"Aye, lass, a fine one ye are." The oldest of the group complimented her. "We're settling our tabs. It's time we're making our way home before the weather turns again." He nudged a pile of coins in her direction. "There's a bit more than needed. Keep it. Ye certainly earned it, lass, putting up with a bunch of louts like us."

She bobbed a curtsey and earned another round of chuckles.

"It was a grand day when the Boar and Rose hired you, Miss Beth. If I weren't married already—"

"Go on with you," Beth enjoined. "Sally will be wondering if you're frozen on the side of the road."

"Right ye are, lass." He tipped his hat and corralled the others, and headed out the door as the other men greeted her a good night, in various states of sobriety. Smiling to herself, she turned back to the table and swept up the coins into her apron's pocket.

"The Knightmare. Truly?"

Beth froze as a chill of dread chased down her spine. She slowly pulled out a rag and started to wipe at the empty table, as she eavesdropped on the two men left in the bar.

"Aye, heard from Tanner. All but a done deal."

The first man cleared his throat and then spat on the floor. "Nay, I don't believe it. They'll never capture 'im."

"He's wily, no doubt. But they've five thief-takers plus the Constable. Beech's Bend is prime for the Knightmare. Mark me words, they'll stop him tonight, if'n they haven't already."

Beth's heart pounded. She knew the place. They had ridden past it on the way to York. She couldn't let them capture him. Oh God, he'd be hung! Terror made her limbs tremble. She had to warn him. Clutching the rag in her fist, she straightened, and with her back to the last customers, she crossed the room and pushed her way through the door to the kitchen. Never pausing, she ripped off her apron and grabbed her cloak from the peg.

"What do you think you're doing, Miss Beth?" Mr. Landon asked, entering the kitchen as she reached for the outside door.

"Emergency! Gotta go!"

"It's too—"

Beth never heard Landon's warning as the door

slammed shut behind her. She might lose her job, or hell could be freezing over along with the countryside and she wouldn't care. What she needed was a car, or better yet an ATV. How the hell would she get to Kit in time to stop him? She started running.

Dashing around the corner to the main boardwalk, she was about to push up the hill, which led her past the smithy, when suddenly she screeched to a halt. God and his miracles, or perhaps this was Remiel's secret way of helping? Whatever, she didn't care. Because across the street lay the answer to her need, as she watched the obviously drunken man trying to mount his horse, slip and fall, landing unconscious to the ground. Behold, the ultimate all terrain vehicle!

She smiled. Checking out her surroundings to find herself alone on the road, since both the late night and severe cold weather had cleared the streets, Beth darted across the frozen mud to reach the drunk and his horse, conveniently near an alley. *Thank you, Remy*! If it was his work or simply coincidence, she'd take her lucky breaks where she could. Surveying the street once again, ensuring she was truly alone, she grabbed the drunk by his ankles and dragged the poor sod into the alley, happy the men of this century were way shorter than in hers, making them weigh less. He didn't so much as twitch.

Squatting down by his legs, she yanked off his boots, tossing them aside. She needed more warmth, and exposing her legs in this weather because her skirts were hiked up was not an option. Next, she unbuttoned his breeches, and pulled them off. She stood, then toed off her fuzzy lined boots and when her wool stocking feet hit the icy dirt, a soft squeal escaped her at the cold ground. She quickly tugged on the breeches, tying the front in a tight knot instead of using the buttons in hope they'd stay up, and then stamped her feet back into her warm boots.

She jogged to the horse and gave the bay mare a pat on her neck, then checked and tightened the girth. About to put her foot in the stirrup to mount, she glanced over at the man in the alley in his stockings and bare legs. Damn it, he'd freeze, especially if he didn't wake until the morning. She turned back and nudged him with her foot. Nothing. Crouching down, she slapped him. Nothing still. Growling to herself, knowing she was wasting time, but also knowing she couldn't leave him to the cold, she went for hard slaps to both his cheeks. This earned her a moan as the man began to stir. It would have to be enough.

Quickly, she spun and raced out of the alley and ran to the horse so he wouldn't see her and be able to identify his attacker and thief. In a fluid motion, she swung up, with her skirt bunching up around her thighs, exposing her purloined breeches, she grabbed the reins and kicked the horse up to a canter. The stirrups were a bit long, but she'd manage. The mare pushed into a gallop as she turned her up the hill. Heart pounding, she hoped she wasn't too late.

Chapter Thirty-Nine

"Easy, lad." Kit quieted the jigging Dante back to the walk. Though his horse had better eyesight in the murky bitter dark than he, Kit wouldn't chance an injury to his partner. There would be time for running later. For now, by the sliver of light the new moon allowed, he could pick out a safe path. Once again, both Dante and he were disguised, as he rode out to meet his fate.

Blast this cold. His feet were numb in his boots, and he had to continually flex his fingers in his thin leather gloves to keep their circulation. He wished for thicker gloves, but then he wouldn't be able to handle his pistols. Maybe he should retire until spring? He hunched deeper into his greatcoat. Some highwayman he was turning out to be tonight. The infamous Knightmare knew no discomfort, striking whenever he chose, regardless of irritation or the weather.

Perhaps he should turn around and call it an evening. He was losing his mind. Though the amount of gold coins and pretty baubles traveling by coach this black evening was certainly a temptation, his gut was tumbling, and the pricking on the back of his neck was an irritating distraction. Warnings he'd normally heed, but this night he was feeling more reckless than usual, regardless if he was slowly freezing to death.

Damn her! Kit wasn't sure if his churning gut was

a warning he and Dante were riding into a trap, or if he was worried about Beth. He should have left her to be shot at the side of the road on the fateful night of their first meeting. She had been nothing but trouble from the first moment. And yet…he missed her. It was like a part of him was lost since the morning she walked out of his door.

Dante carefully left the path to maneuver around a fallen log, before reclaiming the narrow trail cutting through the woods. What was wrong with him? He hadn't had this aching pain and loneliness since… Dear God, it was not. He stiffened in the saddle. Had he fallen in love with the chit? Twice in his lifetime he'd felt this pain, once upon losing his mother and the other, his half-brother and best friend. He recognized an aching heart when he felt one.

Kit mulled it over as Dante strode on. It seemed obvious now he admitted it to himself. He was in love with Beth. Gone these past days, he realized he missed her as if one of his limbs were gone. He worried constantly about her safety, while all the time forcing himself to keep his distance, though he wanted nothing more than to be by her side. It had taken all his vaunted willpower not to spy on her. At least he wasn't so bogged down in decline he was begging her to return. He couldn't afford this entanglement.

Sophie was the closest he'd ever come to crossing the line, with his vow created after getting his brother and friend murdered. He'd reminded himself all the time Sophie was a whore, but just the same his protectiveness and caring grew, but he hadn't crossed the line to love. His guilt blossomed with her death and the odd relief it brought in the darkest corner of his mind, knowing he still held true to his vow of no involvements or personal attachments.

Thinking his heart was well-guarded and his mind strong, how had Beth snuck past his time-tested barriers? Perhaps because she was like no other person, male or female, he had ever met? Strong and feisty, odd and puzzling, plus caring and open to a fault. She didn't hesitate to call him on his shite, or support him unconditionally where others never had. Beth made him feel. Rare indeed, since before meeting her, robbing was the closest he came to feeling alive, which was far from ordinary.

His breath misted into the night air on his frustrated sigh. He was a mess, which led him out on tonight's adventure. Kit needed to regain his sense of self. Though he now freely admitted he was in love with her, he held no doubt it was purely one-sided, and how pathetic was that? Pushed into the figure of unrequited love, the tragic love-struck figure ripped from one of those novels the young ladies were swooning over these days.

Anger pierced through his self-pity and frustration. Tonight was his chance to dare Fate to strike and claim her far overdue payment, or to slip her grasp and live another day, feeling alive and unfettered once more. His brother bid him to live, but he laid no claim on how such life should be lived. When he was riding the bandit's road, surviving on the sword's edge, he was beholden to none. The numb depression, his constant companion since Julian and Adisson, was blasted away like a ball fired from his pistol.

Closing on Beech's Bend, he halted Dante who trembled with eagerness beneath him. At least someone was excited about events this night. He dropped the reins and then pulled Julian's pistols, checking to make sure the double barrel flintlocks were primed and ready. Next, he pulled the black cravat up, covering his mouth and nose, which gave him some respite from the freezing weather, as well as hiding his misting breath. His last ritual was to press down on his tricorne hat, assuring himself it was tight to his head and low to shield his eyes.

Nerves jangling, he forced himself to pick up the reins and nudge Dante to a walk, where he again halted by the edge of the woods yet still shadowed in the trees. Listening intently, nothing disturbed the night except the whistling icy wind. All silent. No owls hooting or foxes yipping. It could simply be his and Dante's presence...or not. Finally, the clip-clop of the approaching coach broke the eerie quiet. Blood pumping, Kit studied his surroundings one last time, before squeezing with his legs and trotting Dante to the center of the road, where once again he halted and dropped the reins.

He reached inside his greatcoat and his hand wrapped around the ivory inlaid handle of one pistol, when a blast and a scattering of sparks shattered the cold dark night. Kit jerked in the saddle as a sharp pain lanced into his side. He managed to grab a handful of mane just in time, as Dante reared and spun in the road. He barely kept his seat. As the gelding's front hooves touched ground, Kit realized he'd been shot.

"We've got 'im!"

"Close in!"

"Don't let him escape!"

Overlapping cries encircled him, and he flinched

when another shot rang out, and his upper arm jolted with a stinging burn. Move or die.

He hesitated, but Dante did not. His horse plunged off the road into the woods, building to a neck-breaking gallop. Another horse crossed into their path, but Dante barreled into him; with a squeal the strange horse was shoved aside, and in tandem with his trusted equine, Kit's well-placed elbow connected, flinging the rider off his horse and into the brush.

With one hand Kit clenched to his side and the other holding Dante's mane once more, he ignored the reins and gave Dante his head, trusting in his gelding's superior night vision and sure-footed talent to get him out the trap someone had devised for the Knightmare.

"After him!" The pounding of multiple horses in pursuit sounded their headlong charge.

Dante galloped, and Kit braced himself as he felt his horse's haunches bunch beneath him. The powerful gelding leapt into the dark night, sailing across an unseen culvert. The landing jarred Kit, making his vision swim as pain lanced up his side.

Trying to clear his mind, he listened frantically to the sounds cutting through the rushing wind in his ears. With an equine scream and a shout from a rider, at least one of his pursuers fell victim to the culvert. Though by the pounding of hooves behind him, the majority did not. Kit released his hold on the mane, to flail for a pistol. Managing to grip one, he pulled and fired blindly behind him, hoping to scare and back off his pursuers. He doubted he'd be lucky enough to hit one.

Keeping hold of the gun since there was a shot left and he might need it, Kit relaced his fingers through the coarse hair of mane and urged Dante on, which was about all he could do, as a draining weakness plied through his limbs. It took what was left of his strength and balance just to stay on. Each jolt of Dante's stride and shift of direction caused searing pain. Kit willed himself to stay conscious, lying low and clinging. If he fell, he was done for and Fate would have her day.

Chapter Forty

Beth dashed through the woods on her stolen horse. She rode as the crow flew, deciding to skip going to Kit's home, and gallop across country to Beech's Bend in hopes of reaching him before he stumbled into the ambush. Her heart raced along with the quick pace she pushed the mare to, all the while praying she wouldn't be pitched into a ditch or the horse snapped a leg. Please let Remy be watching over her.

A gunshot broke through the rushing wind and pounding hooves. *Damn it*! In an instance, Beth nudged the mare to the right, to close the distance in the direction of the shot. It had to be Kit. *Let him be alive, let him be alive.*

Out of the gloom a four-foot wall of brush appeared, blocking her path. She had no idea if her borrowed mount had the scope to clear the obstacle, after only jumping some logs and ditches on her pell-mell run. Too late not to commit, regardless of what terrain surprise was held on the landing side, she needed over that hedge wall. Stretching tall in the saddle, she squeezed her legs with a crushing force, hoping not to face-plant into the bush. She'd never jumped this height before, but her friends all claimed she was a reckless rider, and her fear for Kit made her braver than usual. When the mare took the brush wall out of stride and launched herself into the air instead of stopping, Beth gave a joyous hoot, and an adrenalin rush pumped through her veins, as they landed safely on the other side to gallop on.

She pulled the game mare up, trying to orient herself. The sounds of running horses were directly ahead. "Come on, girl!" Beth urged her horse into a canter. As they built speed, they passed a deadfall branch sticking out of a tree in their path. Beth went to bat it out of her way, but grabbed it instead and tucked it tight under her arm as she galloped toward the horses. The branch was thick and sturdy; at least she had a weapon now.

The thudding hooves closed in, making Beth realize they were heading directly at her up the same path. Quickly, she slowed and trotted off the trail, hiding in the dark shadows of the trees. The mare's flanks heaved beneath Beth's legs in testament to her effort. Stroking the mare's neck in comfort, Beth leaned forward and whispered, "one more time, girl, then it's home for you."

She sat up in the saddle as Dante and Kit galloped into view. Kit lay prone on Dante's neck, but he was still in the saddle as they galloped past. Several lengths behind, but still in pursuit, was a single rider. Beth readied her makeshift lance and prayed her timing would be good.

"Hye!" Beth shouted and kicked the mare forward into a charge while holding out the branch. The mare's chest struck the pursuing horse's shoulder as the rider's head connected to her wooden lance. Both horse and rider crashed to the ground as Beth's mare danced in place. The rider's horse scrambled to its feet, but the man lay still. Seeing the bloody gash on his forehead,

Beth hoped she hadn't killed him.

She looked down the path and didn't see any more signs of pursuit. Hopefully there were none. Beth swiveled her mount and kicked the horse once more into a canter in order to chase down Kit.

It didn't take long; Dante and his rider appeared out of the murky night. But at the sound of her approach, Dante picked up his head and broke into a trot.

"Dante, no! Whoa! Stop!" Beth yelled, and the big gelding slowed down at the sound of his name to a walk, then finally stumbled to a halt. She hopped off her mare, afraid of startling Dante into running again. Leading the mare, she reached him and grabbed hold of his rein. She patted his neck, taking in his lathered sweaty state, sides heaving and nostrils blowing.

Her attention rose to the man lying on his horse, still as death. He faced her, but with his highwayman regalia shielding his face, she couldn't tell if he was awake or even alive. How on earth had he kept his hat on? "Kit?" Standing on tiptoes, she reached up a hand to grip his shoulder. "Kit?"

She was answered with a groan, and he stirred. "Ah, luv," he mumbled. "It might be best to leave." His eyes opened, causing a glint in the dark slit between hat and mask.

Thank God, he was alive. "It's all right," she assured him. "We're alone."

"Hmmm." With effort, Kit managed to sit up in the saddle. She watched as he unclenched his fingers from the mane, and with a shaking hand slid the pistol inside his coat. Motion done, he groaned and started to slide from the saddle.

"Hey!" Beth braced him and pushed him back upright, where he managed to steady himself. Her hand came away sticky and wet. Blood. "You're hurt!" *Damn it.* She looked around, still no sign of pursuit. She needed to get him home and check the extent of his injuries, because she certainly couldn't call 911 for an ambulance.

Decided on a plan, she looped the reins over her borrowed horse's head, gave a stroke to her soft muzzle. "Thank you, girl. It's best for you to make your way home." She stepped aside and slapped the mare's hind end. "Go on, git."

The mare gave one backward glance before lowering her head and plodding off back down the path. Beth watched as the horse disappeared into the night. She turned to Dante.

"Okay, big guy. I know you had a rough night and you're tired, but I don't think your buddy here is going to be able to stay in the saddle by himself."

The slouched highwayman grunted at her statement. "Sorry if the truth hurts," she replied to Kit, as she led Dante over to a fallen log. She clambered on top of the tree; there was just enough height to let her get on the tall gelding.

"Please don't buck me off." She swung a leg over, settling herself behind the saddle. "Good boy." She reached her arms around Kit and picked up the reins and gave a slight squeeze with her legs. "Take us home, Dante."

The gelding continued up the path at the walk. "I sure hope he knows where he's going," she mumbled into the back of Kit's coat.

"Give him his head. He'll get us there."

Surprised by Kit's mumbled words, Beth dropped the reins and curled her hands around Kit's waist. "How bad is it?"

"Not sure…"

Worried Kit was slipping into unconsciousness, she knew she had to keep him talking. "For fuck's sake, what the hell did you think you were doing?"

A low chuckle confirmed he hadn't. "Such language," was his breathy response.

"Stay awake, Kit, or I'll poke you where it hurts most."

"Ah, luv…such…kindness."

"I mean it. And you still haven't answered my question."

"My…job…how?" He didn't sound great. His words were mumbled, and she could tell he was having difficult time breathing. *Come on, Dante. Get us home,* she willed.

"I overheard at the tavern they laid a trap for you. What I don't understand is how you could have fallen for it, asshat."

"Didn't care."

Her blood chilled. "What?"

Kit slowly shook his head. Beth was so done with his death wish. "You need to stop trying to kill yourself."

This earned her a coughing chuckle. She prayed he wasn't bleeding out. The freezing night should help slow any bleeding, but until she could examine the wound or injuries, she had no idea how close to death he was, which sent a chill chasing up her spine.

"Might not…have to try anymore."

"Oh no, you don't. You are so not dying on my

watch."

"Stubborn wench."

Dante continued to pick his way through the forest, and a gusting wind blew wet against her face. Glancing up, she saw snowflakes swirling in the air currents. Great. It was starting to snow. She shoved her bare hands into his coat and buried her face against the dark wool of Kit's back.

Realizing she was in danger of falling asleep just as much as Kit was of passing out, Beth knew she had to keep them both talking.

"So, how many were there, you know, at the trap you deliberately rode into?" She gave him a squeeze, to get his attention.

He grunted. "Didn't really stop to count…four…maybe six…"

"Wow. There was only one behind you. I took him down with a branch to his head."

Kit didn't respond. She nudged his back with her chin. "I believe you owe me at least a thank you." He remained slumped and silent. "Kit?"

"Sorry, luv." He stirred, trying to sit up taller. "…my thanks."

"Try and stay awake, will you?"

"Aye…I'm trying."

She hugged him a little tighter as she checked out their surroundings. Were those clumps of trees familiar? They had to be close; it felt like they'd been riding forever. Dante turned onto another path, the wind dying down so the snow fell gently down. It was beginning to thicken, and at this rate, might turn into a white out. She could only hope, for the snow would hide their tracks if it fell fast and deep enough. How had he managed to lose all those men? She said a silent prayer they were truly lost and Kit's identity safe.

Dante stepped out into a clearing and Beth's heart began to pound with a burst of much needed adrenalin when she noticed Kit's cottage and stable. "Good boy, Dante!" She exclaimed as the horse plodded to the stable entrance and halted.

Beth carefully dismounted, pain lancing through her numb, cold feet as they touched the hard ground. She ignored it. "Okay Kit, come on down, and don't you dare fall and pass out."

With a groan, he slowly slid his leg across the front of the saddle. He swayed before slipping from Dante. Beth managed to steady his landing, but it was a close thing. She helped him over to the fencing of the outside corral where she propped him up.

"Stay here. And standing," she admonished. "There's no way I could carry you to bed."

"If you're taking me to bed," Kit managed a small smile. "I can…manage to be erect."

His barely breathed words and the pasty gray of his complexion spoiled his joke, but at least he tried. Beth smiled back. "See that you do."

Quickly, she led Dante into the stable and took off his bridle. "Sorry, boy. I promise to come back and take care of you." He nudged his sooty face against her arm, smearing wet ash on her damp cloak and revealing some of the wide white blaze hidden beneath. She undid the girth and pulled both saddle and pads off together and laid them on top of an empty stall.

"Come on, you." Dante followed deeper into the stable and into the open deeply straw-bedded stall next to Root. Finding fresh water and hay, Dante set to work on his meal. Luckily the long walk back after finding Kit had cooled out the big gelding. He was a grooming mess, but at least cool enough not to colic from his night's efforts. She shut the stall door and with a final pat to the courageous horse, retraced her steps and headed out of the barn.

Kit was still standing, but dangerously slumped against the fence boards. Beth walked over and slipped under his limp arm to brace him with her shoulder. "Hey there." She wrapped her arm around his waist and straightened as much as she could under his weight. "Let's get you indoors."

He grunted as he tried to take some of his weight off her and started to shuffle toward the door barely seen through the thick snowfall. Beth was sure it was sheer willpower keeping Kit on his feet and upstairs all the way to his bed, where he collapsed with a moan.

She threw off her cloak and went immediately to the hearth, starting a fire in order to warm the chilled room. Next, she crouched down by the bed in front of Kit's dangling legs. She pulled off his boots and wool socks. Standing, she discovered his eyes closed, looking dead to the world; she couldn't even tell if he was breathing, just like when she found him lying so still on Dante. Panic rushed through her veins, and she shook him, getting a groan, and his eyelashes fluttered.

"Come on, you've got to help me." She tugged on his greatcoat as Kit found the strength to sit up, swaying. Somehow, with his barely there help, she got his coat off. She found a bloody gash on the sleeve of his upper left arm, but obviously not the cause of all his blood loss. Shucking off first his jacket, then vest, she thought, who the hell *dresses* for a robbery? It was when the dark-vested coat was removed she found the true wound. His right side was caked in blood, soaking both the front and back of his shirt and staining his breeches as well.

Beth grew light-headed at the sight, only to be steadied by Kit's hand to her arm. "Sorry for the…mess." Kit breathed out, pulling Beth out of her panic.

"No, no, it's all right. We need the shirt off." She untied the mask cravat lying loose around his neck, then undid the strings at the neck of his shirt. She was about to pull the shirt over his head and paused, realizing it might just be better to cut it off. Before she could drop the hem, Kit covered her hand with his, and together they lifted the shirt over his head. Dropping the sodden material, Beth turned to stare at his wounds. His upper left arm had an angry red streak, mostly crusted over, apparently just a graze. She forced herself to look at his side and felt her eyes widen as she gasped. There was a round hole between his lower ribs on his right side, still leaking blood. How could it still be bleeding? His skin was a pasty gray and cold to the touch. She caught Kit staring at her.

He tried for a smile, but it was more of grimace. "I'm afraid the ball is…still inside."

Chapter Forty-One

Oh, God, no. She couldn't possibly, but she highly doubted Kit was up for the task either. It would have to come out for any chance of healing or curtailing a severe infection. Beth met his dull green gaze.

"Sorry, luv."

She pulled her shoulders back and brushed her hair off her face. "Right then. I'll be back. Try to not die while I'm gone." He managed a nod, but Beth didn't miss his white knuckled grip on the bed covers. She turned quickly and strode out of the room, hoping he didn't read the emotions crossing her face. She could do this; she *had* to do this.

What she wouldn't give for a twenty-first century hospital. Even if she managed to clean and close the wound, the threat of infection and no antibiotics made her physically ill. He could easily die. Beth made a mental list of what she'd need, obviously towels and water, some form of bandage, needle and thread. She started to ransack his home; it wasn't large, just the two bedrooms upstairs and the first floor contained the main sitting room, kitchen with pantry, and a small dining room.

As she was tearing a tablecloth into strips, she racked her brain for disinfectants. She'd need flame and alcohol for the needle, but what about something for the wound? What was available in this century? Had penicillin been discovered yet? *Honey*! Beth ran to the pantry and started rummaging. She lifted a crock of nature's wonderful remedy. In the past, well future, she'd used honey on open wounds of her horses with great results. It was a natural topical antibiotic and anti-inflammatory. Thank God for her equine first aid skills. The stickiness would help seal the wound, and maybe she could even pack it in the hole before stitching?

Supplies gathered, she juggled her load, jogged upstairs, and enter Kit's bedroom, surprised to find him still upright. She unburdened herself and turned to face him.

"I couldn't find any sewing—"

He loosened one grip on the bed to wave weakly at the bedside table. "Drawer…"

She opened the drawer and found a needle, and a spool of coarse thread. Pulling it out and placing it on top the table next to the candle, she wondered how many times Kit may have used it to patch himself up. The proof lay with the various scars on his body already. And now there was going to be at least one more for his collection. She forced herself to let go of the vivid image and turned to her erstwhile patient.

"Right. Let's get you cleaned up." She noticed his returned death grip on the bed as she approached him with the bowl of water and towel. Dunking the towel to get it wet, she pulled it out, wrung out the extra moisture, and started to tackle his bloody skin. "So, you want to tell me why you purposefully entered a trap?"

He shook his head. Stubborn fool. Now with the wound revealed, the bile rose in her throat. How on earth was she supposed to remove the bullet? He must have read her mind.

"At least...small hands."

Shit. He was probably right, since there were no convenient forceps around. *Fustercluck.* Girding herself, she grabbed the decanter of scotch and slug a shot back, the burn centering her as it made its way down. She offered the bottle to Kit, holding it for him as he managed a healthy swallow. Next, she poured some into an empty bowl. Placing the decanter down, she plunged her hands into it and scrubbed them together, hoping not to add to any germs to what he already had.

Approaching his side, she saw his shocked expression. "You'll thank me later." Before she or Kit could think or brace, she plunged a finger into the hole in his side. She gagged as he gasped and lost yet more color, but she was impressed he hadn't screamed or she hadn't vomited. Feeling for the bullet caused Kit's breath to come out in pants until he bit his lower lip. Seeing his determination to stay strong, it was the least she could do as well, even though the thought of retching was forefront in her mind.

There! Her finger grazed metal; now to get underneath it. Kit's shoulders hunched, and he grunted behind clenched teeth as her index finger curled around the ball. Slowly, so she kept it in her grasp, she withdrew her finger, and the ball popped out. They both exhaled in unison.

She plunged her bloody hand into the bowl of water, bullet and all, to rinse the blood off her skin. Grabbing another clean cloth, she quickly pressed it to his side and applied pressure on the wound, trying to stop the freshly flowing blood her digging created.

"I believe we deserve another round." Beth picked

up Kit's hand and pressed it to the dressing. "Hold this." When she was sure he had it, she offered the decanter to Kit. With her help, he took a swig, which she followed with another for herself. Next, she grabbed the crock of honey. She removed the lid and scooped a generous handful. As she approached Kit, he raised a weary eyebrow in query. "Trust me." How was she supposed to explain antibiotics and stuff?

"Hold still, I have no idea if this will sting or hurt. It never seemed to bother the horses…"

She tossed away the bloody cloth, and Kit grunted again and braced himself, as she started to pack the wound full of honey until it could take no more. It mustn't have hurt too much, because Kit bore it with grace.

It was now time for some needlework. She unspooled a healthy amount of thread, not knowing how much she'd need since this was all new to her, and quickly did up the needle. She passed needle through the candle flame a few times, before putting it down. Grabbing the scotch, she took another healthy swallow before rinsing her hands and then dousing both the needle and thread. Satisfied she did all she could to keep things sterile, Beth sat on the bed next to Kit.

Nothing more than stitching up some leather, she encouraged herself. It'll have a bit of resistance and then punch through. She could this, she had to. Beth stabbed him with a needle.

Kit hissed. "Bloody hell." He exhaled harshly a few times, before he regained control as she set about sewing him closed. "Waste of…good…scotch, woman."

"Ha! You'll thank me when your wound doesn't

become infected."

"Infected?"

Well, she supposed she could tell him, give him something to think besides the needle in and out of his flesh. "You know, um, festering?"

He hissed again when she tugged a bit too hard. Oops. "Both the honey and the scotch will keep bacteria from growing."

Kit sighed, and she almost laughed as he bit out, "Bacteria?"

"Think of them as super tiny bugs, invisible to the eye. They're drawn to wounds and if one sets in, they multiply like bunnies having a party."

He grunted, but appeared intrigued enough he didn't notice when she knotted off the thread and cut off the remainder with a knife. To distract him when she took a scotch-soaked towel to his side, she continued. "If the population gets large enough, these bugs lead to inflammation, err, puffiness, you know, swollen? Then you get a fever. It's your body's way of trying to kill the little bugs."

She slathered on some more honey, before pressing a linen napkin against the wound. She didn't even need him to hold it when she picked up the strips of tablecloth. Let's hear it for the sticky stuff! Beth was tying off her makeshift bandage when she realized she was so close to Kit he'd buried his nose in her hair. She tilted her face up and kissed his chin. "All done, and even a kiss to make you better."

Kit's mouth curled into a weak smile even as his eyelids fluttered closed. Exhaustion from blood loss and the escape claimed him. God knows how he had lasted this long. She bent and grabbed his ankles to lift his legs onto the bed. He wasn't so far gone, because he managed to help a bit. But that was all, as he finally passed out.

Beth tugged at the sheets and blanket, covering him and tucking him in. She sat on the edge of the bed, next to him. What was she going to do with him? She gently pushed a lock of his hair off his forehead as she studied him. They made a good team when they worked together. She had to get him to help her with the Viper's Eye. Maybe it was time to tell him the truth, regardless if he'd think she was crazy. When she thought she'd lost him to the ambush, Beth completely panicked, not sure if it was her lost chance for returning home with his help, or simply the thought of losing the man himself.

Kit challenged her. Frustrated her. But a world without Kit… No more lies. It was time for the truth.

Chapter Forty-Two

Kit woke with a yawn and careful stretch. He once again felt like himself, a bit tired, but not ill. Despite Beth's best efforts to keep the invisible bugs away, some had set in for their party. The past few days he felt like Dante should have, rode hard and put away dirty. Last night his fever broke, and he had his first truly restful night's sleep. He was ready to be out of his bed.

He tossed aside the blanket and sheet covering him and gingerly sat up. Naked except for the clean fresh bandaged wrapped around his midsection, he wondered where Beth was. Probably asleep, since she had taken care of him, tirelessly, single-handedly nursing him back to health. He owed her. Warmth filled him as he thought of her care. Perhaps, she did feel something toward him. Maybe not the love he had for her, but something he could work with?

Finding a clean pair of breeches, he tugged them on and reached for a shirt. Dragging it on over his head, it settled loosely around his hips. He was happy with only the slight pull to his wound—a bit of tightness and no pain. Plus, the graze to his upper arm was all but healed. Satisfied and pleased to be out of bed, he went in search for Beth.

As Kit prowled down the stairs and into the hallway, the front entrance door opened. Beth blew in with the gusting cold gale, struggling with her cloak and trying to close the door. He reached over her shoulder and added his strength to help, getting a surprise squeal from her as she jumped and spun around. The hood of her cloak fell back, revealing a rosy-cheeked beauty with her golden locks falling from a messy knot high on her head.

"What are you doing out of bed?"

"Hmmm." He reached out and pulled a piece of hay from her hair, then played with the loose curl, twining it around a finger and then letting it spring back. She'd obviously been caring for the horses as much as she had been tending him. "Looking for you."

"Well, I guess you found me," she pushed past him and removed her damp cloak, hanging it on a peg. "Now you can get yourself back to bed."

He ignored the order and padded barefoot after her, following her into the sitting room. He snuck up and was right on her heels when she realized what he was up to and spun around to confront him. No cute squeal this time, as they stood almost nose-to-nose as he looked down at her upraised face.

"Seriously, Kit?" She stood her ground.

"I'm bored and realized I've been most remiss—"

"Too bad, you lost a lot of blood and just got over a fever…wait, what? Remiss?"

"Yes," he reached up and brushed his thumb across her cheek. "I haven't thanked you for rescuing me." He stepped closer, wrapping an arm around her waist, pulling her flush against his front. "For nursing me." His other hand dove into her hair as he tilted her face upward.

He kissed her. Starting out gently, just a brush

against her soft lips, until he felt her stiffness loosen, and she leaned into him. When she opened her mouth, he took her invitation. Their kiss deepened, languid and unhurried. He left her lips to trail kisses along her jaw and trail down her neck, and was pleased by her sharp inhale, which bordered on a moan.

"We should stop." Her breathy words didn't enforce their meaning. "Seriously, you just got over your fever…"

He sucked hard on her pulse, and then gently grazed with his teeth before reclaiming her sweet mouth. Slow and sensual, he walked her backward toward the hearth. When he lowered them to the rug to kneel before the fire, she broke the kiss on a protest.

"No, you're wounded, healing—"

He placed a finger across her lips, silencing her. "I'm fine. I promise to lie back and let you drive the bus."

A laugh escaped her. "You really are good with languages." She placed a hand on his chest, pushing him gently to recline on the floor, where she then straddled his thighs. "So, you're simply going to think of England? Do your duty for King and country?" She started to unbutton the front placket of his breeches.

Hell, no. Why would he do that? He'd be thinking of his luscious Beth. His hand trailed under her dress to find her under her clothes. Their mutual groans greeted each other as he cupped her hot wetness, and she gripped his shaft firmly, then started stroking. No matter how lovely it was to have her hands on him, he needed to sheath himself inside her.

With his free hand, he gripped her hip and pulled her forward. Blessed angel, she took the hint and guided him to her entrance and slowly impaled herself on his length. Another shared groan sliced through the room.

"That's right, luv." She gave a shimmy to her hips, settling him deep inside her, his new favorite place to be. "Give us a kiss."

Beth leaned forward, bracing her hands beside his head, and kissed him hard and deep as she moved her hips again. She was magnificent. His hand under her clothes moved to grip her arse, squeezing in time with her motion. She broke the kiss and braced her hands on his upper chest, rising up to give herself more leverage, as she continued to slide up and down. Her pace increased, and he found he couldn't remain motionless, surprising them both when he thrust as she came down. She flung her head back and moaned. He was close and needed her to be with him. Watching her take her pleasure while riding him was too arousing. The only thing better would be if they'd removed their clothing and were skin to skin. He felt his balls tightening and grew a bit desperate.

He moved his hand between her legs and fondled every woman's magical spot. A slight pinch to her nub, and he sent her flying. Her tight contraction squeezed and trapped him, holding him deep while he shouted his own release. God, he loved this woman.

With a sigh, she collapsed against him, draped across his body. He was feeling a bit boneless as well. This probably wasn't the cleverest idea he had. His side was throbbing, but there was no way he'd let on. If he were bleeding out again, he'd die a happy man.

Beth stirred, her eyes fluttering open. "Mmmmm," she hummed as she raised a hand to push her hair off her face. "That was ridiculously great." She shifted and groaned when he slipped out of her. On a sigh, she propped herself up. "Are you okay?"

"Fine, luv." He took her hand, the one reaching to hoist up his shirt to check on his wound, and raised it up to place a kiss to her palm. Before she could protest more, he twisted them to their sides, where he spooned her from behind on the rug before the fire.

She snuggled deeper against him. He felt his eyelids closing when Beth sighed and tensed in his hold.

"Kit?"

"Yes, luv?" He placed a soft kiss behind her ear.

"I haven't been exactly honest with you."

Truth in fact, he already knew. It was odd; he had shared more of his life and secrets with her than any other, but he barely knew the woman he believed he loved. Perhaps she was ready to open herself to him.

"You know, I haven't lived the most innocent of lives," he consoled her. "I doubt there is anything you can confess to change my opinion of you."

"Well, that's the thing. I'm afraid it will. I don't…" She started to tremble in his hold.

"Hush, now." He reached across their bodies grasp her hand and gave it a squeeze. "It can't be all that bad."

"You'll think I'm crazy." Her hushed broken words sliced at him.

"Ah, luv." He turned her so she faced him, and pressed her against his chest, holding her close, trying to afford her some comfort. "You know, I think you're already a bit mad, being an American and all."

He felt her chuckle, more than heard it. "Beast."

Kit kissed the top of her head and tucked her under his chin. "Out with it, luv. You'll feel better for it."

"You promise to keep an open mind?"

"I give you my word." His hand stroked her back, as he wondered what she was going to tell him.

She exhaled another soft sigh. "I'm not from here—"

"Already established—"

"No, no. I mean…no…fine. I'm just going to spit it out." Beth propped herself up and looked him in the eyes.

"I'm from a different time. I'm from the future."

The future? He burst out laughing.

She slapped his shoulder before popping up to her feet and glared down at him. "It's not a joke. I really am from the future."

He managed to get his mirth under control in the face of her anger and frustration. "Perhaps you hit your head while rescuing me?" Kit sat up, sitting cross-legged on the rug. He was afraid he'd laugh again, if he opened his mouth, so he simply quirked an eyebrow at her.

"Oh my. God, no! I didn't hit my head. I knew you wouldn't believe me." She started pacing.

He stared at her, confused. She apparently believed she was a time-traveler, no matter how impossible it was. He did promise to keep an open mind, so he'd hear her out. He cared for her, even if she was mad. If he played along and let her think he believed her, maybe her agitation would pass as well as this silly idea. "I'm sorry I laughed, luv. Why don't you tell me how you came to be here?"

She froze momentarily, before starting up at a

slower pace. A brief look of anxiety crossed her face, before she wiped her expression clear. Interesting. He wondered if he'd hear the *whole* story, or only a particular version.

"I...um...I'm not exactly sure how it happened," she faced him. "I'm from the twenty-first century. I was helping a friend, find," she waved her hand in the air. "It doesn't matter. What does matter was, I was shot in the chest, in the heart, actually."

"You'd be dead." A chill raced up his spine at the thought of her death. He soothed himself with the consolation he'd seen her chest and there was no scar. She couldn't have been shot.

"I was." She started pacing again. "All I know was I died, but I woke up here, in the woods, healed with no wound. I had no idea where I was, just started walking, when I came upon your robbery."

"The night I first rescued you?"

"Yes," she snapped her fingers. "That's it! Proof! Remember my clothes? They were strange, right?"

He frowned, thinking back to the thin soft shirt she wore and the strange rugged breeches. "You were dressed as a man."

"No, not really. In my time, women wear jeans all the time. Oh!" She clapped her hands and turned to face him. "All my strange, unknown words! Cell phone, bus, asshat. It's not another language, but future words...well I guess it's sort of a new language..."

Beth dropped to her knees in front of him. "Please tell me you believe me, Kit. I really need you to trust me. That's why I need your help." Her sky-blue gaze implored him.

Did he believe her? No doubt, unconscious in the

forest, she attained some sort of injury. Did it matter? He loved her, quirks, temper, caring, and all. He gathered up her hands in his. "Aye, luv, I do. But what help are you needing?"

"The Viper's Eye,"

His spine stiffened at the name of the cursed jewel. He shook his head. There was nothing the gem could do except bring death.

"No!"

She squeezed their joined hands. "I need it. The stone can take me home, to my own time."

He stared at her, shocked. She wanted to leave?

"You have to understand. I have family, friends—"

"A husband." His words cut through him like knife.

Beth frowned and shook her head. "No, no. Grant's dead. Killed by the same man who shot me."

A guilty relief flooded him. He wanted no competition for her heart. But what was he thinking? He didn't have her heart—she wanted to leave him. Now her obsession with the black opal made sense. It was apparently her ride home. No wonder she wouldn't listen to him and heave off.

"Will you help me, Kit? I can't get home without your help." He saw the desperation in her eyes.

Kit met her gaze and another piece of his heart broke. "Fine, luv, I'll help you steal the stone." Beth flung herself at him, and he opened his arms to embrace her. Whether she was crazy or not, she'd keep going after the jewel. She was set on this path, feeling it was her only option. Plus, he owed her his life. He'd help her steal the Viper's Eye, because she might die in the trying, and if her story *was* true and the gem could somehow return her to the future, he'd lose her, but she would at least be alive—away from him. What had he been thinking? It was for the best, having her far away from him. Kit was nothing but a danger to her. Over two hundred years was a vast distance if her claims were real. It was better to be apart than end with her death here, even if the rest of his heart was destroyed in the process. It was the price he'd gladly pay to keep her safe and alive.

Chapter Forty-Three

Constable Jeffries slugged back the last of his ale, before gesturing to the barmaid for another. He stared at his shaking hand and clenched it into a fist. Lord Renweard was a scary bastard. With his failure to capture the Knightmare, Renweard had exploded with raving madness and dire threats, which Jeffries was sure Renweard was quite capable of fulfilling. The man was insane and dangerous. The proof lay in his entire staff abandoning him except for his butler. It was bad enough Jeffries was becoming the laughing stock of the county, with the Knightmare running circles around him and eluding him all this time, but he had the slight consolation it wasn't just him and ineptitude; the surrounding counties had no better luck than he. The Knightmare was the devil himself, appearing and disappearing at will. He took some pride in the fact this latest trap almost succeeded. He had come closer to arresting the bastard than anyone else. Yet, any satisfaction was quickly ripped away with Renweard's crazed outburst upon finding the highwayman had slipped the noose.

Some of the Constable's tension escaped as he watched the Scottish thief-taker, Erik, stride through the Boar and Rose's door. He was the best and smartest of the hired guns Renweard had enlisted to aid him in hunting the Knightmare. His black eye and the welt on his forehead expressed his encounter with the Knightmare. It was with Erik's information, Jeffries was able to finally appease Lord Renweard with a new lead.

The barmaid, the innkeeper's daughter, placed a new tankard in front of him. He gave her a warm smile. "I'll be needing one more, Miss Claire." He stated as Erik joined him at the table. She nodded and sauntered off.

"Erik." He nodded at the blond thief-taker. "I'm here as requested. Any news?"

"Aye." Erik sat after shrugging out of his coat and draping it on an empty chair.

Jeffries blew out a breath of relief. *Thank God.* Maybe there was still a way to salvage this disaster. It all hinged on tracking down the unknown accomplice who worked with the Knightmare.

Erik had been the last man to keep up with the fleeing highwayman and his demon horse. He not only confirmed the wounding of the bandit, but also the use of a partner. Just as Erik had been about to close in for the capture, out of the darkness, his horse was body-checked by another horse barreling onto the path; its unknown rider clocked him out cold. Coming to, half frozen and now horseless, it had taken Erik the remainder of the night and part of the morning to arrive back at headquarters.

Jeffries was taking down a report from a man accosted in the alley, where the victim's breeches were stolen along with his horse, when Erik returned. The waylaid man claimed it was a woman.

The blond mercenary became Jeffries' secret weapon. Erik burned with an inner fire to find the highwayman's partner after he had gotten the best of him. Nothing like an axe to grind to get results. The disjointed puzzle pieces of that night began to assemble and form a picture. Which was why, days later, Erik asked him to meet in this tavern, stating he had the identity of the Knightmare's partner.

The young barmaid returned with the extra ale and placed it on the table. With a saucy smile, she turned to leave, when Erik snaked out an arm and wrapped it about her waist. He gave a tug, and she landed in his lap, all giggles and smiles.

"Can ye spare us a wee bit of your time, lassie?"

"For you, always." She gave Erik a wink. "Can't be too long. My da will get angry."

"We won't keep ye long," Erik reassured her. "I just need ye to tell Constable Jeffries, what ye told me. About the missing barmaid…"

"Hmpf. She's always disappearing. I don't understand why Da lets her continue to work," Claire groused. "The first time she left, she ran out without a word. She was gone six nights and returned without nary an excuse and my da took her right back in."

"When was this?" Jeffries prodded.

"She was just back five days before running out again. No one's seen her in days. Again. I've had to work twice the shifts."

Claire pouted, and Erik ran a hand down her back, to land and grab her bottom, causing the girl to squeal and squirm on his lap.

"Will ye tell us what night she last left, my pretty lass?" Erik focused on the young barmaid, resulting in a rosy blush brightening her cheeks.

"The night of the new moon."

Jeffries felt his mouth curling up in a smile as he exchanged looks with Erik. The man certainly had earned his fee. Nothing like revenge to feed the fuel of results. Jeffries almost chuckled, thinking how angry the thief-taker must be now knowing his assailant was a mere woman. "And her name, Miss Claire?"

"Miss Beth. Beth Leighton."

His smile turned into a grin. Erik must have been done with Claire, because he pushed her off his lap and swatted her on her way. The barmaid gave another cute pout before giggling, and with swaying hips, sauntered away from their table.

"I've got men watching this tavern," Erik informed. "She hasn't been seen since the night of the trap."

"She's nursing that accursed highwayman."

Erik nodded. "I've searched her room upstairs. Her belongings are all there, so I'm counting on her returning. It can't hurt to keep a watch. She did return in the past. It would be the easiest way to grab the lass."

"I don't like those odds. Not with Lord Renweard breathing down my neck." He grimaced. "We have no way of knowing if she'll return or when. You have a description of the wench, no doubt?"

"A pretty thing, if the accounts are true." Erik took a sip of ale. "Curves in all the right places, bright blue eyes, and long curly blonde hair, and just a bit shorter than Miss Claire."

"Keep watch on this inn, but we need to search the area. She couldn't have gone far. The horse she stole returned a day later, and there's no way a slip of a girl could handle an injured man by herself."

If he could find the girl, she'd give him the

Knightmare, especially with some well-placed threats. Jeffries couldn't just sit idly by, not when he was worried about what the mad aristocrat would do.

"I don't think she's in town."

Erik's words jarred him out of his thoughts. "I think it would behoove us to start a search of properties outlying Tredford. We don't have the time to wait for her return. We need to start this hunt. I want every shed, home, and barn searched, from the lowest shack to the grandest manor. They're holed up somewhere and I mean to find them."

"A lot of ground to cover."

"It is." Jeffries pointed his finger at Erik's chest. "That's why you're going to gather up more of your compatriots. Offer a bonus to the man who finds the chit."

Erik slugged back the rest of his ale and stood. "I best get on it." He shrugged into his coat and pressed his hat on to his head, before striding out of the Boar and Rose.

Jeffries stood and tossed some extra coin to the table. He wasn't anxious to leave the warm room for the blustery freezing night outside, but he had business to attend to if he wanted to live. He needed to be on Renweard's good side and with this latest update, hopefully he would.

Truth be told, he could taste how close he was to capturing the Knightmare. The highwayman had made a fool of him too many times to count, but the tables were about to turn, and all he needed was Beth Leighton.

Chapter Forty-Four

Beth slipped the bridle off Root and handed it to Kit, who hung it on a branch. "Are you sure they won't run off?" It seemed crazy to leave the untacked horses loose in the woods.

"Root won't leave Dante," Kit replied as he hung Dante's bridle next to Root's. He turned and patted Dante's gleaming copper neck. "And my good lad will stay until I call for him or I return. It's best they're free so they can eat and move at will."

Kit, decked out in what Beth liked to think of as his highwayman regalia, checked his weapons, making sure his sword was secure and his pistols were ready. She felt under-dressed in her normal clothes, well, normal for this century clothes. She wanted to disguise herself as well, but there was nothing at his house to fit or hide her. Besides, as he elegantly argued, she was leaving once they had the Viper's Eye, so her identity didn't matter, whereas his did. He bent and plucked a knife, still in its sheath, from inside his boot and passed it to Beth.

"Take this. I'll feel better if you have something to protect yourself with. Breaking into the manor during daylight is daring even for the Knightmare. It goes against the grain."

Beth bit back her smile as she slipped the knife into her skirt's pocket. It had taken a massive argument to convince him to come this morning and not wait for the cover of darkness. Everything Kit had tried since agreeing to help her had failed. Renweard was elusive and none of Kit's informants had been helpful. Every time they thought they had the bastard, by the time Kit arrived, the man was gone. Beth argued, searching the manor might give them a clue to where Renweard was or perhaps even find the gem itself. They had nothing to lose since they were at a dead end.

She was worried they were running out of time—how long until the stone was full of souls and Renweard imploded and the opal disappeared? She'd miss her chance to get home. Beth never was good at sitting idly by. These past few days of Kit trying to find the stone on his own had driven her slowly insane. It was time they partnered up and became the well-oiled team again, enough of him trying to protect her. An argument ensued, but she won on the simple merit everything he'd done hadn't worked and they needed a new plan.

"As I told you, the house is empty. Not a soul to be found. I scoped it out myself." It was eerie. The big house should be bustling with people, but it was quiet as a tomb. Hopefully not a bad omen.

Kit took her arm, guiding her through the forest. With her skirts, she was a danger to herself. The woods conspired to trip her, and last night's snowfall certainly didn't help as it covered many a hidden log, even though the snow was melting now. They had dismounted about a quarter of a mile from the manor so the horses wouldn't be discovered, and after a few stumbles, Kit played the gallant. At least the weather was in their favor. Yesterday's storm had finally dissipated, leaving a crisp, clear, but cold day. She was tired of being frozen. Central heating sounded so good right about now. Or a warmer climate, say, Hawaii or Florida.

It was hard to believe her adventure was nearing an end. In perhaps less than twenty-four hours, she could be back home with her family and friends in Chicago. After Grant's betrayal and death, she couldn't stay in Scotland. There were too many painful memories, too many ghosts lingering. Home. Back to the windy city. She could take a hot shower, watch some television, and read on her Kindle. She missed the conveniences of a simple toothbrush and toothpaste, the Internet and cell phones. Toilets.

She glanced over at Kit. He looked so much larger and intimating in his greatcoat and tricorne hat, then when he was prowling around in just his breeches. His lithe body hidden away and replaced by the formable highwayman. So talented and smart, not to mention smoking hot, he could be doing so much more with his life than waste it chasing his death wish. She worried what would happen to him after she was gone. Too bad she couldn't take him with her. A shame, really. She could totally see him rocking tight low-slung jeans and a chest-hugging T-shirt.

"Why don't you hang up your mask and guns?" She really didn't want him to die. Imagining his body swinging from a rope had ants crawling over her skin. Another thought chilled her on its heels. When she returned home, Kit *would* be dead. Over two hundred years would have past. Her chest ached and her mouth went dry.

"And it matters to you, why?" Kit countered as he helped her over some deadwood. "After all, you'll be well good and gone."

Beth stopped dead in her tracks, causing Kit to come to an abrupt halt beside her. "Do you really think I don't care?" His shrug cut to her heart. How could he think that? She'd risked her life for him, stolen a horse, attacked a man—all for him. She'd dug a freaking bullet out of his side with her own finger! Her face heated as she felt her anger rise. How dare he think so little of her.

He tugged on her arm. "We should be going."

"No. Wait." Beth dug in her heels. "Seriously? You think I wouldn't worry what will happen to you?"

"I do not presume to know your thoughts or feelings." Kit retreated into his haughty aristocratic accent. The one Beth had come to realize he used as a cover to protect himself. The one where contractions and his endearing *luv's*, along with his lilting tones, disappeared. She hated when he transformed into his act. She cared for the unrepentant rogue, with his charm and laughing eyes.

"Oh no, you don't." She stomped her foot. "You do not get to hide yourself from me. We're friends—"

"Are we?"

"Of course we are, you stubborn idiot. I don't sleep with men I don't care about."

"How am I to know? You have barely shared anything about yourself. As for me, I have told you things…things I have not shared with anyone."

Oh, my God! He did so not go there. The role reversal was shocking; he was acting like such a girl. *I shared my feelings, but you didn't.* "Fine, what do you want to know?"

His cat green eyes blinked at her as she stared back

at him, not giving an inch. His exhaled breath misted in the air, and he shook his head. "It matters not. You are leaving. There is nothing further I need to know." He turned on his booted heels quickly enough for his greatcoat to flare, as he continued through the woods.

Beth stood there, stunned for a moment before she gave chase. She grabbed the back of his coat and tugged him to a halt. "You don't get to run away from me!"

His gaze narrowed, and his mouth pinched into a thin line. "Yet you can leave me?"

Beth felt her jaw drop open as she stared at him in shock. "I don't belong here. This isn't my time."

She swore she glimpsed a flitting shadow of hurt crossing Kit's face before he schooled his features into the menacing Knightmare scowl. "Then all has been said. Pray." He held out a sweeping arm. "Let us continue so you can return home."

He once again strode off. Beth hesitated an instant before following. Was he trying to tell her he wanted her to stay? Was he upset with her choice? Stunned into silence, she decided to shelve the matter, not wanting to anger him any further in case he decided to renege on his offer to steal the jewel. Beth had to get home, didn't she? It's what she wanted and strove for since waking up and finding herself adrift in the past.

Confused and lost in her thoughts, she stumbled over a tree root and almost face-planted on the forest floor, except a strong arm wrapped around her waist and pulled her upright, trapping her tight against his hard body. She relaxed into Kit's unyielding hold, and breathed in his scent of leather and outdoors, taking comfort in his actions. He wasn't so hurt or angry to let her fall.

In turn, she felt the tension in his taut muscles loosen as he rested his chin on her head and embraced her in his woolen warmth. She buried her face into his coat as tears flooded her eyes. It felt so right being held in this man's arms. If time could stop, she'd stay here forever. It was hard for her to believe how comfortable and how close she'd grown to Kit in such a relatively short period of time, almost as if he had been made for her. Which was utter nonsense, of course. She thought Grant had been the love of her life, and look out how that turned out—betrayed and shot. How could she trust what she was feeling? No matter how she felt, her life was elsewhere, back in the twenty-first century, not in some backwoods time with a rogue highwayman who left her confused and wanting things she had no right desiring.

It was as if Kit read her mind and he eased himself away from her, and tilted up her chin with his finger. He studied her intently before giving her a sweet smile. "We should tarry here no longer, luv. It's time to get you home."

He dropped his hand, and she nodded, confused once again as her stomach soured at his words, yet happy to be back in his good graces. Who would have thought she'd miss his casual term of endearment so much? The joke was on her.

Chapter Forty-Five

Edmond blinked, and his surroundings came into view. He lay curled on the bed of his rented room in the Royal Tredford Inn, clutching the Viper's Eye in his hand. So much time lost and wasted again. His last remembrance was sitting by the fire contemplating his next course of action. There was no recollection of going to bed. Between the endless chaos of the incoherent voices screaming in his mind and the stone's reprimanding physical punishments, Edmond spent too many hours of his days and nights in a stupor of pain. He must be stronger if he was to save his Anna.

He sat up and snatched his dressing gown from the foot of the bed. Standing, he slipped into the silk cover and tied the sash. He dropped the black opal into his gown's pocket.

Edmond

The stone whispered his name into his mind. He patted the pocket in comfort. The jewel must be pleased with his next choice, for there was no lancing pain and agony; even the voices so prominent in the forefront were regulated to background noise. He felt such relief, he almost felt normal. A good omen, indeed.

He walked to the wardrobe and opened one of its oak doors. Reaching inside, he found yesterday's long coat and separated it from his other clothing. Opening the coat, he pulled a glass vial from its inner pocket and slipped it into the same pocket holding the Viper's Eye.

He closed the wardrobe's door, and crossed the room to take a seat at the small table the room offered. His gold pocket watch lay open on the table, and he glanced at the time. He wouldn't have long to wait. Charles knew he preferred to break his fast by eight.

Edmond smiled when a light tapping at his door was followed by it opening, and his manservant entered carrying a tray. Punctual as ever. He snapped shut his watch and slid it to the side, clearing a space for the food-laden tray. Charles placed his burden down. The butler picked up the folded linen cloth and snapped it open.

"A good morning, my Lord," Charles placed it on Edmond's lap. "You appear in fine shape today."

"I am, indeed, Charles."

"Very good, sir."

Next, Charles poured a cup of tea and commenced to add cream and sugar in just the way Edmond preferred, and then placed the cup and saucer next to his plate filled with eggs, steak, and potatoes.

"My Lord, would you like the blue or the brown for today?"

"The brown."

"Very good, sir." Charles turned his back and walked to the wardrobe.

Taking advantage of his servant's position, Edmond quickly withdrew the vial from his pocket and emptied its contents into his tea, promptly pocketing the ampoule out of sight. He lifted the china cup and pretended to take a sip as Charles turned away from the wardrobe bearing in his arms Edmond's outfit for the day.

As Charles laid out the clothes on the bed, Edmond clattered his cup back onto its saucer, drawing his servant's attention.

"Is everything to your liking, sir?"

"No, it is not. Come here."

When Charles reached his side, Edmond picked up the cup and saucer and thrust it at his butler. "Drink this."

Charles frowned, but did as he was ordered, taking the saucer, he lifted the cup and sniffed, and then took a sip. He grimaced as he swallowed.

"My apologies, sir. Perhaps the cream has gone off." He placed the tea back on the table and as he took a step back, he swayed.

Edmond launched to his feet and steadied his manservant, and guided him to the chair he'd just occupied.

"It was not the cream, my good man." Edmond pushed him into the chair and watched with amusement as Charles tried to lift his arm and couldn't.

"I…" The butler's lips flapped twice, then failed to open a third time as the paralytic froze not only his limbs, but his vocal chords as well.

He studied his long-term and faithful manservant. The poison he used was fast-acting, but not lethal; that would be counter to his goal. Edmond leaned forward, untying and removing Charles's cravat, and then he unbuttoned his waistcoat. Grabbing the sharp steak knife from the tray, he used it to cut an opening in Charles's crisp white shirt, exposing the man's chest, but more importantly giving Edmond access to his butler's heart.

The Viper's Eye required a greater sacrifice, and

Edmond had come to the conclusion last night; the forfeit of Charles, who was Edmond's right hand, who helped him in so many ways and through so many trials, would be one of the most ultimate souls for the stone. Charles's death would be his greatest achievement to date. He would miss his manservant's unflagging devotion; it would be hard to go on without his help, yet anything for his daughter. Somehow he would make do.

Edmond removed the Viper's Eye from his dressing gown's pocket and stared into its black yet colorful depths, feeling hopeful. The bumbling Tredford constable had given him a name. He would find this Beth Leighton and after she told him everything about the Knightmare, her soul would go to Anna's cause. Victory was close at hand, but first he needed to appease the stone if he wanted to remain clear-headed and achieve his dream. Afterward, he'd take a short visit with his little poppy before he started his search for the barmaid.

Edmond met Charles's frozen gaze and read his butler's resignation. A good man to the end. Charles understood the importance of his sacrifice. Edmond smiled and raised the Viper's Eye in the flat of his palm, and began the incantation.

"Astaroth, *ego obsident vos*, Astaroth *exaudi me.*"

Chapter Forty-Six

"What on earth is that smell?" Beth stood by the tall, opened window she'd just stepped through after Kit had picked the lock and entered.

His gaze glared back at her, and he raised a shushing finger up to his mask-covered mouth and nose. Well, he was the one to bid her quiet while his cravat help filtered out the noxious odor.

"Seriously, it smells like something crawled in here and died," she added in a whisper, covering her mouth and nose with her hand as she fought not to gag.

Kit shook his head and silently gestured for her to stay put as he stalked across the room to the study's entry. He eased open the oak paneled door and peered into the hallway, then slipped through the opening, disappearing from her sight.

Beth sighed before stepping closer to the window, thankful for the chilly breeze wafting in. She was so intent on the clean air, she jumped and stifled a squeal when Kit appeared magically by her side.

"Stop sneaking up on me," she hissed.

He tugged down his mask, revealing his handsome grin. "Sorry, luv. It looks like you're were correct; the manor appears empty."

"Empty and smelling of death."

Kit nodded and grimaced. "It still behooves us to move quickly and quietly." He took her arm and led her across the room.

"What if the opal isn't here?"

"One bridge at a time, luv."

He guided her into the hall and to the base of the grand staircase before releasing her arm. "Take the second floor, while I search this one. Remember to check all the places I taught you for hidden safes. Come get me if you find one and I'll get it open."

"Do you think it's wise to split up?"

"I wouldn't let you go if I didn't think it was safe. Now up you go, luv. Be safe and clever. I'll be with you as quick I can."

His pat to her ass sent her on her way. Halfway up, she glanced over her shoulder and saw her highwayman slip into a room across the great hall. She hoped he was right and they were the only two in the house. Reaching into her skirt's pocket, she pulled the knife from its sheath and gripped it in her hand. She held the small blade forth as she reached the second landing. The hallway split to her left and right, revealing multiple doors. This was going to take a while. She broke right and opened the first door she came to and entered. It appeared to be what they probably called a sitting room, one decorated in gold, white, and blue. Trying to push aside flashbacks to how a similar search of MacKenzie's house ended, Beth got to work opening drawers, looking into cubbyholes, and peering behind paintings. She hoped to find the Viper's Eye quickly so she could return the gem to Remiel and go home. It's what she wanted, right?

****

After searching over half the rooms on the second floor, she had nothing but growing frustration and anger. The idea of *quick* had morphed into *some time today*. Couldn't anything be simple? She hadn't found a single safe, let alone a locked jewelry box. She knew Renweard wouldn't make it easy by just leaving something like a demonic soul stealing jewel just lying about, but come on! It had to be somewhere in the manor, or they were so screwed.

Moving on to the next door, she twisted the doorknob and entered briskly before freezing in her footsteps, as the smell of rotting flesh blasted over her. Beth had entered a child's bedroom—one embellished in pink and lavender, and containing a dead girl's corpse—the apparent cause of the stench permeating the house.

Bile rose up her throat, and she quickly covered her mouth and backed out the room, until she collided into a body. She whirled, lunging into Kit's arms, but discovered it wasn't him. In his place was a balding man much closer to her height than Kit's, yet bulkier and wider than either of them. Her shock left her speechless. *Renweard.*

The man stepped forward, crowding her and forcing her back into the dead girl's room. It was then Beth remembered the knife in her hand, and raised it between them.

"Get back, I warn you."

His hand lashed out faster than her eyes could track, and her wrist was captured in his iron grip. He squeezed, and pain shot up her arm. Her fingers involuntarily opened, and the knife fell from her grip and clattered to the floor.

Ignoring the stabbing pain, Beth raised her left hand, clawing at his face, but once again he was faster and snagged her wrist in a death grip before she could scratch him. He twisted her wrist, forcing her to turn as he wrenched her arm behind her back. She hissed in pain as he marched her into the room until her thighs hit the mattress. This close to the corpse, she tried not to inhale, but the pain of her twisted arm had her breath panting, and she choked in the foul decaying odor.

He pressed into her, crushing her arm between her back and his chest as he whispered into her ear. "My beautiful Anna will suffer no longer, especially from the likes of you."

"She's dead, you creepy idiot. She's beyond suffering, probably thanks to you."

"Lies! My, Anna sleeps peacefully."

Beth started to struggle in earnest. He was insane. There was no way anyone could mistake this rotting corpse for a healthy child. Suddenly, she was thrust face down onto the bed, bent at the waist as she fought a gag reflex. She flailed with her free arm, but to no avail as he yanked her trapped arm higher up and felt his knee land solidly into the small of her back. Her cry of pain was smothered into the stinking comforter.

"The interfering barmaid, no doubt. You've caused me no end of problems, but I have a use for you. The vile highwayman you serve. Is he close? Tell me!" He pressed his weight into her. "Answer! Who is he? I know you're working with him."

Crap. He knew about her. She had to get out of this, but Renweard was strong for his size, and she was trapped no matter how much she tried. She couldn't even scream for help with her face buried in the bedspread.

"Tell me!" He shoved his knee harder into her back

and twisted her arm again. "Where is he?"

There was no way she'd answer him. Beth only hoped Kit would arrive and shoot the bastard.

"Who is the Knightmare?" He lifted her arm higher, and she felt something pop in her shoulder. Her scream was stifled into the bed. "You waste my time and my daughter's. Your silence is useless. It's time for you to help her. I'll find the Knightmare. I'm sure he'll show, just too late for you."

He had no idea. Kit was just downstairs. How did Edmond get past him?

"*Ego obsident vos*, Astaroth *exaudi me.*"

What did he just say? Was that Latin? Her futile struggles stopped as fear sliced through her.

"*Virtute tua te invoco.* By your power, I invoke thee. *Mea voluntate ego te invitem. Potes me animam tuam.* By my will, I invite you. Your power to me, my soul to yours."

Oh, God, no! He was going to use the opal on her. *Remiel! Help me!*

"Astaroth, *datis tuis libenter recipio, quod optas, gratis date.* What you grant, I freely accept, what you desire, I freely give. *Infundere tua receptaculum, dona mihi tua virtute et studio.*"

Before Beth realized what was happening, he flipped her onto her back, driving his knee into her stomach and shackling both her wrists in one meaty hand. With the breath knocked out of her and struggling for air, her eyes widened and fixated on the now glowing jewel pulsing in the open palm of Renweard's free hand. He calmly placed the opal down on the bed next to her, and with his now free hand, yanked and tore her bodice, exposing her chest. He grinned down at her, while picking up the Viper's Eye.

"*Sum offeramus hostiam huius mulieris animulus.* I offer in sacrifice this woman's heart."

As he started to lower the pulsing black gem to her bare chest, Beth found her voice and screamed.

Chapter Forty-Seven

With a shaking hand, Kit closed the door to the root cellar and then wiped his sweaty palms on his breeches. There was no doubt in his mind Renweard had the Viper's Eye and was using it. The pile of parchment ash he'd found in the cellar, was so reminiscent of Sophie's disintegrated remains in the York Shambles, made him wonder how many poor souls had given their lives to this madman. He had a bad feeling about this.

With his search of the ground floor complete, finding only one safe located in the study, the first room they had entered, he needed to find Beth. Kit had just reached the grand stairs when a piercing scream rent the air.

He flew up the stairs, taking four at a time. He never should have left her alone. Reaching the landing he ran for the only open doorway. Taking in the horrific tableau before him, he didn't hesitate; there was no way the opal would touch her flesh.

He lunged. His outstretched hand closed around Renweard's, trapping the gem in their combined fists as Kit's momentum slammed them both off the bed, tumbling them to the center of the room.

"Kit!"

The bastard was stronger than he appeared, and Kit struggled to keep his hold on Renweard's hand. The punch to his jaw rattled his teeth, causing him to growl as he smashed his own unhampered fist into Renweard's gut in answer.

Renweard lurched to his feet, dragging Kit up with him through their combined hold on the gem.

"You!" Renweard grinned. "You're a dead man!"

Kit didn't reply as he tried to wrench the stone from the madman's grip, to no avail. He saw Beth cross behind Renweard, but couldn't spare a thought when the bastard's free hand closed around his neck and squeezed. Kit reached up and grabbed the man's thick wrist, but much like their struggle for the opal, there was no dislodging him.

Dark spots flecked into his vision as the need for air assailed him.

"You are no Knightmare." Renweard spat into his face. "Just a man who will burn in hell. And soon your whore will join you like the last."

Never! Renweard would never lay hands on Beth again. Kit dropped his hand away from Renweard's choking hold. He would not fail her as he had so many others. His hand closed around the plain ivory handle of his left pistol and drew it from the holster as his vision went dim. He didn't need sight when he was this close; he couldn't miss. Pressing the gun against Renweard's chest, he pulled the trigger. The bang was muffled as the flash of sparks burned his bare hand, when the pistol's ball fired and slammed into Renweard's heart.

Beth's scream reached his ears as the room flashed bright white, blinding him as Renweard fell, leaving the Viper's Eye clutched into Kit's fist when everything went blank.

****

Beth groaned and clutched her pounding head. Worst. Headache. Ever. She really needed to stop drinking so much. Her eyelids fluttered open, and she gazed directly into an unblinking dark gaze of a bald man lying only two feet away in a pool of blood. Reality came crashing in and with a squeal, Beth scrambled backward on the carpet until her back slammed into a wall, clutching her torn clothing to her chest.

Her breath came in heaves as she stared at the horror in the center of the room. Where once there had been a vibrant, albeit evil, man, now was a shrunken corpse of someone decades older. Age spots had bloomed on his wrinkled skin, covering his bald scalp like spots on a leopard. The saggy skin of his neck made it look like he had double chins. Everything about him was small and corroded. In death, his villainous vitality was striped away, leaving an old broken man behind.

She blinked and finally registered the black tricorne hat lying on the ground beside Renweard. Her gaze swept the room but didn't find Kit. Beth pushed away from the wall and crawled across the floor. She picked up his hat and cradled it in her lap, before burying her face in its dark contours. Where was Kit? Why would he leave?

She started shaking, no doubt with the delayed shock of almost dying and losing her soul and fearing Renweard would kill Kit. Oh God, they had both come so close to dying again. Kit was right. The Viper's Eye really was cursed.

Beth jerked upright, clutching his hat to her chest. The stone! Her eyes flashed to Renweard and both of his empty hands. She scrambled to her feet and frantically scanned the room, the black opal was gone. As was Kit.

The invisible ants started marching over her skin and up her spine. Her mind flashed to the vivid picture of Kit appearing out of nowhere, tackling Renweard and stopping the stone from touching her chest by mere inches. *Oh, no, please.* His hands hadn't been gloved. Remiel's warning popped in her mind. Renweard had empowered the stone; it had been pulsing and Kit touched it. She had to find him.

She dropped his hat, clutched her torn bodice to her chest, and ran from the room of corpses, fear for Kit giving wings to her feet. Beth flew down the stairs, and she raced across the marble floor of the grand entrance to the front doors.

In her panic, she struggled with the heavy door, her shoulder screaming in pain, but she managed to pry it open. Lunging through, she darted across the porch until she was pulled to an abrupt halt by the sudden grip on her upper arm.

Fire lanced through her injured shoulder, and Beth screamed in pain as she was spun around, and her unseen assailant now gripped both her upper arms and shook her.

Her eyes widened at the sight of the towering blond man sporting a crusted gash across his brow and a fading black eye.

"Nay so fast, lassie." The Scottish accent rolled at her. "I've gone to a lot of trouble to find ye." His eyes perused her, taking in her torn clothing with barely a blink. "You're under arrest."

Chapter Forty-Eight

The fire simmered in the hearth. The low flickering flames highlighted the man seated in the chair. He stared, mesmerized by the darkly glowing opal lying in the open palm of his hand. Astaroth smiled from his concealment in the dark shadows of the hallway of Locke's house, admiring his soon-to-be new human tool and was pleased.

The demon thought he had failed when he felt Edmond Renweard's untimely death, believing once again to have been thwarted by the meddlesome Archangel. He had been so sure. But imagine his surprise when his soul-imbued gem didn't release its treasure, and Astaroth then knew there was still a chance for success.

And for his stone to land in such hands? A miracle indeed, if such things were granted unto him. He almost chuckled. The boy had such pain and guilt, the perfect leverage to gain the human's acceptance and become the new wielder of the Viper's Eye.

His smile grew to a grin. This should be easy. He straightened from his casual lean against the wall and stepped into the room.

Chapter Forty-Nine

The blinding slap snapped her head to the side. Beth tasted blood and blinked tears away as she slowly turned her face forward, running her tongue over her lower lip. It was definitely split. She glared up at Erik, who calmly smirked at her. He was such an asshole.

"My patience is at an end," Constable Jeffries said, as he paced into her view. "Tell us who the Knightmare is and where we can find him."

Beth kept her bloody lips sealed. After politely introducing themselves, they had started their interrogation. It was like some weird mixed up game of good cop versus bad cop. The two of them had been at this for a while now. At least Jeffries had given up his jacket before tying her up so she wasn't so exposed. She couldn't feel her hands, which were tied behind the chair she was currently strapped to, and her injured shoulder throbbed in time to all her other hurts. There was no way she was going to betray Kit. They could beat on her as much as they wanted, but she knew they wouldn't kill her. Unlike MacKenzie, who had another source in Laurel; Beth was the only one they had. She alone held the information they so desperately wanted. She would just have to find a way to deal with the pain.

"Give him up, or we will be forced to hang you for Lord Renweard's murder." The Constable threatened.

She couldn't help her snort. "Seriously? Do you

think I'm some magical vampire? Did you see his corpse? He looked like he could stand in for the mummy."

"Aye, lass," Erik retorted. "I saw the hole in his chest."

"Then you weren't looking close enough. Besides, you caught me with no guns or knives. I didn't kill him, as I've said a million times now."

"Give us the highwayman and we can be lenient on you, Miss. We know he was there." Jeffries gestured to the black tricorne hat sitting on the table behind him.

Beth's heart clenched. These bastards were wasting precious time she didn't have. Who knew what the Viper's Eye was doing to Kit. She had to get out of here.

"Charge me with something, or let me go. I've got rights."

Erik frowned. "You have no rights." He leaned forward and grabbed her chin, his grip tight. "Where is the highwayman? Who is he?"

She met his gaze and braced herself. It didn't help. His punch landed squarely in her stomach. All her air rushed out on a moan of pain. She would have bent over double, but the ropes held her securely upright. Oh God, that hurt.

"Enjoyed...that did...you?" She panted out.

"Nay, lass, I dinnae." For a moment, sympathy filled his gaze, before their blue depths turned icy. "I'm paid to get the job done."

Beth spat a glob of blood to the floor. "You need a new employer. Better yet, a career change." What she wouldn't give to see any of Laurel's brothers right now. They'd beat the shit out him for her, and then we'd see how the cop enjoyed that.

"This is getting us nowhere," Jeffries started pacing again.

Erik grabbed a fistful of her hair and yanked her head up, forcing her to look at him. "Why don't ye step out, Constable?"

Beth couldn't stop the full body shudder; it sliced through her as his words hit. Erik saw her fear. She'd never been in a fight in her life, never even been hit; she wasn't sure how much more she could take.

Jeffries placed a hand on Erik's shoulder. "No, Erik."

The Scot released his hold on her hair, and she dropped her chin to her chest, hiding her relief, though she couldn't disguise the trembling of her body.

"Put her in a cell. I'm sure a night with the rats and no food will soften her up," Jeffries ordered. "I need you to pull your men watching the Boar and Rose and set them searching. Now we have the girl, the manpower is better spent on locating the Knightmare."

"And where will ye be?"

"Updating the Magistrate." With those words, Constable Jeffries shrugged into a long coat and grabbed his hat, and without a backward glance, left the office. Beth wasn't happy to see him go. She really didn't want to be alone with the blond psycho.

Said psycho was standing in front of her, glaring down. "You going to take advantage of your boss leaving? Hit me some more?"

"Nay. I don't enjoy hitting lassies, I told ye."

"You could have fooled me."

Erik shrugged and squatted down, while pulling a knife. Maybe he enjoyed cutting them? She tensed until she realized he was slicing through the ropes tying her legs to the chair. He stood and crossed behind her.

"Dinnae try anything, lass." He grabbed her lashed hands and lifted. Beth whimpered as fire sped up her arm and through her shoulder when she stumbled to her feet.

She wished she could fight back or flee, but she barely had the strength to stand. Pushing her from behind, with a grip on her wrists, he force-walked her to a door located in the back of the office. He reached around her with one hand and twisted the knob. He shoved her through into a dark hallway illuminated by one small window, set in the wall at the end of the hallway. There were three jail cells lining the far wall. He led her to center one.

Stopping, he pushed her to his side. "Don't move." She stayed there swaying before the iron bars, as he pulled out a wrought iron key and unlocked the prison's door. She wished she could break free. Nothing she tried worked when he caught her at the manor. The stupid Scot wasn't bribable or seducible and no matter how hard she fought, she couldn't escape him. As beat up as she was and on the verge of collapse, there was no way she'd get away from him now. Erik exchanged the key for a knife and cut through the ropes, releasing her bound wrists.

She pulled her hands in front of her and rubbed her chaffed wrists, trying to get the circulation flowing to return feeling to her fingers. All the time trying to ignore her throbbing shoulder. Erik grabbed her upper arm and forced her into the cell, then slammed the door shut, locking it as she grabbed hold of the bars to support herself.

They exchanged silent gazes before Erik turned without a word and left via the door to the office, which he closed behind him, casting the prison into a shadowy darkness. Her strength left her, along with her bravado as soon as she knew he was gone. She collapsed to the wood floor in a boneless heap.

Everything hurt, her mouth felt swollen, her cheek ached, not to mention her ribs, stomach, and shoulder. She was powerless to move, until she heard the squeak and scratching of claws. Beth dragged herself across the floor and pulled herself up on the simple cot against the wall.

Huddled in a heap, she shivered and tugged the jacket tighter. What was she going to do? *Please hold on, Kit. I know you can.* But what if he didn't want to?

Chapter Fifty

Kit stared, entranced by the pulsating black opal in his hand. The vibrant colors swirled deep in its dark depths. Fiery red chased dark orange, entwining with violet. His heart beat in time with the rhythm of the jewel, seeming to suck him into its deepest center. It wanted something. He strained to hear; if he only tried hard enough, he would know.

"Christopher."

Kit blinked, and the pull of the stone was broken. Raising his head, he saw an elegantly dressed man enter the room; his crisp white cravat was neatly folded and tied, the only brightness in his wardrobe, except the gold and silver embroidery on his vest and a blood red ruby stockpin. The rest of the man's expensive attire was black, his over-coat, breeches and boots all dark like the opal Kit held in his hand. Even the stranger's hair was black in its fashionable short cut. His face held an aristocratic look with all sharp angles and pale white skin, making his dark eyes appear to match the ebony of his hair and clothing. And he was tall, at least a hand above Kit's own height. To add to his façade, the stranger was refined. Not hulking large for his height, but lean and muscular. He mirrored Kit's own build.

"Ah, Christopher, it is truly a pleasure to meet you."

Kit blinked again and realized he was inside the

main room of his cottage and wondered how he got there. Confused, he looked around the sitting room. Hadn't he'd been somewhere else? His pulse pounded faster. His mind was fuzzy, his thoughts scattered. "Do I know you?"

"Not yet, but you will." The stranger's cultured accent alluded to wealth and secrets. "You may call me Roth."

Kit shook his head, trying to clear his mind. There was something important…his body started shaking with the need to remember.

"Now, we can't have that." The man who called himself Roth, was at Kit's side without him seeing the man move. "Let's look what you have in your hand, shall we?"

Against conscious thought, Kit turned his wrist so his palm faced upward, and he slowly uncurled his fingers wrapped around the stone. He stared into the dark translucent depths and was lost.

"Ah, much better, my boy." Roth's words entered Kit's mind as well as his ears. There was nothing but the opal and the stranger's voice. A calm settled over him.

"Such guilt. Quite the burden for you to have carried all these years," Roth's voice held compassion and understanding. "Wouldn't you love to be released from your angst? It's been part of your life for so long, defined who you are; wouldn't it be a relief to feel it gone?"

Kit would give almost anything to have the deaths clinging to him not be his responsibility. It's why he gambled so freely with his life. But Fate so far had been fickle and hadn't extracted payment. The guilt was overpowering.

"Answer me."

"Yes." The word was forced past Kit's lips, his voice ragged and hoarse.

"You hold the answer in the palm of your hand; all you need do is accept. Listen closely. I'm sure you can hear…"

Christopher.

His name was whispered deep into his soul. His hated name. The name of the man who caused extreme pain to those he loved. The person he tried to hide from. Deep down he knew there was no hiding, regardless of who or what he called himself. Years may have passed, but he was trapped. Kit just wanted to find peace. Was the black opal, as dark as his soul, the answer?

"It will release you from your pain. All you need to say is, yes."

A simple word, just three letters. Was there a reason to say no?

C J Bahr

Chapter Fifty-One

"You can't keep me here!" Beth's hands gripped the jail's bars. She pushed away from the locked door and started pacing. Her frustration and anger reaching epic proportions, helped to eclipse all her aches and pains. Kit was in danger. She had to get out of this cell. As the day passed and her stomach growled, the little light the small window at the end of the hall afforded her told her it was late. She didn't have time for imprisonments or more interrogations; she needed out.

"Damn it! What about my free phone call?" Too bad this wasn't modern times. She plopped herself onto the bare-bones cot, bracing her elbows on her thighs as she buried her aching face into her hands, while ignoring her wrenched shoulder. She needed to think. There had to be a way out of this.

"Beth."

Her head shot up, and she lunged to feet. "Where the hell have you been?" She marched over to the Archangel Remiel, who was standing *inside* her prison. "Get me out of here." Beth stopped inches in front of the towering angel, glaring up at him. "Air Archangel needs clearance for take off. Right now."

"I'm sorry. I can't." His words and a shake of his head caused her stomach to clench.

"Can't or won't?" She stomped her foot. "I need out of...wait!" She grew excited. "Kit. He has your

314

stone. If you won't take me to him, go yourself."

"It doesn't work that way. I can't reveal myself to him."

"Damn it. What good are you?" She spun and strode back to the cot where she sat. Fear began to replace her anger as tears filled her eyes, but didn't fall. "He touched the stone with his bare hands..." Beth whispered as she stared at her feet.

Remiel entered her view as he crouched down before her.

"You've got to help him," she pleaded.

"I can't interfere, Beth. You know that."

"But what if...what if the stone claims him?" She looked up and met his level gaze.

"There is hope. The stone can't claim him if he refuses. He must willingly accept."

"And the demon?"

"Yes, Astaroth is in play. He sees this as only a small setback, another opportunity to gain a good soul and finish filling his stone."

This time she couldn't stop a tear from dropping and trailing down her cheek. "He doesn't think he's good." She took a deep breath. "Kit doesn't believe he deserves to live."

"But you know differently, don't you?" Remiel gifted her with a small smile. "Perhaps your faith is strong enough for the both of you. There's great power in the human heart."

"But how..."

"As in all great trials, there is sacrifice." Remiel stood, stretching to his full height. "Trust in yourself." He placed a comforting hand on her shoulder, and she felt warmth suffuse her. "And remember, God helps those who help themselves."

Beth blinked, and the angel was gone. Well, that was unnecessarily cryptic and utterly useless. What was she supposed to do with his anti-pep talk? Nothing changed. She was stuck in this freaking cell as a demon was trying to tempt and subvert Kit. She'd never felt more helpless in her life. There must be a way.

Beth stood and swiped a hand across her cheek. Now was not the time for tears. As Remiel hinted, she needed to somehow help herself because no one else would. Not one to give up, she approached her jail door and glared. Too bad she didn't know how to pick locks, a skill that would come in handy right about now. Kit had made it look so easy, but it was fruitless anyway since she had no tools to try. Her frustration mounted.

"Let me out," she shouted and thrust out her leg, launching a kick at the lock. Her foot impacted, shooting a tremor up her leg. The door popped open, off balance from her strike. Beth crashed to the floor and landed on her ass. She stared up at the open door in surprise. *Remiel, you sneaky bird.*

She leapt to her feet and scrambled through the door before skidding to a halt. With a slight smile, she turned back and closed the cell's door. Giving it a tug, she found it locked once more. Good. Let them wonder about her escape. The Knightmare's legend continues.

Beth crept to the door leading into the constable's front office. Slowly, she opened the door separating the area from the cells, mere inches, so she could peer inside. Empty. She pushed the door wider and slipped through, before closing it behind her, hoping when the men returned and not anytime soon, nothing would clue them in to anything being amiss.

316

There was no back door, much to her dismay, so she boldly crossed the office and went straight to the main door. No time to be shy since she had no idea when anyone might return. She quickly exited and paused only a moment to get her bearings as she hunkered down into the constable's dark jacket for warmth. She turned left and strode down the boardwalk, thankful no hue or cry followed her as she made her escape. Beth headed in the direction of the Boar and Rose; she knew it led her in the direction out of town nearest Kit's home.

Beth had no place else to go. She could only hope after killing Renweard and holding the opal, he went back to something familiar. Because if he hadn't, they were both lost. As she approached the Boar and Rose, she slowed. Had they really removed the watch? Perhaps they thought Kit might come to the tavern and look for her having no idea what trials he was going through at the moment. She stopped in her tracks, not knowing what to do when she spotted a recognizable bay mare tied to the hitching post across the street from the inn. Her heart raced. The horse was an answer to her dreams.

Throwing caution to the wind, she darted across the muddy wide path. She reached the mare and gave the girl a comforting pat on the neck. *Just helping myself, God...* Trying to be casual, Beth checked her surroundings as she untied the horse and with her good arm, looped the reins over the mare's head. Thankfully, no one was paying attention, and she definitely didn't see the owner of the horse she was stealing again, nor any cops. What the heck? They couldn't hang her for the same offense twice, and there was no way she was walking to Kit's home. It was too far by foot and time was running out.

She swung a leg over the saddle, her skirt bunching up, but she didn't care. Giving the mare a solid whack with her boots, the horse pricked her ears and took off in a canter. As they hit the hill leading to the smithy, she was in full gallop. She glanced behind her and her heart sank. The blond Scotsman was riding in chase.

Chapter Fifty-Two

She knew her luck was too good to be true. Had Erik set her up? Had he been staking out the tavern or was it pure dumb luck? It didn't matter. Beth sent up a silent prayer as she leaned lower on the mare's neck urging her on. She blew past the smithy and continued on the path, before checking behind once again. *Shit!* The asshole was closing.

Leading him to Kit was not an option and there was no way she was stopping. She had to get to Kit. In a split-second decision when the trail to Locke's home appeared on the left, Beth galloped past and turned right at the next fork. *Let's see just how good a rider you are and how brave your mount is.* She urged the feisty mare on. They've been down this path before in the pitch dark, so the late afternoon light held more advantage then the last time through. Hopefully, it wouldn't aid Erik.

Approaching a sharp blind bend, Beth added more leg, accelerating out of the turn, and the bold mare, after a forward three strides, jumped and cleared the fallen tree in their path. The night of the Knightmare's trap, with the darkness, the mare had slammed on the brakes, refusing to jump, but there was no hesitation from her this time. She rode on, hoping Erik's horse would stop, gaining her extra time and distance to lose him.

Beth didn't wait to see if Erik made the jump. The wooded path turned sharply again; her pursuer was out of sight, and she had a rushing river to cross next. Feeling the mare lengthen her gallop and tuck her haunches, Beth realized the horse knew what was coming next as well. Instead of sliding down the steep bank and plunging across the rapids like their prior ride, it appeared the mare was going to jump the ravine instead. She grabbed mane and held on as the horse launched herself over the open space. The mare almost cleared it, except her back hooves missed the ledge. They started to slide backward. Beth's heart ran to her throat, and she threw the reins forward giving the horse her head. She swallowed a curse just as the game mare managed to pull them onto solid ground.

Both horse and rider paused, breathing hard from their near fall. All of Beth's injuries came to the forefront, her battered face, aching shoulder, and sore ribs. Exhausted and hurting, all she wanted to do was lie down and sleep. The thudding hooves approaching had Beth straightening in the saddle and urging the bay mare back up into a canter. If she could get to the next bend, before Erik saw which way she turned, she might lose him yet.

When she reached the fork, she took the right path, and her gut wrenched. This direction led her farther away from Kit, but to a possible escape. She pulled up at the next bend, listening for Erik's horse. Maybe she'd lost him already? Or, maybe she should hide and let him ride by? Whack him with a branch again? She picked up a trot, hoping to let the little mare gain a second wind. It didn't matter. She needed to lead him further astray and had to assume he was an accomplished tracker. The woods were getting darker by the moment with the quickly setting winter sun. Both a curse and a blessing; Beth was conflicted. Too much time had passed, and she was freaked out about Kit, yet it would be all that much easier to lose the Scot in the dark.

She kicked the mare up into an easy canter, knowing what was coming up. They quickly cleared two more logs and a ditch. The crash of brush to her side made her look. *Shit!* Erik broke trail out of the gloom on a side deer path and was almost on top of her. Her pulse kicked up another notch. Her hands turned clammy with sweat, as she urged the mare into a gallop.

The loud bang had her flinching and laying low on the mare's neck. Was he really shooting at her? She didn't stop. He wasn't going to kill her; he must be trying to frighten her into halting. Wasn't going to work. He needed her. Oh God, but he could shoot her horse! Pressing for more speed, she made the next turn and jumped another log, at least taking her out of his line of sight momentarily, and galloped on.

Where the hell was the huge hedgerow? It had to be close, just like the bastard cop hot on her heels. Another bang had her ducking again and cursing. She added a prayer to her mad gallop. How many bullets did his gun have? She knew from watching Kit prime his own pistols, it wasn't as simple as slapping in another clip. Beth also knew Kit's guns were special, holding two shots apiece. It didn't matter; she still wasn't going to fall back into the Scot's hands.

Then out of the darkness, the four-foot wall of brush appeared, blocking the path and making it into a T-intersection. *Yes!* Beth found the strength to sit up tall and urged the mare on with confidence—experience the greatest motivator. She only had two thoughts as the mare gathered herself and jumped, a prayer that Erik's horse wasn't brave or athletic and the huge hedgerow went on for miles in both directions so he couldn't easily go around.

Landing safely on the other side, she gave her mare her head, as Beth glanced behind, while crossing mental fingers. Her prayers were answered when there was a loud crash of an object hitting the brush, hopefully the rider and not the horse, followed by what sounded like a Gaelic curse. Now she needed to make herself disappear. The darkness would help.

She slowed the mare to a canter, and when she finally hit the large crossing path, she turned left and started to make her way back to Kit—now from the opposite direction she originally intended. She only hoped she could find the trails Dante had taken them on, because the day was wasted away. Beth couldn't get her heart to slow down as fear coursed through her veins. She couldn't be too late. Life wouldn't be that cruel. Right?

Chapter Fifty-Three

Christopher.

The reviled name brought Kit back to himself. His given name only held memories of the dead he'd failed. He wasn't that man anymore. He'd spent his life distancing himself from that name. What was he doing? There was something important, someone important. Why was it so hard to think? His hand holding the opal started to shake.

"A fighter, it would seem. It's only a name, boy. Yours to embrace or discard. What my gem has to offer is so much more. Look deep and find your answers."

Pain lanced through his skull, and Kit squeezed his eyes shut on a groan. When he opened them, he was no longer standing in his home, but in a summer field, watching as three young men ran. A cold dread speared through him as he recognized where he was, when he was, just as a report from a rifle rang out. Once again, he witnessed Adisson as he staggered and dropped dead in his tracks—his head blown open from the long-range ball.

"No!" Both present and past Kit cried out together. He watched Julian grabbed his younger self and drag him away, racing for the woods.

"Make this stop. I will not live this again!" He shouted at Roth when he realized the stranger was standing next to him.

"Alas, one must *know* his deepest sins if he wishes to atone." Roth swept out an arm, gesturing to the fallen and bloody Adisson lying in the field.

"Damn, you. I know my sins. I've lived and breathed them."

Roth smiled at him. "Would you like to set this day right?"

Kit shook his head. "It's the past. It cannot change."

"True," Roth answered. "But what if you had the power to avenge their deaths, perhaps make the world a better place?"

"Impossible."

"Not on your own, but with the power of my opal." Roth gestured to Kit's hand, and he realized he was still holding the jewel tight in his fist.

"If you accept the stone, you'd *have* the power. You could punish the people who prey on the innocent. You could accomplish what you set out to do so long ago. The deaths of Julian and Adisson would finally mean something. Their lives would not be wasted."

Was it true? Kit opened his hand and stared down at the gem.

"Your wrong set right. Remove all your pain and guilt. All you need to do is accept."

He was tired. Kit looked away from the stone back to the field where Adisson lay shattered and broken. He hadn't meant to lead his brother and best friend to their deaths, but he had. His actions had resulted in Sophie's death. Had he just kept the jewel, she'd be alive today. Wouldn't it be better to start helping people instead of robbing them? Accepting what the stone had to offer may eventually end his life, but wasn't that what he'd been trying to do for years? His thoughts whirled. He could balance out his life, make his worthless existence mean something.

Kit gazed down at the Viper's Eye. All he had to do was say yes.

Chapter Fifty-Four

Beth galloped into the yard and was relieved to be greeted by Dante's whinny. The site of both Dante and Root gave her hope. If they were here it boded well that Kit would be here also. She pulled her stolen ride to a halt and kicked her feet free from the stirrups. Swinging her right leg over, she barely managed to clear the mare's haunches—getting tangled in her skirt as she dismounted. Trying to use her right arm more to take the weight off her injured left shoulder, she slithered off and as her feet touched the frozen mud her legs collapsed, and she fell. Beth laid there, breathing through the pain. She stirred at the warm huff of air in her ear. Cracking open her eyes, Dante stood over her, his refined chestnut head lowered as his soft nose nuzzled her face.

"Hey, big guy." She stroked his bright white blaze. "I know, I know…" She struggled to her feet. Urgency coursed through her veins, blocking her pain as she stumbled away from the horses and crossed the yard, halting as she saw the open front door. Someone was home at least. Crossing the threshold, she entered the hallway and heard the murmur of deep voices. She slowed, wondering if it were more cops or if Kit was with someone or something else. A chill shuddered through her. There was only one way to find out.

Stopping outside the sitting room, she pressed

herself against the hallway wall and carefully peered around the opening. Kit stood by his chair near the fire, gazing intently down at the Viper's Eye held in his bare palm, while a classily dressed stranger stood way too close to him.

"Why are you waiting?" The man stepped even closer to Kit. "You can salvage their deaths, atone for your crimes."

Hearing the cajoling upper crust accent, Beth was in no doubt who the stranger was. Temptation rolled off his words. Astaroth. There was no way he was sinking his claws into Kit. Emboldened, she stepped into the room.

"Get away from him, demon! He's not yours!"

Astaroth slowly turned, a smile on his handsome demeanor. "I beg to differ, my girl. He was mine the moment he touched my empowered stone."

"No, he isn't. Kit!" Beth tried to push past the demon, masquerading as a gentleman, but Astaroth blocked her with a thrown-out arm.

"I think not, dear."

Beth met the demon's black gaze. "You can't hurt me. It's in the rules. You may be great with jumping through all the loopholes, but I *know* you can't personally harm me. That's why you use an intermediary. So drop the act and let me pass."

"My, my. Quite the feisty girl." Astaroth broke her gaze as he deliberately perused her body from head to toe, taking in her disheveled state. She clutched the jacket tighter. He inhaled deeply and took a step back, practically colliding into Kit as his eyes widened. "And full of surprises. I was wondering how you knew who I was."

"Yes, I know who you are, Astaroth. And you're not getting Kit."

"You may be angel blessed, but you're in my domain now and what I desire, I claim. He is as good as mine. You're too late."

Angel blessed? Too late? He's lying. That's what demons do, right? She wasn't about to lose this fight because no matter how much Kit might think so, he didn't deserve damnation.

"Kit, can you hear me?"

The demon chuckled. "There's nothing you can do, little girl."

Beth shot a dirty glare at Astaroth. Just watch what this girl can do. "Kit, seriously, stop being an asshat and look at me. You *hate* the Viper's Eye. You wanted nothing to do with it. Don't do this. Drop it. Just turn your hand and let it go."

Her heart clenched when all Kit did was stare, immobile, the black opal entrancing him. There must be something she could do; there had to be a way to break him away. The demon couldn't win. She swallowed the lump in her throat, pushed past her pain.

"Kit, you can't do this. Please, you have to listen to me."

"Choose now, Christopher. It is time." The demon ordered.

Kit blinked, then blinked again. *Yes!* "Kit, look at me. It's Beth, please."

At her voice, Kit looked up, confusion written across his face as he stared at her. "Come on, you stubborn idiot. Drop the stone." Kit started to look down at his hand. "Stop! Don't look, just drop it."

With a full body shudder, he tossed the Viper's

Eye, where it landed near the hearth. "Beth? Luv?" His voice whispered, raspy and low.

She stepped toward Kit, but Astaroth was between them. He pushed Kit in the direction of the stone and shouted, *"In te virtutem meam*! by my power," while flinging out his other arm, blindly connecting to her injured shoulder. Beth gasped. White filled her vision as pain coursed through her. She struggled through pain and saw Kit stiffen and take a step toward the gleaming gem.

"No, you can't have him. He's mine!" Beth launched herself, shoving past the demon to reach Kit's side. She threw herself forward as Kit reached out for the stone, bumping into him. Her hand closed around the Viper's Eye, snatching it; she curled her fist tight to her chest and somersaulted until her back hit the hearth's stone siding.

"My, my, aren't you full of surprises."

"Beth?" Kit's hoarse voice croaked out.

Both the demon and Kit stared at her, one in horror, the other grinning. The demon chuckled.

"Beth Leighton Murray, open your hand. *Ad videndum in lapide.* Gaze into my stone."

"Beth, no!"

Her eyes widened, and her body began to shake as her wrist turned without her command, and fingers uncurled around the jewel. Her gaze was drawn down, then trapped. She felt her mind fall into the black depths swirling in violet, orange, and red. Lost in the spinning, beating darkness, everything fell away.

Chapter Fifty-Five

Beth stood on the edge of a cliff, clutching the demon's black opal. The sky held no stars or moon, just a swirling darkness mimicking the jewel. The ground beneath her feet was barren, a dry dustiness that the arid wind stirred. Beyond the cliff's edge was a bottomless pit causing those despised ants to reappear—crawling over her skin. A black hole set to devour her, suck her in, never to spit her out.

"You have a choice."

Beth snapped her head to the right and found Remiel standing next to her. He appeared to her in his true form, towering over her. Reaching over seven foot, everything about him was extreme, his face chiseled looking sharply carved from marble, bright blue eyes, lightened to almost crystal-clear diamonds, his long black hair pulled into a tight warrior's queue. His broad chest was encased in a tight linen shirt, gauntlets covered his forearms, and black breeches sheathed muscular legs shod in tall leather boots. A cloak of midnight blue snapped in the wind beneath furled cobalt wings.

She blinked, her eyes filling with unshed tears. "I think I messed up, Remy." She held out the stone to him in her bare hand. "I wasn't thinking. I just reacted. I needed to protect Kit. Here." She held out the stone. "Take it."

He shook his head and smiled gently at her. "With great trials come sacrifice. What are you willing to give?"

"I don't understand."

"Of course not."

Beth spun to her left and found Astaroth standing next to her, but unlike Remiel revealing his true form, the demon chose lies and remained in his human disguise of a handsome British gentleman. She closed her hand around the stone and clasped her fist against her chest. Great. She practically had a demon and an angel sitting on her shoulders.

"What are you doing here, demon?" She challenged.

Astaroth chuckled. "I have more right to stand beside you than this feathered bird. What games are you playing, Remiel? You tread close to a dangerous line."

"Just taking a page from your own playbook," Remiel replied. "I haven't broken any rules and I don't plan to."

"She's mine, angel. She's touched the stone."

"If that is all that was necessary, you would have won a long time ago, Astaroth."

Beth, tired of playing ping-pong with her gaze, decided to take the reins in her hands.

"Enough, gentlemen. Though calling you a gentleman is a bit of a stretch," she locked gazes with the black-eyed demon, who merely shrugged. "You said I have a choice." She turned back to Remiel. "What do you mean?"

"Free will."

The demon snorted. "That old line."

Both she and Remiel ignored him. "What do I do?"

"You need to choose."

"Choose what? I choose both Kit and I are free of this stupid jewel and that asshat." She flicked a thumb at Astaroth. "He can go back to hell."

"Not so simple, my innocent mortal human," Astaroth countered. "Nothing is for free; all must pay a price."

"Price?"

"Either, you give up the stone and I claim Locke, or you don't, which will make you mine. Now choose."

Beth's heart started to race. Those couldn't be her only options; they both sucked. She turned her pleading gaze to Remiel.

"The demon is correct." Beth's heart sank. "Those are choices. However, I gave you a different currency, your heart's desire."

She noticed Astaroth stiffen beside her.

"I should have known. I smelled your angel stink upon her. You *have* crossed the line, Remiel. I'm surprised your pretty wings are still attached."

"Have I?" Remiel countered. "Her free will is intact. It is her choice that will decide the end results of this game. You may be a powerful duke in hell, but I think time has made you rusty."

"I don't know what you think to gain, angel. My stone is bursting full of innocent souls, and when I deliver them, I'll be crowned Prince."

"Perhaps. Or soon you'll be a laughing stock."

"Can someone just speak plainly? How can I possibly make a choice if I don't know my options? Stop sniping at each other and tell me what is going on."

"Please." Astaroth gestured toward the angel. "Tell

her and let this be over."

Remiel inclined his head. "You have three choices. First, you can hand over the stone, return home, and damn Locke. Second, you accept the stone's offer and become its new wielder and save Kit's soul by destroying yours. Or...you can use the power of your heart's desire and end this game permanently and destroy the stone, trapping you in this time."

Astaroth laughed. Beth frowned. Why did the demon find this so amusing?

He wiped a dramatic hand across his eyes as if erasing tears. "Oh, Remy. Seriously? I thought lying was my domain?"

Remiel stood silent—crystal eyes glaring, and his full lips pressed into a thin line. Doubt trickled through Beth, and she shot a questioning glance at the demon.

"Oh, my precious little girl, you are so doomed. I win either way." Her confusion must have clearly been written across her face, because Astaroth smiled and continued, "Your precious Christopher wants to die. Why stop him? Let the feather bird take you back to your family and dear friends in Chicago. Stop their mourning. It's what you want and you'll give Locke what his heart has ever desired."

Her stomach physically clenched. Kit didn't deserve to die. He was amazing. She couldn't let the stone drive him insane as he took souls. It wasn't right, not for him or the innocents trapped in the Viper's Eye.

Astaroth must have read her mind. "It is up to Locke who he uses the stone on."

But that made no sense. If Kit went for the guilty, weren't they already condemned to hell? It didn't gain Astaroth any bonus points. He must be lying. Again. Or she hoped.

She turned to the Archangel. "What do I do? How do I destroy the stone?"

The demon chuckled once more. "You can't. My creation is indestructible. If it wasn't, don't you think he," Astaroth pointed to Remiel, "would have destroyed it eons ago?"

She was so confused. There had to be more to this. Astaroth made it out to be two choices. Take up the stone, or go home and condemn Kit. She loved her family, but hadn't she given them up already when she married Grant? True, they were a plane ticket away, but she still managed a happy life without seeing them. They thought her dead already, so she wouldn't be hurting them anymore if she chose not to return home, thus saving Kit, who very much deserved saving. His life was filled with such tragedy it broke her heart. But if she saved Kit, she doomed herself to insanity and death while taking innocents along with her.

"Remiel?" She stared at the angel who could have been a marble statue, which he appeared to be carved from. "Please?"

He granted her a sad smile. "You have free will and your heart's desire. It's all you ever needed."

"But how—"

"Beth Leighton Murray, *nunc iam elige*. Choose now!" Astaroth commanded.

She gasped. The stone burned in her hand, yet she couldn't drop it. The hot wind gusted, blowing her hair back to stream behind her as she gazed out over the pit. Remiel said she could destroy the Viper's Eye and back in the prison told her to have faith. She didn't want to die, and she certainly couldn't let Kit die either. Her heart's desire. It wasn't really a choice at all. With all her might, she threw the stone away from her and lobbed it into the bottomless chasm.

Chapter Fifty-Six

A bright white light flashed, filling the room. Kit was blinded as he heard Beth cry out. He blinked, his sight returning to see her curled on the floor. He dove and cradled her in his arms before the dying embers of the fire. He gathered her protectively into his lap as he looked frantically around the room, but the strange aristocratic man was gone.

"Beth, open your eyes." He brushed away the hair from her face and then caressed her cheek with his knuckles. He studied the deep bruise on her cheek, the black eye, and the swollen and split lip. What in the hell had happened to her? "You stubborn chit. Why did you have to take the stone?" This couldn't be happening. Her death would break him. He felt for her pulse and was so relieved to feel it steady and strong beneath his fingers, he felt light headed. He reached up and tucked a curl behind her ear, trying to get his racing heart under control. "Please, luv. Wake up."

Her lashes fluttered, and she opened her eyes. Kit was never so happy to see her summer-blue gaze. "There you are." He gave her a smile. "Are you all right?"

"Kit?"

"Yes, luv, I'm here—"

"Astaroth!" She jerked upright in his arms glancing anxiously around.

"It's all right," he assured her. "There's no one here but us."

"Oh, thank, God." She collapsed into his embrace, resting her head on his shoulder. "What happened, Kit? Why did you leave me alone in the manor?"

He frowned. Everything was still a bit muzzy headed and surreal. "I remember your scream…"

"You saved me." Beth tilted her face up and smiled at him. "You stopped Renweard from using the opal on me."

"I can't… I remember the struggle, choking, and then firing my pistol." He pinched the bridge of his nose, before lowering his hand pulling Beth closer. "It's a bit of a hash afterward. I can't remember a thing. How did I end up here?"

"I don't know either. There was this bright light when you shot Renweard, and I blacked out. When I came to, you were gone."

Icy tendrils flooded Kit's veins, and his body gave a full shudder. There had been a man and he was offering to remove Kit's pain and guilt. He remembered almost giving in, not thinking it was worth the fight and not knowing why it was so wrong. He remembered Beth's voice. Staring down at her in his arms, he knew why. He had so much to lose if he accepted and used the stone. He'd live with his guilt if it meant Beth remained at his side.

"What happened to you, luv? You're a bit of a mess…" He ran a finger softly against the angry, dark bruise on her cheek. Taking in her injuries, it looked like she'd been beaten. His relief of her being alive quickly morphed into anger. Who the hell had hurt her?

She sighed. "Yeah, I'm pretty banged up. A cop,

um, thief-taker caught and arrested me. He dragged me to the Constable. They kind of wanted to know who you were, and where…"

His anger flamed into rage but was brought up short when Beth pressed her left hand to his chest.

"Hold on there, lover. No need to go all Cro-Magnon. After all, I did manage to pull one over them and escape. I'm fine. I'll live. I'm just happy I got here in time."

"You went through all that and still managed to find and save me?"

Her eyes twinkled up at him. "I did."

"You're amazing." He couldn't imagine anyone going through that for him, and he dropped a quick kiss to her forehead. "It's becoming a habit between us. Saving each other."

"I noticed."

Suddenly, she looked down at her closed right hand and frowned. He followed her gaze as she slowly opened her fingers. The Viper's Eye sat upon her palm. Kit sucked in a breath at what he saw. The jewel was a danger no more. It no longer pulsed and didn't glow with an unearthly light. The cursed opal was broken into several shards, burnt, charred, and no longer translucent, not carrying the vivid swirling colors that used to lace through it. The stone lay dead.

She shook her hand, dropping the pieces to the floor, and wiped her empty hand on her skirt. His gut twisted, and he felt shame at his relief of the destruction of the stone. Though nothing good could have come from the gem, it had been a way to return Beth home.

"I'm so sorry, luv." He reached up and stroked her soft hair.

"I'm not." She turned her face and buried it into his chest.

"It was your only means to go home. It was your deepest wish."

Her slight hiccup gave him concern she was about to start sobbing, so he tightened his arms around her.

Her hands pressed against his chest, and she pushed herself away, putting a slight distance between them. She was teary-eyed, but not crying. Beth gave him a watery smile.

"I may have lost my family...but I haven't lost my heart's desire." Her liquid-blue gaze held him entranced. "I am home. It just happens to be wherever you are, whenever you are."

His heart leapt at her words. "Are you saying you love me?"

"Yes, you idiotic scoundrel. I'm not sure how you wormed your way into my heart, but there's nothing I think I won't do for you. Even live in this barbaric time. You have *no* idea what you've made me give up. Hot and cold running water, cars, Amazon, smart phones..."

"I guess I have my work cut out for me making sure you never regret your choice." He tucked another curl behind her ear. He would do everything in his power to show her how much he loved her.

"Yes. Yes, you do. Think of it as a new career."

He grinned. "I had given up hope you'd ever care for me as I do you. You are my life, luv. If you had left me, I'm not sure what would have become of me."

"Then it's a good thing I came to my senses. Now, shut up and kiss me."

Kit gathered her close, thanking fate for his deliverance, and he gently kissed her.

Chapter Fifty-Seven

St. Brendan's Church, near Durness, Scotland, March 1795

Father Colin McPhee crouched down next to the plain wrapped package left beside the door. Tied with twine and wrapped in brown paper, the box was unlabeled. Picking up the package, he stood and entered the church he was in charge of watching over. Located in the far north reaches of Scotland, he was the sole occupant and so, he mused, the mysterious gift must be meant for him.

He entered the small library in the back of the church behind the altar. The little room had shelf-lined walls holding leather journals of various ages. The only furniture was a plain wooden table with four chairs, placed upon a bright blue woolen carpet. He placed the package on the table and then untied the bow. The paper fell open. Lifting the lid, he found a small card sitting on top of a red velvet purse. McPhee picked up the card and read.

Father,

It has come to my understanding you are the keeper of certain items. As I am told, you will know the meaning of my next words: For Remiel.

Intrigued, the priest put down the card and lifted the velvet pouch. Loosening the cords, he upturned the sack and let its contents spill onto the table. Several blackened shards of stone spread across the wood. McPhee crossed himself before he gathered up the pieces and placed them back inside the pouch, making sure to pull the strings taut in order to keep the contents inside.

Clutching the purse, he left the library and entered the church proper; pausing at the altar, he genuflected and then walked up the aisle until he reached the crossing, where he turned and in a few long strides entered the Archangels' shrine. The chapel held seven statues standing in a half-circle. St. Michael with his sword stood in the center, on his right was Raphael, the healer, and on the left was Gabriel, the messenger. The remaining Archangels, Uriel, Raguel, Sariel, and Remiel formed the rest of the half-circle.

McPhee walked to the far left of the circle and stood before Remiel's statue. As with all the statues, they appeared dressed for combat, with gauntlets, armor, and cloaks. Yet, instead of a weapon, Remiel held a set of scales. He knelt before the statue and pressed his hand against a decorative section of the base's molding. A hidden panel opened and a hollowed chamber was revealed in the statue's base.

Reverently, the priest placed the red pouch with the broken shards inside and closed the panel, sealing the base and hiding its treasure. He stood and walked to the center of the ring of statues and bowed. As he was straightening, his eyes were drawn to the base of Gabriel's statue, where its secret compartment wasn't quite aligned. Quickly, he walked to the statue and dropped to his knees. He fiddled with the hidden switch until the compartment slid fully open. He gasped. The space lay empty, except for the crushed blue velvet and the indented impression of the missing artifact it once held. With a shaking hand, he closed the compartment, concealing it into the base of the statue. He stood and stared at the Archangel's statue. Gabriel's horn was missing.

Chapter Fifty-Eight

Northern Scotland, Near Durness

"What shall we do now?" Beth asked as she tightened Root's girth. "We seem to be footloose and fancy free since we delivered the Viper's Eye to St. Brendan's. The world's our oyster, which I suppose you'd probably plan on stealing for the pearl."

When Kit didn't reply, she looked up from her task and found Dante without his master. "Kit?" When he didn't answer, Beth frowned and stepped around Root heading over to Dante. She gave the copper gelding a pat on the hip. "Where's your guy?" She propped herself up on her tiptoes to peer over the tall gelding, but found nothing of interest on the far side of the barn.

She dropped back to her heels, but before she could turn around she was trapped. Beth stifled her squeal, not wanting to reward his sneakiness. His arms surrounded her as he laid his black-gloved hands flat on Dante, caging her between horse and man. A smile curled up her mouth; they'd been in this position once before.

He bent, his body enveloping hers. The slight warm breath against the back of her ear was the only warning he gave before he spoke.

"So." He drew the single word out.

She shivered, with the lingering whisper of the

343

lengthened syllable.

"What are you doing alone in this stable, on this cold and frosty morn'?" His soft words tickled her ear. "Dressed as you are?" He slowly removed one hand from his horse. His hand slipped inside her cloak to land at her waist, just above the band of her men's breeches. She felt a light caressing of his thumb on her hip.

"What are you doing?" Beth's words came out low and throaty.

"What any good highwayman worth his ilk," Kit murmured.

"And that is…" She swallowed hard, as his fingers caressed higher beneath her cloak and grazed the side of her breast.

His hand dropped back to her hip and was joined by his other as he gripped her sides. "Robbing you, of course."

"I thought you gave that up?" His fingers tightened, and he spun her so she faced him with Dante warm against her back. "You promised to take me to Spain. Some place warm."

Beth had to fight back her smile. Kit was decked out in full highwayman regalia. Greatcoat unfastened, revealing his sword and pistols, his hair pulled back in a tight queue, tricorne hat firmly affixed. He even had a black cravat pulled up over his mouth and nose, allowing only the glint of his cat green eyes to peer out.

"You dare to taunt? Here stands before you the notorious Knightmare."

"What? You're not Mysterio or Nightmask?" She asked, playing along with their reenactment. Beth never suspected he had a romantic streak.

His eyes danced with his hidden smile. "Enough. I have places to be. Your valuables, if you please, my lady." He released his grip on her hips and took a few steps back.

"I have no valuables, o' dread Knightmare. I'm afraid you've picked a rather poor person to rob."

He cocked his head. "I think not, my lady. Turn out your pockets. I would hate to harm such a lovely lady."

"Suit yourself." Beth reached into her cloak's outside pockets and came out empty handed. "See, no treasure."

He *tsked* at her. "Now come, my lovely. You have another pocket. There is no use denying your fortune. I have a sense for it." He tapped the side of his nose with a leather-clad finger.

"You're going to be disappointed." Beth reached into her inside cloak pocket and froze. There was something in her pocket, which she could have sworn had been empty. She lifted her hand and saw a tiny black velvet pouch tied with white satin strings. She darted a glance up at Kit, a question surely written across her face.

"As I said, you cannot hide treasure from the Knightmare."

Beth untied the bow and reached into the bag. Her mouth dropped open on a silent *oh* as she pulled out a ring. It was tasteful, yet simple. A brilliant heart-shaped sapphire, no more than half a carat surrounded by diamond pieces, and set in a white gold band. The ring was offset where it gripped the gem in what appeared like small hands, lovingly holding the top and bottom of the sparkling heart. It was as if Kit was telling her he held her heart, or she held his. It was perfect.

She looked up at him and watched as he pulled his mask down to lay loosened around his neck, and next he removed his gloves dropping them into his greatcoat's pockets. He reached out and plucked the ring from her hand. Gently, he took her left hand and slipped the ring onto her finger. He lifted her be-jeweled hand and pressed a kiss to her knuckles.

Not releasing her, he asked, "Will you be mine?"

"Did you steal this?"

Kit glared down at her. "I'm offended you asked."

"I noticed you still didn't answer my question."

"Well you haven't answered mine, either, luv."

She tilted her head and raised an eyebrow.

"I purchased it in Edinburgh on our way North," he gave her a roguish grin. "Of course, the money to buy such a ring…well."

She smacked his arm and laughed. "Scoundrel."

"And you love me for it."

"I do," she rose up on tiptoes and gave him a kiss. "Yes. I will be yours, as long as you know you'll be mine."

"Always and forever, luv." He gathered her into his arms and sealed his vow with a kiss.

If you missed *Walking Through Fire*, the first book in The Fire Chronicles Series, please turn the page for a sneak peek…

Walking Through Fire

by

C J Bahr

The Fire Chronicles, Book 1

Chapter One

Northern Scotland, Near Durness, July 1809

The first tingle of fear raced up Simon MacKay's spine as he found himself alone in the pitch dark—kneeling on rough, wet granite. Waves thundered and crashed around him in the gloom. He must be in one of the sea caves on his estate. A blast of salty, cold air struck him, clearing his muddled, throbbing head to frightening awareness. He staggered clumsily to his feet, pain shooting through his arms and shoulders. He couldn't move his hands.

"Nay!" His shout echoed in the darkness. He was bound to the cave's wall. He struggled, arms stretched tautly behind him, his muscles strained against the ropes tying his wrists. Ignoring the bite of the coarse fibers and the pain of his tortured joints, panic set in. He had to get free. He had to get out. His family was in danger.

A wave slammed in close, spraying water onto his face. Sweat mingled with salt water as he thrashed. The metal mooring ring trapping him clanked against the limestone rock, as his heart raced with equal parts dread and exertion. Clasped hands turned sticky with blood from the rough bindings biting into his flesh. Simon ignored this too.

Ice water drenched him as the next wave crashed

against the wall. The chill soaking froze him in place. The tide was coming in, and the cave was rapidly filling. He hung his head and water dripped from his long hair to streak down his face, mimicking the tears he couldn't shed. His body started to shake as shock and disbelief speared his mind. If he didn't free himself, he'd drown and his family would be left unprotected.

"I canna die like this. I won't!"

He lifted his head and peered into the shadows. Another wave hit him waist high before he felt the dragging pull of the ocean's retreat. He could now hear lapping water.

I will die here, his traitorous thoughts declared, *and for what?*

A choked laugh escaped Simon, and he shook his head. "Never!" He strained once more against his bonds, but they held fast. Whoever tied the knots had done it well.

How had he gotten here? His last recollection before waking in the cave was leaving the manor and walking to the stable. He entered, but then it all blurred together. His throbbing head held the missing clue. He'd been struck. There had been no warning, no telltale movement.

The next wave hit him chest high, slamming him against the wall, crushing his arms behind him. This time however, as the wave retreated, frigid water remained clawing at his ankles.

Simon prayed the high-water mark wasn't above his head. With no light, he couldn't tell. In his soul though, he knew. He was meant to die, and at the rate the tide continued to rush in, his fate would soon be sealed.

"Damn you to hell, you bloody devil!" His cry was lost in the booming darkness. He should have known better, should have anticipated. There had been threats. He ignored them all. More fool he. Now he would pay the ultimate price.

He shook with rage as the icy water swirled about his waist. Numb to his physical discomfort, his inner turmoil was dagger sharp. Who had done this to him?

The thoughts of his tormentor fled from his mind when an incoming wave crashed above his head, submerging him. He instinctively held his breath until the arctic wash drained away to chest level. He braced and waited in the darkness for the wave set to finish. He knew the sea's rhythm, it was in his family's blood.

Three. Four. Five. The last wave pulled him from the wall, stretching his arms painfully behind him. He floated back and his feet found ground. The sea now reached his neck.

Regrets flooded him. Who would care for his family? He would be leaving behind a little sister and a sick mother. Sadly, the sea had already claimed his father, and now she would have the son. Were the men in his family cursed? Simon would disappear, and the MacKay name would die with him. Would the sick bastard who killed him now go after little Jean or his Ma? Who would stop him?

A sob escaped his throat, and he ruthlessly bit his lip. He would not die a sniveling coward.

The water lapped his chin and reached higher to caress his mouth.

The bastard would pay. Though he knew not who his murderer be, Simon saved his last thoughts to curse his enemy.

The water closed over his head, submerging him into a liquid world. He held his breath, willing the water to retreat, but the sea would not be cheated.

His lungs burned, tears squeezed from his closed eyes, and mingled unseen in his watery prison. He bit his lips, drawing blood in his effort not to breathe, but his body betrayed him.

Purely reflexive, his mouth gasped open sucking in air for his oxygen-starved lungs. All they received was the cold water of the north Atlantic.

On the second inhalation, his body started to convulse when the ocean filled his lungs.

On the third, Simon MacKay drowned.

A word about the author...

First published in Marion Zimmer Bradley's "Sword & Sorceress" anthology, CJ was bitten by the writer's bug and hasn't stopped since. The Wild Rose Press published her first novel, *Walking Through Fire*, book one in The Fire Chronicles.

When her pen isn't scribing, you can find her busily cutting and tracking music for film and television. With close to twenty years of music editing experience, her credits range from "Northern Exposure" and "The Muppets Christmas Carol" to "The Kill Point" and "The Middle."

She currently resides in sunny southern California with her two cats, great friends, and her horse.

Thank you for purchasing
this publication of The Wild Rose Press, Inc.

If you enjoyed the story, we would appreciate your
letting others know by leaving a review.

For other wonderful stories,
please visit our on-line bookstore at
www.thewildrosepress.com.

For questions or more information
contact us at
info@thewildrosepress.com.

The Wild Rose Press, Inc.
www.thewildrosepress.com

Stay current with The Wild Rose Press, Inc.

Like us on Facebook

https://www.facebook.com/TheWildRosePress

And Follow us on Twitter
https://twitter.com/WildRosePress